OUR LADY DARK COUNTRY

STORIES

SYLVIA V. LINSTEADT

Wild Talewort Press
December 2017

"You, full of sources and night."

- Rainer Maria Rilke, "Antistrophes"

CONTENTS

INTRODUCTION

Women of America, of Europe, women of my blood and mothers of my ancestors, women of all the lands of this Earth: the words in this book are needles. Thread them where they need to go: through your body, through your life, into the ground as roots. They have come from a true place in me, from the place where forgotten stories have been buried, and I give them to you in these pages gladly.

We have come to an epistemic crossroads, a crisis of the "real." I will not be able to win an argument with an archaeologist, an academic, a business man, or possibly even an old friend, by trying to state facts about the indigenous feminine traditions of Europe, about the Neolithic, about the work of Marija Gimbutas, about war, about peace, about menstruation, about sexuality, about freedom, about truth, about the heart, about the reality of magic, because facts have become a slippery thing and it seems that these days what matters is who fears what, and who gains what, and not What Is True. A fact is not What Is True. A fact is only an arrow that points toward who has the power and what story they want to tell.

A dozen times a week, sometimes a day, I want to write angry essays, immaculate in articulation and bombproof in argument, essays that are swords, cutting through two thousand years of tyrannical, imperialistic, misogynistic, life-denying narratives—the ones that are presently calling climate change a "pagan" notion, the ones that allow big oil and big gun lobbies to persist even in the face of the deadliest public mass shootings in history and a planet on the brink of devastating environmental chaos, the ones that enable the exploitation of just about everything and everybody remotely exploitable and objectifiable—but if I write angry essays like I am beginning to do here I will be dismissed by many as an angry feminist. Hysterical. It's just her womb talking.

Well, actually, it is, and I'm proud to say it. I'm bleeding today. My womb is shedding like a snake. It is windy outside and just started to rain, loud and sweet on the roof. It is dusk. There's a cake of quince, saffron and almond flour baking in the oven, and wood pigeons roosting in the bay trees, and I am indeed an angry woman writing but it is time, women of my blood, women of America, women of this Earth, that we were not ashamed. That we no longer believed anybody who told us our bodies and the wisdom of our bodies was not true. It is time we were proud and not embarrassed to say "I am bleeding today." It used to be that a woman bleeding was sought for what she knew, for what she thought, because she was closest to something bigger. A moon, a tide. It is time we started at the very snake-center of our bodies and saw again the birthright of our strength, our power, and of a knowing that is older and vaster by far than the life-destroying cultural story we are currently living in.

You don't have to know all the details about what happened, and who did what, and why—the series of Bronze Age invasions from the Russian steppe, the rise of the Roman Empire and a fanatical Christian state, the Inquisition and witch burning times, the colonization of the "New World" and onward—and how all of it is still embedded in the legacies we enact today, to feel what is beneath, in the dark country of our bodies, out of sight. All you have to do is begin at the center of yourself and listen. Earth's language and the language of the living world will speak directly to you there, and tell you What Is True, from that wellspring which has long been associated with the womb (if you have a female body), and the center of yourself and your lifeforce (if you have a male body).

I want to pause here and make it clear that this book, though deeply feminine, is not only for women but for men too, and everyone between, around, above, below and sideways from those gender designations. I want to make sure you know I am not disparaging the male gender here as such, but only an aggressive manifestation of it—called patriarchy. There is little good in hate, and especially something so silly as the hate of an entire gender. Over-simplification, as my good husband often says, is rarely useful. And I have been blessed in my life with strong, caring examples of masculinity. I am married to a wonderful, respectful man. I was raised by a wonderful father, with a wonderful brother, kind and protective uncles, two loving grandfathers, and am now blessed to have a generous and good-hearted father-in-law and two brothers-in-law I am proud to call my family. Some of my most cherished teachers have been men, and some of my loveliest friends.

The violent objectification inherent in extreme patriarchy affects men as much as it does women. Differently, but terribly too. As I heard Lyla June Johnston (the Diné and Tsétsêhéstâhese poet, musician and activist) say in an interview last spring, the witch hunts damaged the men of Europe as much as the women. The witch hunts broke them too, for there is no faster way to destroy a man's spirit (besides enslaving him or sending him to the trenches of a senseless war) than to take away and kill the women he loves—mother, wife, daughter, sister—and leave him with the horrific belief that it was his fault, that he didn't do enough, that he could have done more. That he failed them. So while this book may appeal more to those who identify as "women," it is not only for women. I write these words for all, in celebration of what the feminine might look like untrammeled and in balance with the masculine—in the past, in the present, and in the future.

I believe we are walking around with the witch trials still burning in our blood, and it is time to turn and look. There are lies still branded in our culture and the story of what it means to be a woman in the West, put there by the ancestral memory of breast ripper and hot rod and iron maiden and shackle and pyre, put there by forced marriage and forced silence, corset and shame. No manner of rhetoric would save you if the men of the Inquisition wanted you dead, even when you confessed to a mythology made entirely by them. Satan and the Devil do not belong to witches or to women, but to the life-denying story that says: to be born of a woman's body is to be soiled. This is our original sin, they say. You must spend your whole life atoning, paving your path to elsewhere, away from Earth. To be a woman who practiced the old indigenous ways of Europe, who knew her power and the power of earthfast stone and holy spring, bird and knot and hare and womb, a woman who was a priest in her own right, a doctor, a seer—this was to be a direct threat to male Christian power. Some women were carried to "trial" in baskets, so their feet wouldn't touch the ground, because the men feared that they would get power from the Earth that way.

But the worst part of it all is that the Inquisition worked so well it not only killed hundreds of thousands of women, but actually erased the truth of the witch and her (or his) indigenous roots from the old land of Europe. Erased them right out of the field of history. It is only very recently that this narrative is being amended. The story of the witch replaced the reality of the witch and we are left in its ashes still, alternately scoffing at the notion that a witch was ever a real person, or caricaturing her as a terrible old woman with warts who deserved to be killed by a young hero because she put babies in her oven and ate them.

Imagine if we spoke of the Holocaust with a snicker—"well, I mean, Jews weren't *real*, it was just a mistaken hysteria, and that's over now, don't be silly." And then we dressed up like them for Halloween to scare each other, and to laugh. *Don't be fantastical, witches were never real anyway, and if you want to talk about it, about women's oldest knowing and a time when we were not objects under the hands of more powerful men, well, that's some weird goddess shit, go ahead, suit yourself,* but you will immediately be written off and shoved into a women's studies department or the occult shelf. Meanwhile the rest will go on calling the real thing History and not men's studies, starting with the earliest so-called "real" civilization, Mesopotamia, and the old Epic of Gilgamesh in which a man clearcuts a forest and builds a city, or the Enuma Elish, in which the newer gods kill the older gods, including the dragon-creatrix Tiamat, using her body to make the world. *This is how you do it, this is how you build a civilization, see?* they tell us. But if you read between the lines and into the more marginalized texts (the ones called "Women's Studies," for example) you might begin to suspect that to be built upon the carcass of dragon might be a metaphor for the overhaul of an older mythology by a violent, patriarchal one—the conquest of a peaceable, fecund, matrilineal agrarian culture that had been flourishing for the previous five thousand years or so without trouble or resource depletion.

Don't get me wrong. I spend a lot of time in the bookstore in the Women's Studies section. I make a beeline straight for the mythology shelf and the science fiction and fantasy wing. Deeply intelligent, important things are being written and published and placed in these sections, and I feel most at home among them. *Here be dragons.* But I think there's something inherently troubling about the way this genrefication of both fiction and historical studies creates a hierarchy that looks a whole lot like the hierarchies of the Roman Empire, the Christian state, the US government, the workplace, and in many cases the home, whatever we say about feminism.

The eminent Lithuanian archaeologist Marija Gimbutas provides a fascinating, and to me very frustrating, case study. After enjoying great esteem among her male colleagues for many years of work on Bronze Age Proto-Indo-European culture in the 1950's and 60's, she began to point out that there were an awful lot of female-shaped figurines in the ancient substratum of sites across southern, eastern, and central Europe long before said Indo-Europeans arrived. She went on to suggest, based on decades of study not only of ancient Neolithic cultures but also the folklore of eastern Europe, that they might have had religious value, possibly as representatives of goddesses in a matrilineal clan culture. She noticed what she thought were many small temples and a remarkable lack of weaponry or ornate burial mounds with kings in them, having dug most of the sites herself and read the reports for the rest in one of the eleven languages she was fluent in and her male colleagues were not. As if this wasn't apparently bad enough (using the word "goddess" and "matriarchy" seems to immediately make the academic community uncomfortable) women who weren't academics got excited about her work in the 1970's because they felt she was uncovering at last a feminine heritage that was empowering, a new narrative that honored women's bodies, women's ways, and returned to them a millennia-long tradition of goddess worship across the ancient western world.

As far as many of Gimbutas' colleagues were concerned, this was the equivalent of digging her own scholarly grave and burying her academic reputation alive, although her work was no less thorough, thoughtful, or well-researched than before. But she had begun to adopt a more interdisciplinary approach, weaving in her knowledge of folklore and linguistics to interpret the figurines she was uncovering, and probably a bit of imagination and intuition too. A more feminine way, maybe, but still founded upon thirty years of study and thought.

I'd be curious to know if the reaction would have been the same had she noted a remarkable number of male figurines, and suggested the worship of predominantly male gods. I have little doubt that there would have been no academic outcry. But a goddess is a very different thing than a god. Today, her work is much beloved among feminists and goddess followers, but generally dismissed by the academic community, and while we can laugh it off as a big loss to them, I think it's actually quite chilling. An essay by a man who'd clearly not read all of Gimbutas' work and certainly hadn't thought very much about it is the only one included in the best contemporary volume on Old European culture. In his piece he dismisses all of Gimbutas' conclusions with a writerly sneer and says not much of anything else besides that they might have been sex objects, pornographic in some way, maybe dolls or maybe just female bodies but, *come on people*—you can feel his sarcasm between the lines—*let's not be ridiculous here, let's not be fanciful, sacred? Religious? Wide-hipped female figurines with possible snake heads, how could they be sacred or religiously important in any significant way? Let's not get worked up about this, that's just what the women want them to be and they can't be right because, well—*

And here we come at last to the terrible crux of the problem, and my diatribe. They cannot be goddesses with central significance to the cultures they were found buried within because— because—

It's subconscious at this point, deeply so. You can see the trend. Why should we be so outrageously embarrassed when a woman suggests matrilineal goddess-worship that we won't even consider it a real possibility?

Because it upsets the entire narrative of academia, of "progress," of what we think we mean when we say "civilization."

Because it takes us straight back to the woman beneath the apple tree speaking to the snake in the garden. Whatever she knew, whatever the snake was telling her, they've been trying to silence for at least the last two thousand years. And we've been trying to silence her in ourselves.

But I think something is changing now. I see it in the news, and it I feel it in the air, and in the center of myself, and in the ground.

Women and men of heart, Earth's snakes are speaking. It is time we listen for the truth they tell us through the centers of ourselves. Women and men of heart, we make a spiral around this planet. It is time to tell the old stories that have damaged us differently. To go beneath what we've been told and into the dark country, into the Earth, where the other side of those stories is hidden, the truth that was carried all along in the roots of the trees despite thousands of years of war.

In this book I offer stories of that place, from the dark country that was never truly conquered or secondary, no matter what they told us. The place that was always the beginning, the center, the root. The place the snakes and dragons went when they had been called monster, and evil, and finally just a fantasy, one too many times.

The rain is falling harder now. The bishop pines roar with wind. Soon the owls will be calling. The house smells of quince and almond cake.

Come in. There are doorways, very near, that the dragons will walk through if we listen, and thread, and have the courage to stand up in our bodies and call them home.

SYLVIA V. LINSTEADT

The Bishop Pinewood
Inverness, California
November 2017

A note on some of the stories—"When Dragons Came" was written in November of 2016, just after the most historic and tragic presidential election of our time. "Net" was originally one of my Tinderbundles, sent out in the mail to subscribers in the spring of 2015. "Our Lady of Nettles" was written in 2014, a re-wilded telling of the fairytale "The Six Swans," and one of my thirteen Gray Fox Epistles. The novella "The Dark Country" was written mostly during a two-month visit to the Greek island of Kefalonia in autumn 2016, and is set in a fictionalized version of that beautiful land. "The Pythia" and "Rhea Silvia," set in Greece and Italy respectively, are reworkings of two Classical myths, re-imagined from the perspectives of their women and the possibility of a pre-Hellenic, matrilineal heritage.

THE RED STRING

I .

The moon sheds herself into the water
The moon sheds herself into the sea
The moon sheds herself under the mountain
And all will be red, be red, be red

There is blood runs through
the middle of the world
on the footpath the hooves
of speckled horses leave
crescents in the dirt.
Long after the end of morning
beargirls in yellow with red ocher
on the soles of their feet come
with watertight baskets
to gather up the dust.

A snake has left her skin
made of diamonds and ash
by the roadside.
The first purple iris is blooming today
and it is a woman.
Tell me old road, old moon, old red
how to die
and then how to midwife
onto the birthing floor
where the beargirls have grown up
into grizzlywomen and are
scattering hoofdust
across the rushes which grow
at the bay edge where
you are shedding and shedding
your name.

Tell me, speckled horses
who bear the milk of night
where did you come by your hooves?
And tell me young moon on the water
old moon on the sea, is it that you
were once a woman, and so we bleed
and learn the name for Time?
Or is it that we were once made
inside the ground like you
like iris bulbs
and must die each time with you
to remember our own?

I I .

"Aunt leaf, Aunt humus, Aunt thorn, Aunt rose, how was it they bled in the time Before? Was it that which ended the salmon's coming? Was it that which killed the waters' redd?"

The evening star is big and blue-white in the first dark. Aunt is by the door, watching it rise between the apricot branches. There are white blossoms with red centers. Aunt has a pipe between her teeth. The smoke of sagebrush and poppy rises. It touches the star. In the firwood beyond the dwellings, the first woodrose of spring closes for the night. Nobody but a spider, weaving a small place between thorns, sees.

Aunt turns back to the girl there by the fire in the clay house. The walls are white and round, made of earth and wattle. Fire in the center makes them shift, warmly. The orange embers crackle under the girl's stick. A clay kettle sits on rocks, steaming tea. Aunt chews her pipe. It is hare bone, from the long thigh.

She comes to the fire. The red ocher on her feet flashes. Her hair is a high white pile. At her throat, coming from the back of her neck, the nine fine scars. Lines from the claws of bears whose names are hidden. The girl remains silent, prodding embers. The star is gone from the doorway. Aunt hesitates. The others are asleep on bedmats in the far corner. She begins. Her voice is trained and deep, but even so, it shakes.

I I I.

Blood balled up in
white paper, the plastic and the plush
cotton, easy to trash, to plug, to plunge
up into the red of the body
and keep there, a stoppering,
and at night I was so afraid
my heart would just stop:
some clot, some unholy end.

In the Valley the old silt rivers
got dammed early on
culverts and dykes
and locks in the channels
to release flow for crops.
This, and the drying, and the dying.
How the dust can
carry poison made to help
the almonds grow when the silt
was gone, and the blood,
and the hundred thousand bodies
of chinook seething up the mile-wide
Sacramento.
Once, bears waited on the banks,
fishing them out lazily,
that tide of silver and red.

Listen, to throw away blood
is to throw away
the beginning of the world
and the first shadow on the moon.
To throw away blood

sopped up in paper, bound up
with plastic, a stick of sodden cotton
and a string, is to throw away
the salmon, the redd, the river, the silt.
To throw away blood among
the other garbage and
broken things, the cans and baggies
and rot and tin and tub and
twist and scrap (because
the true name for Vessel
has been buried under Hunger)
is to call it broken too
this salmonred river
this bear-clawed moon
this footpath run with horses.

Listen, there was a time when four
colorless tasteless pills
were my bleeding and I
felt nothing, nothing that took
me to my knees, that laid
me flat, that told me *rest*
that told me *breathe*,
that told me *dream*, that gave me
the iris of my body
a skin to shred and to swallow
and to light into dawn.
Nothing that ached me
into sleep. Only a pink creek,
the locks well-manned.
No flood, no clot, no broom.

But listen.
Beyond the four white days

of bleeding, for those twenty-four
other pink moons, I was a shatter
I was balled up in white paper
awake at night listening
for my heart to end
in terror of my death
at the break of a string, my mind
a scissor snip, the knot, the bind,
a fraying girl hunched
over her own embroidery, her own
immaculate and indigo dreams
worrying and worrying the threads
to terrible bits
a poison of dust under almond trees.

No one told me it could drive
you mad, because no one
told me I was carrying
the Beginning of the World.
The gibbous. The loom.
No one told me what it meant
to lock, and what to flood.
No one told me it is better to fall down
on your knees
and bleed the rivers home
than it is to bind up the strings
in white and throw them
neatly away.

Now.
The cloth soaked in
clear water. The red poured out
onto the roots of trees.
See, they are speaking again.
See, they remember your name.

WHEN DRAGONS CAME

To my future granddaughters beyond the end of the world, where you are gathering laurel nuts and combing out the hair of dragons:

Let me tell you a story. About where the dragons came from. About what it was like when I was a young woman before ever I carried a child.

When I was a young woman a white dust had fallen across the land, and people gathered it in fistfuls, fighting each other to get the most, because its taste was unearthly sweet and it brought on a euphoria that made what was real dissolve in favor of what was desired. A white sleep. Back then, people often loved the simulacra of Things more than the Things themselves, for it was easier to buy a Thing than it was to dig one from the Earth. And because we were all afraid of death, so afraid we would swallow any measure of dust, any strength of oblivion, in order not to look there, until our loneliness and our animal despair were such that we forgot what we feared altogether, and turned to sleeping, calling it Life.

Many of us tried not to breathe in or swallow that dust. And there was still beauty to be found. There always is. I loved many things then. The bay at high tide with a heron walking. Any number of stars. Gathering nuts from the autumn wood. Your grandfather and the warmth of his hand. Food shared with family, with mother and father and brother, with grandparents and uncles and aunts. Music under a moon. A fire in the hearth, tea brewed, and wool. Rain. Always, forever, rain. You could still find such things, if you sought them, but you were often alone in the seeking, bumping into others there only as in a dark wood, each desperate for something whole and old and earthly that none of us could ever find entirely, or name.

In those times, whatever was easiest was called best. And, as always, whatever served the ones who had the most possessions to lose. Not the most life to lose, but the most control over death. For it was not any of us alone, but Earth, who had the most life to lose, and lost it daily, hourly, under the thrall of that white dust, that sleep, that terrible need, and the howling loneliness that crouched behind it all, devouring.

There came a day one autumn when we knew the world would end. Your grandfather and I were clearing the dying oaks from the land we loved, the land where we were making a new home, our round tent of felt and canvas and hearth to stand inside the changing. Votes came in. Everything we had feared, everything we had not believed, began to come to pass in the hands of one too white with dust to rule, and yet who ruled nonetheless, by the will of people and their sorrow; and later, by a will only his own.

No one believed in dragons then, because they had gone into the Earth long, long before. There were stories, broken ones, in which dragons burned towns and men killed them for it. Nobody remembered that the older name for dragon was hidden inside the lava and inside the moon, and that bones kept it safe even unto our day, far down in the ground.

We didn't know we were burning their blood to power our world, not then. We didn't know they might be as small as moths, or as large as the entire night sky, and that they could fly through the Earth just as easily as the air. We didn't know because we had been afraid for a very long time, and asleep, and alone. All of this made it hard to see them, to hear them gathering far, far underground, in all the cavities and all the scars made by all the rigs and drills and blasts that had torn the Earth, searching for what had always belonged to dragons and not humans, the hordes that should never have been taken away.

This is how it happened.

In the middle of the country, in the middle of the end, on a great and sacred plain by a great and sacred river, the first people of that land stood a final stand against that white dust, against tanks and guns, against a hunger too dangerous to bear, against the digging up of sacred blood. Everywhere across the country people woke up at last, struggling, from the dust of their lives, They tried to shout their outrage to someone, tried to make it stop, tried to say what mattered, tried to end the long and unspoken war. But by then it was too late.

An order was delivered. The drilling began. The tanks rolled in for the last time and surrounded the place where people were standing, where people were praying, where people were crying, where the horses had been gathering and gathering for days, where all the white dust was gone from the ground, where everyone's eyes were open, were clear.

They stood in peace, without fighting. They stood with fists raised to the sky and they stood with tears falling and falling and the horses ringed them, ready to die. In the very middle of the people were three young woman with black lines painted on their chins. Three sisters holding hands. Three sisters whose beauty was as old as the world.

The horses began to stampede. Guns began to fire. And a hole opened in the ground where the three sisters stood. They fell in, and before anyone could follow, the Earth closed again. Then it rocked and bucked and the tanks fells sideways and everyone ran for cover together as the river flooded its banks.

For a time, after that, there was a standstill. Machinery had broken. Drilling was suspended. And all the while, the three sisters were inside the Earth, learning the names of dragons, riding the backs of dragons, braiding their hair for battle.

I knew none of this, then. Nobody did. Only three women inside the Earth knew it, and the ones who had taken them there because of their beauty. Don't get me wrong for a moment that their beauty had anything to do with external appearances. Do you think dragons care for the faces of humans? It was the beauty of their souls they saw and took them for, beautiful as the fire at the beginning of the world. They had been waiting all that time for three such as they to stand in that place, in the name of the blood and the land, and not back down, and not turn away.

This is not a story that ends with three men who went out searching, and the youngest who found them and killed the dragons and saved us all. No. Life went on much as before. A shrine was erected in the place where the sisters had been swallowed, and people brought jars of clear water to pour on that ground in grief.

For the digging had begun again, and the smell of oil was in the air, and the taste of oil was in the water.

A year and a day they were gone and mourned for dead. A miracle, but dead. A year and a day and through it the world's weather grew wild. The ones who ruled us called orders on the bodies of women, on the dark bodies of their brothers and sisters, on the bodies of men in love. They filled the ground and the sky with every imaginable poison, as if there was no end to the curve of the Earth. They began work on a wall.

And then, all at once on an evening in winter when the stars were very sharp overhead, every light and every engine blew out at once. In that rain of light the air filled with dragons and with three beautiful women wielding battle axes made of fire, come to take back every last thing that had been stolen. The dragons came to take those thefts back into their bodies and back into the ground. They laid the Earth to rest that night as she had not rested for hundreds of years, in an ancient veil of green.

All we could see of it that night was auroras, those northern lights which had never danced so far south before. But by morning, the ground was covered with ash and with eggshells, the eggshells of the first animals to ever walk the Earth. There they were, crouched in the trees and roofs and riverbeds, on the hoods of cars, the broken telephone wires, the abandoned mines, the quarries, the sky-scrapers, the parking lots, the mountain tops. Not winged, not horned, not clawed, but older still, and stranger.

Some people couldn't see them, not yet. Others could, and could not bear the sight. Still others wept, and knelt for joy. But no one, no matter how hard or how hungrily they searched, could find a trace of that white dust again. Only ash, which by spring made the fields sprout as never before. Only air so clear and eyes so open we could see every crater on the face of the moon for weeks after.

It will be long before we can see everything clearly again. It takes lifetimes to believe in dragons once more. But you are women of dragons, now. You must gather the laurel nuts and the acorns like we could not. You must say the true name of the water, and wait for it to run clean. Forgive us, oh my granddaughters not yet born. I am so sorry, my dear ones, for we have woken the dragons that you must learn to ride.

So may you be beautiful in soul. And may they come courting you. May they swallow you whole and make you theirs again, keepers of the oldest justice. Hers.

THE PYTHIA

I saw a terrible vision the day before the one they call Apollo came.

I saw what was inconceivable then in the days of inno-cence, when a woman's body was as holy and whole as the saf-fron crocus, and her sons beloved for their generosity, their way with animals, their lithe speed in footraces, and not for their cleverness at war. In that vision I saw beyond conquest, far beyond, to another kind of brokenness. I saw into the desolation of a terrible forgetting. When even the names were dead, and the Oracle a ruin visited but not believed. To be conquered is one thing. To be silenced until the silence itself is forgotten is to be left without the dark blessing of rebirth that lives at the center of the world.

But there are daughters and sons coming who need the story of what silenced us, and how. So I will tell it from the beginning.

WHEN I WAS I GIRL I BELIEVED that our omphalos, our mountain cave and the Python within, was the center of the world. So I was taught. But in the autumn of my third season as a young priestess at Delphi, my cousin went north into the mountains of Epirus where the goats are shaggier to visit the oak oracle of Dodona with her mother. When she came home she said it was the same there.

"It seems the world has many centers!" she said when she saw me at harvest time while we peeled the quince for my mother's sweet dessert. I was a little horrified by this seeming blasphemy, so later I thought it over. I sat under the old olives in my father's orchard, thinking, and when I returned to the Delphi I walked among the laurels and listened to their whispering. Troubled still, at lasted I asked the Pythia, our great Sibyl, while we were all out in the late autumn heat gathering the olives into nets. The Pythia was always among us working at the daily tasks of life around the sanctuary and the dreaming caves, save at the times of prophecy. There was little hierarchy except then, when the Python in the Earth called to the Pythia in the silence of her mind that the ground was breathing, that an Oracle was ripe. Then she was our Sibyl, our Mother, and we served her as such.

Out under the olives, she smiled when I asked my question.

"The Earth has only one true center," she replied, sitting up from the net, brushing a leaf and a spider from her gray hair. "And that center no human will ever visit, for it is far, far underground, all fire and darkness. I have seen it in my trances, but never with our bodies could we go there. But love makes other kinds of centers. Anywhere enough love comes together, something whole is made, and all whole things have centers. She laughed at my empty look. "Another way put, child, is that anywhere they speak a different language or dialect, there is a different center of the world. A different holy mountain, stone or snake. And yet the same inside, in essence, invisibly, with a root straight down to the middle of her, the molten core that we may only see in spirit. No better? Ah, it's just as well. A question is a sacred thing with its own center to be sought." She patted my hand and pushed up to her feet. "Now, the oil."

We had our own great stone olive press at Delphi. It looked like an altar but it was just for crushing out the oil. We gathered it from there into fine-necked urns as big as I, which we stored in the cool of an underground chamber, free to eat as much as we pleased. Sometimes, when the moon was dark and my body or my mind weary, I liked to eat a spoonful, and then another of honey from our hives. After that nothing in the world seemed too bad, for I was made of the gold of bees and olive trees.

I was fifteen the autumn my cousin went to Dodona and I began to consider that the world might be bigger than our holy mountain sanctuary. I discovered other centers that year, as the autumn rains filled the earth and the crocuses began to bloom beside the pink tongues of the cyclamen. I had a particular friend among the other girls, Silene she was called, much taller than I and more beautiful. We were inseparable then. Our young bodies loved to be near one another, touching. Her breasts where fuller than mine and I was often looking at them. One day while we were down the mountain looking for mushrooms, she put my hands on them and kissed me.

"Let's practice together," she said, and her breath was warm. She knew more of her body already than I did, and showed me the root of mine with her lovely, hot hands. For a while after that we slipped away often together between our duties. During those times I began to understand how a body might dissolve into something greater, a part of the trees, the red earth, the limestone cliffs, the cyclamen.

I think Silene only ever loved women her whole life long, but I also loved a man. I had a son by him and raised the boy as a child of Delphi, as many did in those times. My son's father was a goatherd, who'd brought us fresh milk up the mountain track from his family's holding a mile below since he himself was a boy. He was like a gatekeeper to us, though in those days no one would dare defile the Oracle, much less the women who kept it. Still, our Pythia taught us, it is good to make people a little afraid, to make sure they come only when they really need to, and not for trifles. For it is no small thing on body or mind to ask counsel of the Python, or dreams from the cave.

But my Aristus could do little against the men of Apollo, who came on the backs of beautiful, long-necked creatures we had never seen, with round shining hooves and long tails. Like donkeys, but much finer and larger. Horses, they were called. Their hooves rang on the mountain stones.

By the time Apollo and his men and their horses came, I was the Pythia of Delphi. Our old mother, the one who had been Sibyl since I was a girl, had died, and I at thirty was her successor, though there were older women who envied me the position. But she had been training me for many years. By then I was a mother, my son a boy of nine, raised among the women of Delphi and the mountain shepherds, his father's people.

Only once or twice each month did the Earth begin her exhalations, the sweet breathing of the Python which preceded prophecy. Then I would prepare myself for three days entire, abstaining from sexual pleasure, from all food save oil, honey and clear spring water. I bathed in the deep spring, and in the smoke of laurel leaves, and sat with my mind empty high up the mountain for a day and a night. Then I descended. My Aristus always knew the day and brought his finest goat for the sacrifice, the one most black of fur. He came no further than the sanctuary's mouth, and one of the girls took the goat from him, bleating on its leather lead, and soothed and praised it until it was calm. Then a pitcher of cold spring water was poured over the goat's body. If he shivered the time for the Oracle was right, and I bowed while his blood was given to the dark ground, then descended with laurel, barley and spring water in my hands to sit on the tripod over the chasm in the stone and call up the Python. If he did not shiver, which happened very rarely, it was not safe within, the Earth's breath too strong for a human to breathe, even a trained Pythia, and I returned the following day to try again.

During the times of prophecy Silene took our son and looked after him, and he grew to be a fine young lad among the women, spoiled by their doting, and a little wild, but always kind like his father, and good with plants and animals. He liked to work in the gardens on the terraces below the sanctuary where we grew our food. He loved the blue flax in summer, the smell of the silver wormwood, the faces of the bean flowers as they climbed, the vines of the half-wild grapes from which we made a simple mountain wine.

Besides those days of prophecy, which for me were intensely bright and dark both for body and for mind, my life and the lives of my priestesses were gentle and slow there on the mountain, the center of the world. Much of our time was taken up with the daily things of life—the spinning and weaving of our cloth, the gathering and tending of plants for our meals, the shaping of clay for our libations, the mixing of herbs for incense and medicine. In and out we wove the pleasure of each thing. This was how the Pythia before me taught us, and the one before her. For every holy cone of smoke we shaped, we made an oil of thyme and saffron for our skin, to smooth on in the hot dawn sun of summer. In autumn we went down the mountain a little way for acorns. The shepherds joined us, and there was always much flirting and chasing and games and laughter, a fire with a goat or a deer on it, rough wine and the many stars at nightfall through the trees. We worked hard but rested often to swim in summer, or tell an old in winter story.

THE NIGHT BEFORE APOLLO'S MEN CAME, I emerged from the Oracle deeply troubled by what I had seen, unable to rest or even to ease out of the trance of Earth for many hours; not until the moon had set and it was almost day again. I should have gone to Aristus and asked to be held there in his bed of sweet straw and goatskins. I should have brought our son, and the three of us slept curled together, he who was body of our bodies, us three a whole. But I was not entirely human that night, and so could not dwell among my kind. Earth's Snake was still in me.

The old Pythia had warned me of this the night she gave the Oracle to me, placing the laurel and the round bowl of water in my hands there in the deep adyton with the great Python herself coiled between us. *Your love belongs first to her, now. And to her mother, the mountain, the stone, the Earth, the one whose oldest name is Ge.* It was true. I could not understand it until I made my first prophecy alone. I became the Snake, the Earth, the Stone. I saw as through their eyes. I was not myself, but only Pythia, she of the Python, she of Ge, my skin no longer human, my womb no longer mother of my boy but a limestone cavern filled with stars. I felt what it was to be a great serpent in those depths, the current of my body running sinuous through the dark between fault lines, between mountains, between ages and seas, through underground springs, among the dead who carry all the seeds of Earth in their gentle arms. In the sanctuary on my tripod, I was Snake and Earth and they were I, and thus I saw the round of things, the shedding skin, the beginning as the end, the end become seed. I knew every root of every plant and tree, the bones of every creature. I do not know what I looked like to human eyes when I entered that chamber of prophecy, but in my own eyes, my inner sight, I was the Python herself, vast and scaled, with eons on my tongue.

That night I saw horses in my vision but did not know their names, and thought them beautiful. I saw a great laurel tree outside the sanctuary, where none had been before. I saw the mountain burning and thought it a warning of summer wildfire, or the need for ash among our fields to feed the soil. But I also saw things I had no words for—many men in strange clothing and dark chariots and a power around them that sucked at the

very life force of the ground beneath their wheels, a crushing hunger of need and force that made me reel. I saw at last the great Python herself cut to pieces and buried beneath the holy stone, our omphalos. This was what broke my trance as nothing ever had, and why I did not take the necessary steps, the slow unwinding of the sight, the careful coming down. I did not let my maidens feed me the grounding honeycakes, the cup of hardy wine, the second cup of goatsmilk, the oil on my skin.

Instead I fled. I cast away my bowl of sacred water and it shattered. I dropped the bay leaves and they burned when they touched the ground though there was no fire there. And the great Python who always went back down the chasm where Earth breathed when it was over, she who would only ever show herself to the Pythia in trance, she did not go away. She stayed all night filling the entire sanctuary with her body, curled around the omphalos, breathing the words of Ge which none could understand. My maidens hid that night, afraid of what it meant that the Python had shown herself and that their Pythia had fled raving to the hills, when there had been no warning of such a danger during the ritual water-pouring over the black goat.

I was mad with trance all night. I was full of Earth's fumes still. I was half-Snake. I could not loose my scales and remember my own name, for what I had seen, though inconceivable to me then, had still broken through, untranslated but clear in meaning nevertheless. I had seen terrible changes that wound not through single lifetimes but through eons, through lineages, through all the centers of the world, and the horror of it near broke my mind. The loneliness of those eons without the Python, without the knowledge of her at the heart of every darkness.

I plunged myself into the spring where we bathed to purify ourselves, the sacred spring that comes out of the unseen, out of the stone in a little canyon gorge where the oaks are young and green and the white clematis blooms. I plunged in raving.

This sobered me a little, until I could sit still, high up tangled in trees. There I tried to sing myself clear, sing myself whole, so I might go down and warn my women, go down and hold my Aristus. That I regret still, that I had no time to hold him or see him again, to be soothed by his warm hands on my back. But I only had strength enough for a single thing as the trance at last faded and I descended with the dawn—to hide my women, and my son with them.

Most would not at first leave me or the sanctuary where the Python still coiled—a terrible, unheard-of thing. She filled the shrine with the light on her scales, the absolute endlessness of her name. I could not articulate to them what was coming, nor why the threat so great. I didn't really understand myself. But Silene, my oldest love, she saw what could not be said in my eyes, and it was she who convinced the other women to go up the dreaming-cave for the day. Then she took my boy and ran to the place where the bears go in winter, very high up in mountain caves where the wild thyme grows thick. I remember his skinny body in my arms when I said goodbye. I tried not to make him afraid with my fear.

"Aunt is taking you for your first bear hunt," I said to him. "Capture a cub and we will raise him together as your brother. Do right by his mother, leave offerings, and take care, my sweet, my wild kid." He smelled of warm barley, of honey, of his father. Silene kissed my mouth and took him, eager with his bow and his best obsidian tips that Aristus had helped him knap the month before. He grinned his eager grin and it was the innocence of it that broke my fear to rage.

When I heard hooves on the mountain path I listened to them come with a hot clarity. I was as cleared as the Earth after the magma, dispassionate in my rage. But when they crested the ridge and I saw their size, their beauty, their terrible potency, I understood more of the danger that had arrived, and was afraid.

I went to the Python's side then and looked into one of her

copper eyes, big as my own palm. I needed neither the Earth's breath nor the laurel burning to hear her now. Her voice filled me, whole as ground.

Run, daughter.

No. I will not leave you.

There is nowhere you could go that I would not find you if you called. Run, now, and save yourself.

Then all I could see in my mind was a great laurel tree. It was enormous, ancient. Around it was Delphi, but unfamiliar, not the simple stone sanctuary, our little terraced gardens, our olive trees, our well, but something vast and white and shining, and many people in fine dress, a whole hive of them, a city around the sanctuary, tall white pillars like bone tree trunks holding up great roofs. It was sharp edged, immaculate, dead even in its colors and its noise.

The sound of metal brought me back. My arms were around the Python. I held her head against my breast, big as a child. It was cool, smooth as water, without end. A man called out from the terraced garden. He had seen the coiled serpent within. I glimpsed his face out there in the light though he could not see mine in the shadowed sanctuary, only the Python's gleaming and enormous form. The sun was on him, high overhead. He shone. This frightened me and awed me both, until I saw he shone not from his own light but from the pieces of fine metal he wore on his chest and forearms.

He held out a very long, very thin, very sharp blade. Not a knife but something else entirely. With it held before him he began to creep toward the sanctuary, waving his men back, as if stalking a great beast on a hunt and not a lone woman and a gentle, ancient serpent, both huddled over the center of the world. At last, when he was at the door and terror of the Python for a moment paused him, I managed to gather myself together, to gather my wits. I stepped toward him. He had yet to notice me.

"Do you come seeking prophecy, my friend?" I said, the

proper welcome for a guest. "What question is it that brings you to our door?"

My voice startled him, and my form. I saw this in his eyes. I saw him take me in, saw my strangeness and my body as I had never seen myself, wholly other, wholly object, untethered from anything known. My black hair that shone as the laurel leaves shine in sun, my skin very brown beneath the yellow of my robes, which were half torn from my night up the mountain, lined with earth, broken by thorn and damp; the Earth still in me, in my eyes and my breath and my voice from that last trance. I was all that he was not, he of the shining metal and golden body. I saw myself as he saw me. I saw his desire.

"So you are the Oracle then?" he said with a little smile. He still held out his blade. He took another step forward. His eyes were hot, sliding everywhere across me. I wanted to run, but knew that in running I would give away what could belong to no one. I saw how badly this man wanted what belonged to no one—the Earth's voice, the Python, my body, my power too.

"I am," I said, standing taller, trying to muster all that was in me, only to find that in his eyes I was already his. "I speak on behalf of the Snake, and of the Earth."

"You are beautiful, priestess. I have never seen a woman so beautiful, so strong and pure of limb, so lithe, a serpent queen, a queen of stones," he said, slipping nearer, making his voice the tone of one trying to catch a goat for slaughter, hypnotic, droning on. "I will make you so, I will make you mine, you will speak for me and not for your snake. Let me show you, let me show you how much better it will be." He reached right for my thighs with skilled fingers but I leapt aside and clawed his face. In the same moment the Python reared up and struck him square on the shoulder. Only she knew truly how much we were about to lose.

I will never forget that, the pure beauty of our Python as she rose as high as the sanctuary roof, her eyes bright, her head a terrible molten planet, rearing, striking him so hard that he screamed and called for his men. Then there was no hope. They came running with long sharp blades and descended together upon the Python, doing what no one had dreamed to do for the unholy curse of it, a matricide of the worst degree. They cut the Python to her death, into a dozen pieces that bled black across the stone floor.

It was a frenzy, a murder. They said no words of prayer or remorse. Their eyes were red, their bodies bulged with what coursed through them, a kind of power I had never seen save in my vision. I recognized it then, huddled over the omphalos stone, over the center of the world, unable to move with what I witnessed. Then I understood, very brief but clear, how what I had seen might come of power such as this.

Black blood flooded the floor of the sanctuary. It covered my feet. The pieces of the Python were no longer reptilian but Earth, great fragments of a fallen planet. The sanctuary reeked of underworlds, of the dead, of new soil. I saw only a single point of light right in front of me. My vision was otherwise tunneled. What I had believed eternal was destroyed. I lay inside that darkness, struggling to breathe.

It was the voice of the one called Apollo that shook me out of my stupor. His voice and his hands, taking hold of my arms, lifting me, running across my breasts.

"Now," he was saying. "Back to my offer..."

With a final, wild burst of trance and of power, I rallied. I wriggled free of his hands and fled him and his men with all my might, screaming Earth's name. My whole body was only one word, Ge, a prayer for Earth to swallow me so I might never be captured by those hands. I was hardly a woman in that moment, mostly animal in flight. But I was woman enough that a part of me screamed mercy from the one I served. I ran, crushing laurel leaves from my robes in my fingers, offering them to the ground. *Please great one, swallow me, change me, save me, I am yours.*

Apollo loved the chase. My body, fleeing, stirred him and

quickened his pace. Once he almost caught me. His hands were on my waist. But already I was hardening. Myself and body would not be his release. I was bark, trunk. I saw with my eyes my long dark legs turn to wood. I felt the roots in agony split open what had been my feet. But the pleasure of their rooting was more total than can be spoken. As if what had long branched in me as thoughts had turned downward and become material, traded thinking for soil, water, sugar; something filamental, essential, manifest, and no longer mental.

I thought in radicles, in earth. My breasts filled the trunk with sap. My arms, reaching of their own volition upward, mirrored my feet. A searing that opened into branches, into waxy dark green leaves. My own fragrance engulfed me, and I was no longer a woman, no longer Pythia, but the laurel tree.

DAPHNE WAS MY NAME when I was a woman.

Daphne, my women called later, circling me where no laurel tree had been before, searching.

It was Silene who recognized me, and Aristus who came every day until he was an old man to touch my bark and speak to me, and after him our son.

THAT WAS LONG AGO. I have not gone, though all the ones I knew have left. I am the laurel at the cavern's mouth, and my roots touch the spring water and the vent far below where the Earth moves and steams. My roots go deeper yet, so deep they know the center of the world the old Pythia taught me of. There in the far darkness, in the molten light, that is where our Python went when Apollo and his men cut her to pieces and buried her under the omphalos. That was also very long ago, and Earth's serpents take an eon, maybe two, to be reborn. But don't think for a moment that they can ever truly be killed.

At the tip of my roots I have felt her stirring.

NET

I.

Time is a net thrown around the universe, though every knot may be loosed. There are winds that live inside knots, and love affairs—solar winds that blow comet shrapnel through the great glinting fishskin of the galaxy, stars bound to the same gravitational spin, like two pumas, golden and circling one another.

Of course there is no saying what cordage was twisted to make that net, nor how dark space may tie a knot, but on ordinary days, when there are low clouds and then rain, when you have to turn on the heat or light the fire, when your slippers are nowhere to be found and there is a hunger for breakfast in your belly, you can just as easily find the netted universe in the fascia of your own body. There are enough stars to last a lifetime, inside. Not all nets are for capture. Some things long to be contained—veins and muscle, fat and bone; stars and moons and striped old planets, a hundred million other suns and all the dust that drifts between them.

All witches know this, how a knot loosed in the fascia of the body, just under the skin, may let in a star, may ease a moment in time into a long slow murmur, may make the spheres creak and ring, may cure a migraine induced by the smell of floor polish. All witches know too that the cords in a net are for walking, and all the empty spaces for slipping through, but only if you know the way back. It's best to tie an extra cord to the knot by which you left, and unspool it from your belt so you can follow it back home.

Cats are the exception to this rule. Cats have no trouble slipping in and out of time, in and out of the fascia of their bodies, in and out of worlds. They never have trouble finding the way back home. The priests of the Inquisition were not mistaken to suspect cats as well as their mistresses for magic. It does not do justice to the women who burned at stakes and drowned tied up like boats to call the whole business a case of religious hysteria; it doesn't do justice to the women who held to the old ways of their grandmothers, of blackthorn and red thread and the power of motherwort and silver moon, of robin song and the leaves in the bottoms of teacups, to say they were never witches at all, to say they did not speak to their cats, or send them out under dark skies to walk through the openings in the netted night. Of course they did. It is only that the Devil never had anything to do with it. He was the purview of priests alone.

I I .

It did not help that she was called Magdalena and her hair was dark and moved like two hands behind her when she walked. It did not help that it had been a bad winter and though it was mid-February the snowdrops were still far down in the cold ground and the hedgehogs hadn't stirred in their burrows, and everyone was hungry, with a murmur low through the dreaming town in the dark-iced dead of night—*will it end, will it end, will it ever end?*

It did not help that Magdalena liked the snow, and trapped fur and food for her family in snare nets twisted of nettle, and that the cat called Stripe—who had followed her out of the forest one day and home, and who might have been a wildcat, one of the last, because he stood tall as her knee and had tufted ears and too much slink for the comfort of the town tabbies—always went hunting with her. Nor did it help that in her kitchen hung the feathers of the birds he killed and ate with his immaculate claws, taking the dark organs in his teeth like jewels.

It did not help that when Magdalena went to check her traps, she stopped to look at rabbit tracks, like long faces through the snow, and how the fox circled them on furred paws, and where the buntings landed and pecked under the snow, their bodies so slight they hovered at the surface, light as snowflakes. Dressed in furs sewn from the skins of the animals trapped in the forest, and soft boots, and wool mittens, at her ease in the middle of winter, Magdalena stopped to sit on logs in the snowy wood and listened to the quiet of that white, to the crease and crinkle of the air as snowflakes fell through from their elsewhere in the sky, to listen for the robins talking, warning one another of Stripe, and the weasel out hunting by the frozen creek. Sometimes she crouched on the ice and made a hole to tempt fish to her hook. These, she fried in their own oil, and sang.

It was twenty-five years ago that the Devil had moved into the woods; a generation, or more, since the last time the Inquisition had come hunting witches there between the forest and the valley hills, in the little town called Grossbreitenbach. It was safer to believe he was there, where before had been only fir and pine trees, rosehips in autumn, woodruff in spring and elderberries in summer, deer with perfectly cloven hooves, the white faced owls; it was safer not to argue, to leave the forest behind, than to walk out under moonlight for herbs, and risk *witch*. It used to be that women tied colored scraps of cloth to the willow by the creek, knotted for healing or for love. It used to be that women left stones with holes in them at the base, for easy labors, for healthy births, but most of those women were dead in fires at stakes paid for out of their own pockets, as well as the ropes that bound them and the price of the upkeep of the jail cell that held them.

But Magdalena still brought cloth to the willow tree—pant cuffs her son tore on brambles, a shirt worn to pieces by her husband, always smelling of sweet wood and varnish and the spice of rosin from the violin shop. She brought stones with holes for women who were about to give birth. She brought angelica root to their bedsides while they were in labor. She brought yarrow for hemorrhage and peony root for pain.

Don't be afraid, her mother had said when they took her away. Magdalena was a girl of seven then. *Be clever but do not be afraid. Some one has to keep dreaming the woods or they will leave our hearts forever, and then we will be well and truly lost.* And so Magdalena was not afraid of the Devil in the woods when she checked her traps and brought home white winter rabbits, when she sat in the crinkle of snowfall and listened to how the sky and the firtops and the birds and the quiet earth were knotted, strand to strand, one net like the net of her body, held together just below the skin, because she knew he didn't live there. She knew he didn't live anywhere but inside people. She knew no matter what might happen to a place, no matter if her whole village burned to the ground because of someone's fear of Devils, no matter if the whole forest were razed to the roots, the Devil could never live there, in the snowfall, in the way the fir tree crown sprouts from a stump, in the way the robins know about the weasel, in the way they are all knotted together, and move, inseparable.

It didn't matter though, what Magdalena feared or didn't fear, what Magdalena loved or didn't love. It didn't matter how clever she was, just like her mother had told her to be. In the end it was as she had always anticipated: her body, at a stake, all fire. Like her mother before her. This knowing had always been there, but she would not have traded her life for a safe one, and winters without the net of snowfall around her in the soft wood, where the foxes hunted the rabbits and the cat Stripe hunted the robins.

In the end it was simply a long winter. The witch-burning fever always caught in the cold, in the dark hard pit made by hunger. Everyone knew how Magdalena walked in and out of the woods with cheeks in high color, like the rosehips, and how she cooked stews that kept her family plump through the winter, with meat from the Devil's forest, wearing the skins of His cocoa-dark minks. It happened because the baker's son walked by her window while she was stirring a rabbit stew at dusk on the coldest day in February. He peered in through the glass at the stew, and at her, because her cheeks were rosy, and her hair dark. She was stirring it widdershins, moonwise, absently. She smiled. He slipped on black ice on the cobbles and cracked his skull. The cat named Stripe sat on the sill, and flicked his tail, as at a bird.

The butcher's wife across the way saw it all, but she never mentioned how Magdalena ran out onto the cobbles with bundles of herbs—comfrey, yarrow—and a great cloth to swaddle the boy's head. Nor how she held him, and wept. By the time the butcher's wife had run for her husband, and then the doctor and the constable, the boy was dead, and Magdalena was standing above him, mute, holding her herbs, holding that cloth with a knot in it where she had meant to tie it around his head.

Stripe sat in the window without moving and watched it all with bright green eyes that showed no sorrow. This, the butcher's wife did not forget to mention.

STRIPE WAS TIED TO MAGDALENA'S LEGS when they burned her in a wicker cage on the top of a pile of brush. When the fire reached its greatest heat, and the ropes fell away from his body, and hers, only one child in the gathering of village folk saw the silver-gold form of a cat, leaping out of the flames, clambering up the columns of smoke.

It was called proof, later, that they could find only her bones on the pyre, and not a single one of Stripe's.

I I I .

At the edge of the valley called Silicon for the mineral hearts of computers, where the latest OS X operating system had recently been named Mountain Lion due to its speed and general capacity, a little male cougar was born tiny and strangely striped. He was the fourth cub, a surprise to his mother when he came out, tucked into the bottom of the placenta, criss-crossed with blood and tissue, like an afterthought. He was conceived in February and born in July, when the hills were dry gold the color of his mother's body.

She taught him to read each strand of the net of scent that all mountain lions live by as he grew up. She taught him where the strands knotted and where the edges were—the long boundary lines scraped and sprayed on fence posts and oak trunks, in little piles of soil, at the edges of human hiking trails, by other mountain lions. She taught him which were female, and which male, and that a female's home might share a corner with a male's, but two males, never. She showed him the cords of scent that led to old bucks, and deer mothers ready to give birth; to rabbits and raccoons and foxes in leaner times. The air is not an invisible medium to a mountain lion, remembered only in the wind. It is a matrix, weft and warp, criss and cross, of the lines left by the lives of every last creature in his particular domain.

She showed him nets of sound, too, and how they changed when the wind did, and the light, and the season—twists of jay call, scolding, knots made by the tentative hooves of young does, crunching through dry summer grass, the way their movements changed the quality of the air, its fabric. During the first year of his life, watched over by his mother, he learned to hunt, he lost his strange, un-cougar-like stripes, he played with his siblings in long patches of sun.

It was not an easy thing to leave his mother one August morning and know that this time, she would not allow him to return. This time, the dry trail where humans hiked by day would only take him one way, his big paws leaving their impressions in the loose earth, fine as powder. He stepped into that net of scent all alone.

A mountain lion doesn't make his home with words, or deeds, or settlements. He can't make it by theft or barbed wire, but it must be big, big enough for him to roam end to end and find many deer without crossing into the territory of another adult male. There, the smaller of the two, he might be killed.

That August, he never stopped roaming. He ate raccoons, and brush rabbits, which were so small and fast as to be hardly worth the effort. He slunk through the territories of two large males in the darkest hour before dawn, the witching time, staying out of the fall of moonlight across open hills, using the shadows made by trees, and ridges, to slip through. There were no deer to be had, with older cougars on each side. At dawn one day in September, he sprinted across highway 280 to find himself on the paved streets of Mountain View, where the houses were neat and enormous and the cars shone like comets, moving just as fast. He crossed back over the freeway again, and this time the headlights of early commuters almost paralyzed him with fear. A woman on her way to work at a small tech startup saw him, the black tip of his tail, the great size of his haunches and paws, disappearing over the cement freeway shoulder. All day long he was in her, all muscle and gold, all silence. All day long, she wanted to cry.

He wandered further south, weaving along the edge of a neighborhood that leaked up into the hills. There was a narrow flush of grassland and coast live oak forest free of the scent-net of other mountain lions, along a skinny finger of land with no deer to speak of but plenty of raccoons, who ate the garbage at the edges of the human neighborhoods at night. Raccoon is a bitter meat compared to deer, and the young mountain lion grew hungry, worn thin from the effort of hunting small prey.

By day he slept on the cool limbs of madrone trees at the edges of an Open Space Preserve. He dreamt, in that absolving sunlight which feeds the grass, and the leaves, and the scrub-brush, of the warm hearts of deer, and of stars, dying and being born, and of all the worlds hinged to this one by the light of stars. By day the souls of cats roam, easy as water, between here and there, yesterday and tomorrow, sun and moon, hunting other kinds of hearts, the hearts in the knots of time. Upon waking, he knew none of this.

At night, he padded the trails nearest the parking lot of the Preserve, making them his territory with a net his own scent—a zigzagging, meandering affair, slivered between the home range of a big male who smelled of smoke and fresh hearts to the north and west, and a female to the south who smelled of streambeds and the sharp musk of milk.

It had been a dry year, the driest in a century. The grass, by October, was grey. The hills were worn and hungry and tired of dust. The deer were prey to other, stronger claws, and the raccoons grew wise and quick and began to raid garbage cans by day, to avoid the young mountain lion.

In the end, he had no choice. He started hunting by day. He was taut with his hunger and with the lines of house and freeway and scent net that hemmed him. He watched the human trail in the daylight, caught rabbits at dawn, slipped out of sight when the sound of human voices cut through the still warp of hill and oak forest.

When a little boy, tall as a deer, ran ahead of his parents one afternoon in late October, the mountain lion was watching from behind a thickness of coyotebrush. It didn't matter that the boy wasn't hoofed, and that he ran upright. The boy was larger than a raccoon, and running, and it was irrevocable, impossible to deny, the way his muscles wound and then sprang, the way he was gold and water in the air for a moment before his teeth snatched that small neck.

But he wasn't expecting the sharp scream, the pounding feet of the taller humans who came running and yelling and throwing stones. He dragged the boy halfway to the cover of coyotebrush, but a large rock hit his back flank; a flare of pain. The young mountain lion saw that this was like stealing a deer from the home of the big male who smelled of smoke: a danger, a boundary he couldn't cross. He let go of that small neck and ran into the brush. The little boy, scooped up fast into his father's arms, had several deep cuts that required stitches, but was otherwise unharmed.

BY DUSK, SEVEN FISH AND GAME OFFICERS had rolled up in the parking lot with rifles, nets, and coonhounds. There was a tranquilizing gun too, but nobody expected to use it. They blocked off the hiking trail with yellow caution tape, as for the scene of a crime, and let the dogs loose. The young mountain lion was so afraid of their smell of metal and smoke, dog and net, that, at the first sound of them, he climbed straight up a tall fir tree and didn't come down for two days. There was no chance to come down. The dogs were everywhere, as were the men and women in green, who camped out in heavy brown tents and talked loudly into the night. His paws ached, and his throat was all fire with thirst. The morning of the third day, a dog caught his scent at the base of the tree and bayed.

In the newspapers, the public was assured that, if at all possible, the mountain lion would be tranquilized and tested, to make sure he was a match with the DNA taken from the saliva on the little boy's neck. If so, he would be euthanized. But in the end, the Lieutenant Officer appraised the tree, called the mountain lion's behavior aberrant, to have remained so close to the place of the attack, so seemingly unafraid of human beings. Likely rabid. Certainly the same cougar as attacked the boy. Looking up into those branches, he said the cat wouldn't survive the fall anyway, and shot him through the head.

The young cougar's body was tested at a laboratory in Sacramento, and the DNA did indeed match. But he wasn't found to be rabid or sick in any way. Only young, and starving.

NOBODY IN THAT TIME, IN THAT PLACE, knew anything about such things as the souls of mountain lions. None of the officers gathered around the base of that tree as the shot rang out and his body fell seventy feet saw that something gold and bright as water stayed up there in the high branches and then, in one long coil of strength, leapt into the knotted sky.

IV.

At the end of the world, there are women twisting string from nettles and knotting it into nets. At the end of the world, women are retting and scutching, spinning and weaving the nettles into cloth. At the end of the world, they are waiting for the salmon to return up the creeks, through the alders. They have laid nets in the water. The nets are there like a promise of abundance, a reminder to the fish of the ecstasy of human cooking fires, that old dance, that old worship—you offer yourselves to our net, and we will sing to your spirits, and we will never stop telling your story, and we will look to the wild creeks of December, when you are coming, as men and women once looked on the figure of the cross, and the man crucified there—salvation. When the salmon come at last the women will leave the nets like quilts along the bottom of the creekbed, so the fish may bless them in their silver-rose rushing passage. Always, praise must come first. Then, in later years, feast.

At the end of the world there is a cloister of women who scutch and spin, ret and weave, from the great thickets of nettles that grow along the alder creek. Their grandmothers knew and feared the word *witch* upon their necks, but that time is over, and they are twisting and carding, weaving and knotting a new world into being around them every day. There is a reason no one but traders of clean heart and weary kind travellers find them in their cloister in the alderwood; all those women, binding knots in string.

IN THE FIRST WEEK OF DECEMBER, in the morning, Sister Matilda watched the nets in the creekbed, weighted down with smooth greywacke stones. That winter, the women took turns holding vigil for the salmon, because Mother Samsin had a dream all silver and scaled, and her dreams were never wrong. No salmon had been seen since the end of the world many centuries before. But the women knew that once a dream was had it was simply a matter of waiting, waiting for the net to call the salmon home. They knew how hard it was to be born, how much easier it was if you knew you were awaited, if you knew someone sat there, hoping for the sight of you alone.

But this morning, Matilda wasn't thinking of fish at all, as she was meant to be—it's hard to keep the mind on any one thing for an entire morning. She was thinking of willow shoots, and how she preferred their thick whipping resistance in weaving to the fine and tangling weight of nettle fibers, and how even now in December new growth was coming, copper colored, and how she had a toothache, and how her grandmother had once said something about the sky being a net, and in the knots souls might pass in and out, and she was wondering if she would learn this to be true when she herself died one day. She took a piece of her hair, black, and began braiding it, a tiny absent plait.

That's when a sound came from the creek, a heaving splash. She looked up from the dark strands of her braid for that dream—a silver sheaf of salmon, muscling upstream toward their birthing grounds. Instead, in the middle of the nearest net, she saw a skinny young male mountain lion stand, as if just having pushed himself through an impossibly tight doorway, diamond-shaped. He was up to his elbows in water. For a moment, he looked startled, just as disoriented as Matilda felt. Then he leapt, gold and water, onto the opposite bank, and shook himself. The spray of silver water around him was, for a moment, a vortex, a warp and a weft her eyes could hardly bear, because in it were suns and moons and knots where time had been born, and died. Inside that beaded net, he looked striped, and tassle-eared. Then the water fell to the ground and he was a regular golden cougar again, already smelling at the air for the cords of others like himself.

"You're no fish," whispered Matilda. She had heard stories of mountain lions, and every year or so one of the sisters found the tracks of a big female along the sandy creek, but she had never seen one. She couldn't bear to look away from his immaculate fur, his eyes which were the palest shade of green, like sagebrush. She knew it wasn't wise to look such a large cat in the eye.

But he was afraid of humans, and looked away first. Then he was gone into the pale trunks of the alders, following invisible cords of scent, his long tail swaying, sensing that home, at last, was near.

Nothing exciting ever happened to Matilda; this was why she hadn't paid much attention to the net in the creek. She was never the one to find the first baby-blue eyes blooming by the ferns, never the one to see the auburn face of a gray fox at dawn, never the one to find a shining thing on the seashore, an old necklace chain or piece of blue glass. But another sound was coming from the net now, and a huge wind moved the alder trees sidelong, and this time Matilda was on her feet, peering down through the rush of December water, wondering how it was that two exciting things might happen to her in one day. Her dark hair blew and tangled.

A large hole had been sliced in the net, by sharp claws. She could see the cut pieces wriggling in the current. Strangely, she couldn't see the bottom of the creek just there—no smooth red and black and grey pebbles, only a whirl of silver water that might have gone on forever, into the center of the world.

A salmon leapt out of it, vermillion. Then another, and another. In a moment, Matilda was soaked with their splashing, with the wind stirring the water, the great silver-red clamor of them everywhere, their bodies humming *home home home*.

OUR LADY OF NETTLES

Offer

For the first year you may not pick the nettles with your hands. Every morning for a year, while the dew still speckles the nettle leaves, you will brush your fingertips to the stalks in order to be stung like She was stung, in order to bring life and blood to your hands for the day's work. The spines shine with dew, delicate as glass, and your fingertips will become strong. You will choose a patch of nettles to touch, to pray beside, to sit with daily. You will learn about more than nettles this way. You may touch the tops of their leaves, and their seeds when they come pale-green and hanging in soft coils, but you may not pick. You may ask the nettles for the story of Nain, but only once you have given them your own story.

Every morning you will touch the nettle-spines with a fingertip, and you will leave white goose feathers at their ankles. You will bring water from the creek cupped in your hands. You will watch every new leaf begin and end at the patch of nettles where you sit, and every small bushtit who comes to eat the aphids from the stems. How, after all, can you cut and kill a thing, before you know who it is?

You will walk the dirt path of offering every day. You will carry alderwood trays of nettle tea into the spinning room when it rains, tonics of nettle seed and the roots of dandelions for your sisters in the weaving room. When the Sisters of the Harvest cut the nettles in autumn, you will watch, and you will mimic how they offer handfuls of nettle seeds to the ground and a dab of comfrey oil to the open wound.

You will learn to leave the new pollen of hazel catkins in the fresh pawprints of bobcats, alder-catkin pollen in the pawprints of the two mountain lions whose territories cross here, when they come to drink from the creek where the nettles are retted, swinging the black tips of their enormous tails.

Leave the scarlet juice of thimbleberries in the pawprints of the gray foxes. Leave shiny pieces of glass from the bayshore at the entrances of woodrat nests. Leave handfuls of spiderweb on tree branches for the winter wrens to make their nests. Leave soaproot stalks wherever the deer have walked. In rain puddles, float the petals of the winter-blooming calendula flowers from long ago gardens. Where the newts with orange bellies cross the paths from the hills down to the creek to mate after the winter storms, leave red stream stones, one in the wake of each newt, so that the next walker might pause, and know the newts are out, and step gingerly.

There is an ancient garden rose gone wild at the front door of the Convent of Our Lady of Nettles. It is as big as the whole wall, as big as an alder tree, branching and twining everywhere. The wall faces the southeast and the summer sunrise. At night, pick a rosebud and put it under your pillow. It is an offering for your own heart, to keep it open, despite everything, despite each day of your life before now which may have taught you that to close off the heart was the only way to survive. It is not easy to learn to soften, to touch each small creek stone with love, when it has been the safest thing to close, to hate, to use fear like a net around the body.

Ask the nettles, and they will tell you.

You have come for a story? Place your hand on my stem, there, where the hairs fringe and spike. Wait until the sting. Think of it like a trade. It wakes up your mind, the sap that moves up and down your straight-up back. We can't talk, not until that little shock, your fingerpad on my finest needles, a greeting. I now know what you are made of, I know now that you are full of wanting for the story of Nain, as are all of you when you first arrive.

We nettles have always been full of Nain. A thousand times around the sun before her coming, she was already in us. We could hear her breathing. Now that we have known her, my ancient grandmothers and grandfathers and therefore I, we have never not known her, because time is a flux of green rising and green falling to us, green spinning and green setting, the spindles of our flowers blooming, going to seed, stalks drying and dying and growing again. There is no start or end to it, just a big circle like the circle of a woman's hips, dancing. A thing which has happened to our grandfathers a thousand years ago is also in us, so Nain has held me though she died three hundred years before I was born.

She was always with us, my grandmothers of a thousand generations past who grew here and are therefore also me, who grew up in thickets around each city and each town, graveyards of stone and plastic and metal, barricaded so that your kind would have to loose all things, and begin again. We grew to protect the city places, the places heavily marked, from you, so they might die, so they might heal. But also we knew she would come, and others who needed refuge, and so we grew for her. We grew so she could cut us, and wet us, and through us remember what it is to spin and to weave.

We had missed—oh, how we had missed!—the dance that happens to us in human hands. It is not the dance of being eaten, nor of wind, nor of our seeds, swelling and swelling their pale pollen. It is the dance of being made into something wholly different. Your hands are two alchemists colored in all the shades the soil and the sand can be.

Our roots can be like your hands. They reach and they gather and they hold. Our roots here touch the body of Nain, buried deep in the mud earth of this creekbed, down there where the scraps of asphalt roads that once covered the creek now lie. It has been three hundred sun-journeys since she died an old lady with fur on her chin like the fur of our stalks, and was wrapped in a fine sheet woven of our fibers. She was buried here in her string skirt—for old women, you must remember, have as much dance in their hips as the young. How else could she dance up to the clouds, past the route on which the snow geese fly, to the place where the rain grows, without her skirt?

She was buried with her favorite deer-bone hair comb, with a spindle dipped in molten gold, with a little bucket of blackberry and passionfruit mead at her feet, with a sprig of yarrow dropped down in the grave. It was a summertime burial, and at the Convent the sisters were wailing under the summer fog, picking and throwing white yarrow down upon their Nain, because they knew the story, they knew of the Mother of Nain, and how it was the yarrow blossoms and the hemorrhage blood of birth that turned her newborn daughter, left out as an offering to the Drought, to a snow goose who flapped and flew away, gone from her forever.

My roots hold the bones of Nain, and the bones of Nain hold the story of Nain, and so you will hear it because you have come to me with white feathers, and you have come to me and spoken, and you have called me friend.

Harvest

Reach out your fingertips as if you are to touch the fur of a wild-cat. You will not wear gloves. The nettles like the taste of your skin, they like the touch of warmth before the bone blade. Grasp the nettle from below, smoothing the glass of those small furs upward. Invite at least one sting. It makes your hand alive.

Lay the goose feathers down, white, then sit and wait before you cut, until your mind is only gentle threads. Wait to be let in. All it takes is a certain glint of light on the dying nettle-spines, or a wind that seems to nod one crown of dry seeds *yes*, toward you, and your knife-hand hums a little, and you know it is all right. She is ready. Cut the stalk clean, at a low leaf node, as if you are slitting the neck of a great blue heron and do not want to cause pain. Hold the nettle stalk after it is cut; do not let it fall. Lower it to the ground, a sweep of fringed and jagged old green. Listen how it swishes.

Sing. It doesn't matter what. Sing something that makes you sway. Nettles like it when you sway, as they do, tall in the wind and ready to let go of the long, silken strings inside their skin. Repeat this all day, crouching in the shape of a woman giving birth. This is good for your digestion, and your hips.

You will smell the autumn in the alder leaves that are just barely starting to dry and wrinkle. You will hear it, when the golden-crowned sparrow returns from the north-country tun-dras three thousand miles away, and lands in the yellow willow branches, and sings—*twee, twa, twoo*, a minor descent. You should be finished with your harvest and your cut when the earliest golden-crowned sparrow returns. The nettle stalks long as women's spines should be laying down with the dew when that first golden-crowned sparrow comes, and sings right into the heart of the first day of autumn, with that hint of winter at the back of his throat. Then you can put your bone knife away, back in your pocket, and clean it gingerly before cutting any other thread, so as not to upset the yarns with the green blood of their daughters.

When you harvest the end-of-summer nettle stalks with your blade, that blade carved with six goose-women on one side and the seventh, Our Lady of Nettles, our Nain, on the other, know that you are also harvesting the old stalks standing still in the meadow-edges of your heart. You are cutting them gentle, but firm. You are laying them down soft. You are harvesting those things which have grown to the edges of their fullness in you. You are listening to the swish of their broad and jagged leaves as they sweep and sway to the ground.

> At the end, it is said, there was dancing. It is said by my grandmothers and by my grandfathers three hundred generations of seed back, it is said by the bones of Nain and the last pieces of her string skirt, suspended in the sharp deep acid of creek mud, that at the end there were seven women, and their hips moved round and swaying the way no woman's hips had danced in a thousand years. It is said that at their hips were skirts made of fine string, and that those string skirts swayed, and in that swaying the threads each spun of nettle lived again, moving against the thighs and hips of women, swirling like coils of rain touched by wind. It is said that the hips of women made spirals, their joints and muscles and bones swiveling like the wheel of stars moving from morning to night.

It is said that at the end, out in the marshgrass at the mouth of the Temescal Creek, which below was once asphalt highway, seven women swayed their hips both narrow and broad in skirts of nettle, and by morning, the slow caravans of clouds had come, and they had begun to open. It is said that six of their shadows were not all the way human yet in the waning moonlight, but still the winged silhouettes of snow geese.

That was at the end, oh my human sister, of the story of Nain. But there was another End, and it is connected to the beginning of Nain. It was the very tail tip of a different world, the world underneath, the world of the buried tar, the city. That ending lasted seven hundred journeys around the sun. It is said that once, human people put all of their knowing into a strange web, into a stranger cloud, and not into their palm pads, their heart-valleys, their sturdy feet. They put their knowing into a web, into a cloud, and it made you naked though you thought it made you vast. Your people did not make a map of blood and iron, of violet-light and earth-curve and story in your sternums, like the snow geese do. The geese forever know the way home, because they have never taken it out of their breasts and given it away.

And so, when the cloud dissolved, as clouds always do in the end, and when the million strings of web fell apart in a single flooding rain, when the cities that the world held together by strands of cloud and web went dark because their people had forgotten even how to make fire with sticks and stones, there were no maps to show them the way home. Instead, the old earth moved, and hissed, and spat, and flooded, and fired, and for seven hundred journeys around the sun your kind only clung on, and lost all the rest of what they might have known.

When it was over, when the water receded, when

the earth stilled, when the creeks started again to run clean of their poisons, though no salmon dared swim them yet, that's when we came, and grew. It is said by my grandmothers and my grandfathers a thousand seeds back that we grew up as if overnight, and ringed each city, each house, with our stalks all furred and stinging. It is said that we grew with our roots in the shit of the past, and that we grew thicker and more tangled than walls, to keep your kind away from those places, to force you to begin all over again. Not to pick up fallen pieces and try to make the same things again. To make you start again with only our hearts and your hands.

It did not begin well, for it is not always a gentle heart that survives when the world has turned violent. It was those vicious of heart and hand who survived, who took to hilltops with guns until the powder ran out, and killed anyone who came near, because there was not enough food or water. The strong, you see, in one sense of the word. The strong of limb, the hard of heart. What they remembered was only how to storm, and slash, and carry on. They knew how to take, and so they did, and when the gunpowder was gone, and every last tin of food, they tried to breach us, they tried to come through our thickets nine feet tall and into the cities, but our stinging was not just a bright and sharp pain, a red rash of blisters. We had madness in our stings for those who came to raid the lands of dead houses and streets and hospitals and offices, that graveyard. It was not a gentle madness.

Ret

Take the retting net down to the shallow and fast-moving part of the creek, to the last bend of the yellow willows before the snaking marsh begins, the tule and then the saltgrass. Carry the bundles of nettle—long as your spine from tailbone to crown—right up close to your chest. The dew has softened them. If they sting you slightly it will only puncture tiny pinpricks against your breast, making you feel the place your heart lives. The net is made in crocheted loops and spirals of nettle cordage, sealed with the resin of bishop pine trees. When laid flat on the ground, the net resembles the silhouettes of trillium flowers, geometrically woven together as one circle. Around the edge is a string that cinches. Lay it out on the sandy flat place among the rank old growth of the wood mint.

Place your armload of nettles in the center of the net, tops facing the stream, roots facing you. Fold the netting over them, like tucking in a child. Pull the two strings until the net makes a sack. Ease it into the creek where the water moves fastest. Loop each end of the string to the retting hooks lashed to the bases of willows, so that the nettles and their netted bag don't float out to sea, so that the water eases and eases the fibers around the pithy cores loose, yet does not rot away the fibers themselves. This is a balance. You must check on them at dawn and at dusk, when the birds give their chorus.

Nettles move water down through your body, washing away the stones, the thorns. Let the water wash through the nettles, chiming, for half a moon, until the earliest snow geese begin to land again out on the bay and in its tules, honking, bringing the rain behind them in swaying strings of wet. Every morning and every evening for the span of new moon to full come down to the creek-place of retting with your other Sisters of the Ret and sprinkle a handful of ash from the fire-pit inside the Convent, where the stories are told at night, onto your own retting-net of nettles. They like the taste of that ghost of fire, as the water takes their stalks apart. They like the taste of human stories.

When you take your bundle of nettles down to the creek and lower it into the moving water to rot the pith from the fibers, to break down the nettle into her parts, bring also a thing from under your ribs which can be laid there in the water too, and washed, rotting, into something new, something that will begin to glint gold under the current.

Three hundred more sun-journeys passed. Men made blades of stone and killed the deer without thanks and without mercy. Camps were formed, led by Masters who commanded the most fear, and whether or not all the men who followed them were the same, it did not matter, because the human communities they made were mean, and hard.

But it is never so simple as a good and a bad. I like to say that your kind, your men and your women were, underneath everything, afraid, and did not remember how to love the world as much as themselves. In trying so hard to live, they had forgotten from whence their life came. They had forgotten because it undoes you— to love the dark eyes of a doe, her narrow jaw and soft nose, moving as she chews, to love her in the place in your chest that loves people, and then to kill her because you must, because you as a human are also a killer, as a mountain lion is. You must kill to eat. You cannot eat sun.

And so when I tell this story I like to say that to the people of Nain, it seemed easier to kill and not to love at once. But to do such a thing is like taking bucket by bucket of water from a creek, only to find it dry and no rain coming. Her people chose to kill without love because it was all they knew how to do, and also because they did not want their hearts to break open when they pierced the doe through her own. Worst of all, they feared she did not love them either. Without love, there are no threads hitching you to each and every thing—

to us, to the woodrat in his nest, to the newts heading
for the creek, to the kestrel as she hunts the meadows,
to the clouds as they travel in a white herd from elsewhere. You are alone.

They had forgotten that dancing and praying are
the only ways to keep your heart from breaking when
the doe's own heart splits in two. They forgot the secret
truth—that it breaks anyway, whether you love her or
you don't. It breaks and it no longer works properly,
when you don't, like one of your spinning wheels whose
parts fall into pieces, and cannot be rejoined. If you
love, it breaks, but you learn how to put it together
again with song, with the swaying of hips, with spider-
webs, just as the hummingbird does to seal together
each bit of nest.

If a doe is only an object for your killing, for your
taking, the world becomes made again of things pos-
sessed, and a woman becomes one of them. When
the killing-fever comes to define the men who live
in a place, in a time, in a land, the shape of a woman
becomes a treasure and in danger of being stolen, or
running away like the does on black hooves.

Nain was born into a place like this. For a time, all
the places where people gathered around the big old salt
bay, after one End and before another, were like this,
and if you felt different things moving in your heart,
you hid them. You gave yourself two faces and you did
not resist, because after all, it is better to have a heart
weary and sore and shredded, but alive, than one cut
in two with a blade. And so when a Drought did come,
and it did not rain for four years, and everything but us
nettles went brown and dusty—we stayed evergreen until the day the girl called Nain came, and harvested, and
spun us—it was decreed that newborn daughters should

be sacrificed on the stones of a dry creekbed. They were left there still wet from their mothers for a coyote or a cougar or a cloud, to eat.

Six little ones were left on the stone in the winter Camp of Nain's people, just beyond the ridge of oak-filled hills you see from here, to the east, just east of where the creek starts, just beyond the place we once made our barricade, beyond the edge of the last house, collapsed to nothing but brick dust and an orange tree. The first of the six daughters given to the creek to bring the rain was Nain's older sister. Their mother went wild.

When that tiny babe, wet and wrinkled as fawn-skin, was taken from her arms, the Mother of Nain began to scream, and in that scream was a breaking of each part of herself. She wailed and she raved, her thick black curls wet with the sweat of labor, and sorrow opened up the secret places under her ribs and in her hips where she had been keeping, all her years, the small beautiful things. They had kept her alive as much as blood and air did. A newt with an orange belly who left feathered tracks on the muddy bank of a creek; the sparkle of a poppy petal when held up to the eye; the calling of two winter snow geese to each other high up in the sky.

That rending made her hemorrhage there in the dark on the birth bed, where she had been left alone to scream. She forced herself to stand anyway, wavering. She left the birthhouse. There was no moon, and so she had no shadow. She smelled the air and followed on it the smell of her baby, as a cougress would. She left the circle of skin tents. She crossed the field, snapping stalks of yarrow in her fingers, the last stalks to bloom until the Drought was done. She ducked through the bare arms of buckeye branches, stepped softly on their humus. She walked the dry creekbed, stumbling on rocks, bleeding heavily, chewing the yarrow flowers and pressing them between her legs to staunch the blood, eating the bitter leaves, reeling.

She heard and followed a sound, a mewling, and at the end of it she saw her baby girl on the flat stone, crying and bare. Her own heart and her womb rent further, so that with the hemorrhage blood came also the geese, calling in the sky, which she had tucked under her ribs. She stumbled, howling in the voices of mountain lions who have lost their newborns, and cannot bring them back, and picked the baby up in her bloody hands, stuck with the white of the yarrow. She knew she could not bring her back home, knew also that she could not live if her little one died here, and as she howled and held her baby, the secret strength of heart and hip that her body had kept hidden unfurled, a coiled strand of feather-white. The baby became a snow goose, just fledged, in her hands. She opened her wings, she reached her neck, newer and softer than any just-fallen snow on the eastern mountains, she looked back once at the dark eyes of her mother, and then, in a panic of feathers, flew up into the night.

By morning, a thirsty coyote had lapped up the trail of blood, and so no trace remained of the thing the Mother of Nain had done. The yarrow stopped her bleeding, but it did not close the secret in her that had been opened. The following rainless winter, when a little girl was taken newborn-wet from a different mother's arms, the Mother of Nain slipped out in the darkest part of the night, and crept to the same greywacke stone with the dried yarrow crumbled in her pocket, and her moon-blood in her. She touched the girl-baby—blonde where hers had been dark, but otherwise no different, another mewling wet thing barely human yet—on all

four corners of her body, and her heart, with that yarrow
dust and that blood. In her mind she held the memory
of her daughter, a snow goose winging north. Under her
hands, then, was a second goose, pale as clouds, and off
it flew, honking.

Stook

When the sky is a wet hinge between autumn and winter, and all
of a sudden cold, when the last stragglers of the golden-crowned
sparrows have arrived from the north, when rose hips are heavy
on the wild rose, when the big-leafed maples turn the color of
embers, when the mountain lioness who stalks the creek weans
her cubs from milk and shows them how to hunt, when the
moon is also full, go out under it and bring your net in.

Using moonlight, gather up your nettles from the water, and
relish that cold splash. Your hands will go green and smelling
with rotted nettle skin. Tie up your bundles no more than twenty-nine stalks per bunch, with the Tying Up Cords. You will
make your own Tying Up Cords when you become a Sister of
Spin, but that is still three years away. They are coated in the
rare beeswax of the black bumblebees who shake the bells of the
manzanita flowers up the ridge-top for their pollen. The nettles
like to be held by a thing of pure sweetness when they emerge
from the water and find themselves retted, rotted, transmuted
to the strings of their bodies, which once held them together.
Bring them, tied into their stooking bundles, in by the firelight
on the Night of Hallowing, as you and your sisters dance in fine
nettle-spun veils.

On that evening, the air is full of other veils. It is the night
to lift them, for she, Nain, might be over the other side, still
spinning. The bones underneath the skin of the world you know
are there, behind the veils. As you dance and lift the veils of
yourself, you will see how you are spun into the web of the world,

and your bones are as white as the milk of brush rabbit does, your bones have the songs of human time in them, and love, and the ghosts of your grandmothers and your grandfathers.

The nettles in their stook bundles must be leaned up against the back wall where your shadows and the shadows of the flames dance, because it is warmest there, and because those stalks are themselves thinned veils who once danced, who will dance again. First, they must be dried by the heat of that fire on the Night of Hallowing, when the sisters dance the veil. They must dry for another twenty-nine nights at least, the passage of a moon and also one of the eggs, moon-round, in your own womb. They must dry inside, leaning against the wall of the main room where you and your sisters eat, and gossip, and laugh through the cold nights.

When you stack and tie the wet nettles, when you lean them in neat sheaves inside the radius of the fire's heat, so they may dry, and shrink, there is a part of you that also leans into the heat, that steams, and dries, and turns a golden-crisp color you never were before, light as feathers.

The Mother of Nain saved all six girl-babies left in the dry creekbed for the Drought this way, making them six snow geese instead who flew away north. In the seventh year, it rained, and she gave birth to Nain, and for some time the hills around the Bay were green again. But the Mother of Nain had a way of walking, after that, which made the Master of her Camp uneasy. She seemed to leave pollen in her wake, she seemed to make the manzanita flowers hum as the bees did, she seemed to glow, too beautiful for her own good. She taught her little Nain how to have one skin, one self, which was quiet and plain and eyes down, and another which was fierce, and hoarded beautiful small sights like the dusky-footed woodrats do pretty glass. She poured all her yarrow-pollen-light, her blood with the maps of snow geese in it, into her Nain.

When it did not rain again twelve years later, the Master—who had tried to take her as his second wife down by the creek rocks as she washed her husband's deerskins, pushing her back to an oak tree with its spiky leaves beneath their bare feet, only to find a spiking pain just as sharp between his legs, and a look in the Mother of Nain's eyes that made him go cold—called it her doing, because he hated her now, and wanted her dead. He wanted her burned so that glow in her, that thorn of fire in her eyes, didn't spark and light the other women, quick as the dry hills under wildfire.

He said that only a fire made of the Mother of Nain and the black smoke from her skin and bones would turn the clouds to rain. He hated her enough that he ordered first to have her heart broken: to take her Nain. He proclaimed that little Nain—an odd, quiet child, slim and prickly as the teasels with their summer brown combs, an unsettling child to look at, for she was all one color, an acorn, except her pale green eyes—who had just begun her moon blood, should be sacrificed. That river of blood in her should be given over to the rivers of rain gone missing far away in the sky.

The Mother of Nain had known it would be her own blood, every drop of it, that would be given over to the dry hills this time. She had, only the night before, tried to touch Nain with blood and yarrow, but no feathers had grown, no long white neck, no change at all, only her pale green eyes big and scared because underneath her rabbit-skin dress, Nain could smell her mother afraid, and her mother was never afraid. *Only a newborn soul is yet soft enough to become a snow goose, not a girl of twelve, and bleeding*, her mother whispered. She told her daughter of the six snow geese, and wept.

Nain never saw her mother again after that night. Her mother gave her a satchel of food, a stolen knife, and told the girl to go straight into the nettles-thickets, toward the bay, for madness was better than death.

And so Nain ran.

In the morning, her mother was burned on a platform of stone, lashed to dry oak branches. They burned her even though a fire was fool's work in that dry time, because the Master wanted to see those black cords reaching up, up, into the sky, and into the hearts of the women watching.

It is said that Nain's father went quietly out to the dry creekbed afterward, and heaved, sobbing. His daughter, his wife, gone, and how he had loved them; they had never known how much. He had been too afraid to love them tenderly, freely, and now he never could again.

Scutch

An egg must be broken open by the hard small beak of the new chick, before the little one can emerge, glowing with the inside world that has yet to be touched by air. It is the same with the sheaves of nettle, fireside-dried, having felt both the shadows of veiled dance and the gossip of women at dinner and over mugs of huckleberry mead. They must be cracked open gently, like eggs with something new inside.

One moon past the Night of Hallowing, the dried nettles must be broken away from their pithy wood centers, the fibers around them a glint of blonde and soft. On that day, with your sisters in the year of Scutch, on the stalk-beating floor packed hard by the scutch mallets and clogs of women, lay the nettles down again with their root-ends at your knees and their tops pointing away.

Never work them upside down. That is like brushing the fur of a wildcat, backward. Hold the stalks at their bases while another sister beats them with an alderwood mallet. Turn the nettles so they are loosed from their pith-centers and their skin evenly.

Take turns—the hold and rotate, the beat. Do not hit the nettles with any of your anger. You may have anger in you somewhere, hiding, that you did not know about, and it may want to spring out. Let your anger be the thing the retting water washes in your year of Ret, the thing the stooks by the fireside dry in your year of Stook. Do not put it back through the mallet into the breaking open of nettles. This is why you must also dance on the scutching floor, and not just beat.

When the nettle bundle in your hand has been beaten once, from base to tip, lay your mallet down. Spread the stalks out across the floor. Leave a little space around you. Each sister must dance on her own nettles. Partly this is so the fibers do not tangle and fly everywhere. Also this is because you must learn to know your ground, and stay standing on it. Put on the alderwood clogs whose soles are carved with the webbed feet of geese. Dance while your Sisters of Weave play the deer-hide drums, and your Sisters of Spin pluck the bobcat-gut strings of turtle-shell lutes. Do not feel envy, or impatience, as you stomp and then sway, stomp and then sway, for the sisters who have done the Eight, and who wear their string skirts now, dancing, thighs bare, those corded skirts giving a sway to their hips that is almost too lovely, too rich, for words. Do not feel envy for the sisters who have done the Eight and get to carry one swathe of harvested nettles from their beginning all the way to their end each year. Your time will come.

That sway of nettle strings at the hips of women is meant to make the heart ache, the very sun and the very soil ache with longing for the making of pollen, of rain, of eggs, of embryos, of bark, of winter fur on the coats of coyotes, mating plumage on the yellow crowns of siskins, of the two-plies of nettle string, spun as one, of the warp and the weft and the birth of a cloth.

Now, today, you are only a Sister of Scutch. All year you have been the Scutch. All year the only time you may handle the nettles is now, when you scutch them. Last year you only handled the nettles for the stook. But all year you have been the breaking open, the shattering of shells, the separation of fiber from chaff. In your thoughts you have been scutching, breaking open each old thing which must be broken to find the fibers inside. By the first day of winter, as you dance on the scutching floor, you are ready, you are watching your own pithy parts fall away, too. You are learning how it is that the dance and stomp and sway of hips is a making, and a memory of seven women, string skirts swaying the rainclouds down to their very knees with yearning.

Gather the coils and strands of blonde fiber now laying about the floor. Shake them, watch the pith fall. Place the uncombed fibers in the willow baskets in the Carding Room, and sweep the floor. The pith will be mashed and sieved into thick sheets of paper for the keeping of the Lives of Nettles, and the Stories of the Nettle Sisters, and the Tarot of Nain, in case all other things fall away, and none of you are left to speak of it.

> Nain followed the creekbed that night, running, glad
> of all her scrambling over the rocks and up the live
> oaks when in the company of women gathering acorns.
> Her mother had never told her to stop, to come down,
> while the other mothers ordered their own children out
> of trees. Nain was always knee-scraped, lichen-dusted,
> moss in her hair, flushed. She ran over the rocks and
> roots now, hardly looking down, trusting her mother, as
> she always had. She ran and her mind flew out around
> her like the six snow geese, one of them her own sister,
> her sister who had never been more than a tiny pink
> wrinkle of wet and human skin. Her mind flew, white-
> winged, to those girls turned goose-feathered, and her

mother turning them, and how she might have become
a snow goose too, flying far up and north, instead of
a girl in a creekbed, running, running, following the
tributaries up a ridge, thinking of her lost sister, wanting
her.

She came to the first ruins of old houses where my
grandmother nettles began, abrupt, our fringe of green
glowing in the dawn light. Nain was afraid of madness
more than of pain, but her mother had told her through
the nettles, toward the bay, and so she hardly hesitated, she went in through our toothed green leaves, our
needles. When we pricked Nain's hands, her neck, her
arms, through her rabbit skin dress, touching her blood,
we rippled though the air was windless. We shuddered
with relief. Nain whimpered, stinging, but felt no
madness, so she kept walking, following a big spur of the
creek this side of the ridge, down steep hills so long ago
lined with tar and house, now a strange forest of lemon
tree, rose bush, maple, palm, wild passionfruit vine, and
the hint amidst them of a path, of depressions where
house foundations had once been laid.

The madness, you see, my human sister, was never
madness at all, but an opening wider of the mind. Some
minds open wide and poison spills in, because poison
is somewhere in the heart. Other minds open wide and
the rest of the world comes in.

Nain stumbled, tired and stinging with small red
nettle blisters, through the ruins of old schools, fallen
freeways, neighborhoods of violence, neighborhoods
of peace, all of them now unrecognizable and part of
one tangle of live oaks and lone redwoods planted at
forgotten intersections, dry grass and dead blackberry
vines and soil, soil pushed up and over all the metals,
the asphalts, the plastics.

Gradually, Nain began to make out the sound of another pair of bare feet on the dry dirt path behind her. The tingling pain of our stings crept up the back of her neck, and she suddenly turned, and with her mind propped open wide by our needles, she saw her, our Lady Nettle. To you, Nain is Your Lady of Nettles. To us, our Lady Nettle is the form we take when we are speaking in the tongues of humans. Right now, my sister, I am Lady Nettle, but you cannot see me, because your mind is not flung open wide like a door, not yet.

The woman Nain saw before her had skin all furred with glossy white spines and hair a jagged sweep of chlorophyll. Her hips were so narrow, narrow as nettles, but they swung with a short skirt of beautiful string. The skirt had a woven waist and knotted edge all glinting and clinking with tiny bits of metal from that older world, soldered into gentle beads. She wore a loose blouse of that same fine woven fabric, palest of white-greens. Nain had never seen fibers spun and woven together, only gut-string. Those swaying strings, gently moving as our stalks in a breeze, the drape of that shirt, were like wind and bird feathers and grace, captured against the body of a woman, coaxing it to dance. For the woman swayed as she walked, hands curving, catching, opening, closing, and as she walked the string skirt moved, hiding none of our Lady Nettle's green skin.

It is said that Lady Nettle took Nain's hand, and her fingers stung the girl, but she did not let go. They walked together until it was late in the afternoon, far around the bay's edge, until they came to a creek. The sun on the water touched them, and when they reached a bend in the creek thick with nettles, and alders, with willows all bare of leaves, Lady Nettle left Nain, saying only: *gather, spin and weave seven string skirts of my fibers,*

of my golden hair, for yourself and your sister geese, and
they will come back to you, women again, with rain under
their wings.

Nain was only a girl of twelve the day Lady Nettle
left her at the creek bank where everything was dry but
the stalks of my grandmothers three hundred seed-births
ago. For many hours Nain's palms stung from holding
the hand of Lady Nettle, but she was not thinking of
her hands. She was thinking of that skirt, and its twined
cords, its woven waist. She had never seen such a thing,
but something stood up in her chest, in the threaded
veins that led to her heart. She saw the skirt in her
mind's eye the way her mother had taught her to catch
with her eyes the tiny beauties, the nuances of each
thing—footprints left behind, small as dandelion seeds,
by harvest mice—and so she saw it and felt as if she had
always known it.

She saw it the way the monarch butterfly, migrating
to the pine trees beyond the ridge for their winter
hibernation, know the exact tree of their ancestors,
though they have never made this journey before, nor
will they again. Nain saw that skirt in her mind as she
crouched alone and frightened—of what it would mean
if someone found her and let all of her blood spill out
on the dry creekbed to call down the rain, frightened
of the new bright moon-blood on her thighs which had
been the reason for her running away, with no time
for her mother to tell her not to be afraid, to find dry
tule stalks, and bundle them to catch the blood. She
thought of the skirt for several days as she crouched
there in the nettles, shivering with the fear and loneliness her life had become. For days she watched our
stalks swaying in a small wind, and then she knew, all at
once, how to begin.

She cut us so tenderly with her little deer-bone knife. She sang child-songs, lullabies, croons her mother had sung to her. But our burning on her hands soon seared too much, like holding fire. She was desperate and scared; she lurched at every small noise. She did not know then to hold us gingerly, smoothing us like fur. Howling, she threw us instead into the water. She plunged her hands into that old muddy flow. She paced the streambank, prodding the stalks of my three-hundred time grandmothers, weeping, missing her mother, missing the rain, missing the sister she had never known, missing her father who had been made hard by the Master of Camp, but who was always as gentle with his girl as with a newborn rabbit, explaining to her how to hunt a thing, in secret, though all she could ever try was throwing rocks at trees.

On the fifth day she was starving. Her blood was dry on her legs. It made her weak, the loss of it, and she craved blood to eat. She had never killed a creature, but she also knew she would not live if she didn't learn to, because in the dryness no tree had fruit, nor nuts, though it was autumn. With a smooth stone thrown lucky and straight, she killed the red-furred squirrel who had chattered at her and kept her company the past few days. She did not really expect to hit him. When he fell, limp, from the alder limb, blood on his skull, she felt her heart lurch and heave. She curled beside him on the ground weeping, weeping, for his small sweet life gone out of him with the strike of one stone.

Then dusk came, and she held him limp in her arms, and she sang a lullaby. She built a fire and she moved with that squirrel in her arms in a swaying motion like she had seen the Lady Nettle make. Then with her knife she made a mess but managed to pull off his skin and cooked him on her fire, crying through her eyes for sadness, through her tongue for hunger.

It is said that a man heard Nain's howling from the nettle-pain. A man who was a hunter, a man who called himself Robin after the red-breasted bird, a man who slept on oak limbs and prayed every time he killed a deer because it was proper in his heart to do so. You see, our nettle barricades had become a refuge for those who pushed through them seeking asylum, for those on the run whose hearts had kindness. Men who wept when they killed, men who could not kill at all. Not women, not before Nain, because women were guarded too close, tethered down.

When the hunter who called himself Robin heard the hooting shrieks of Nain, girlish, shrill, he came quietly, as if upon a doe with her fawn. He sat in the shadows beyond the nettles and watched her as he would that doe and fawn, not wanting to frighten, only wanting to know. He sat and watched her and felt a big sorrow rising, for himself ten years past, her age when he had run from his Camp and into the nettles because he had been too soft.

When she wept at the dead squirrel, and sang, and danced, he looked away, because his heart hurt and he thought of the little sister he had left behind. He vowed then that he would protect her, this girl brown as the dry land and with eyes green-gold as nettles in sun. He would protect her so well she would never know he was there at all. He could see the fear in her, and knew that if she ever saw him, she would run. Inside our stinging barricades, men kept to themselves mostly, hermit-types, but Robin could not say what the sight of a girl pure as any young doe might do to a lonely man who had not been in the habit of reverence and discipline, a man who had been lonely for years.

In the morning, when Nain found a handful of dried blackberries and wild onion roots by her fire, she sniffed them, and did not eat them for several days, until her hunger made her. Nobody came to claim a reward for the favor, and then Nain forgot all about it, because in the creek, two weeks since she'd placed them, the nettles had changed. Their skin was loose. Beneath was a hint of golden hair.

Card

The nettle is a woman and she enjoys her hair combed. If the day is without rain, go outside with the two carding combs and your hanks of nettle fiber. Sit near enough to the creek that you can hear it moving. The alders, bare now, will click and sway their pale-fingered branches. Sit where you can see the old stands of nettle, and how the very first fringe of green may be just pushing up tongues through the soil. You may sit on a blanket dyed with mushrooms in stripes of yellow and of blue. You may bring clay cups of tea that steam, to keep your hands warm, and your throat wet, and you may sit with other sisters as your carding combs clank and muss at the nettle fibers until they are gold clouds of fine hair, ready for spinning.

The teeth of the combs are hard, and sharp, and so the nettle likes to be out in the air, near her daughters and her sons, so that the small pieces that fall away will stay near their root-place. You will begin to make a rhythm with the carding combs—a *brush brush hiss*, *brush brush hiss*, like the *brush brush hiss* of the winter bare alders and the winter-full creek, untangling that which was knotted, letting each hair glint and smooth.

The combs are made with teeth from the thorns of the hawthorn trees gone wild, the last ghosts of the houses once here. They have been dipped in the Convent's one vat of molten Sierra gold, gold brought to Nain from the people of the mountains to the east, and used only for our tools, not for our bodies. The teeth of hawthorn pierce, but in the way of love that pierces, and the gold holds them strong, it keeps them from breaking against the strength of nettles.

During the whole year leading up to the days when you sit in the early winter sun, carding the scutched fibers with your sisters, you will first untangle the knots in your own spirit, carding and carding with strong teeth. You will untangle the quarreling words of others, smooth them flat, all one way. You will untangle fallen skeins for the Sisters in the year of Weave at their looms. You will untangle mysteries you see around you in mud and feather and root—whose footprints are those, walking the creek-edge, and what is their story? Where does the tiny pink-throated hummingbird nest, and what does she use to build it? What parts of the body do the flower and the root of the plant called trillium correspond to, and what is their healing nature?

> For seven years Robin left gifts for the girl Nain, and never once did she see him, nor realize that the reason she did not see another human soul was that he protected her, he persuaded others without a word to veer a different way, planting nettles, scattering bones, always leaving her a freshly killed rabbit, a quail, clams. Nain came to believe it was Lady Nettle, or some other alderwood spirit, and so she left small offerings in return in the places where his were found—a hummingbird feather, a stone with a quartz streak, an odd song, minor and sad as the golden-crowned sparrow's.
>
> It took Nain six years to learn the way of the ret, the stook, the scutch, the card, the spin, and the seventh year to weave. In those seven years it rained seven times, just enough to wet the land, to keep it alive, nothing more. In those seven years, a flight of six snow

geese landed and found Nain each year on the day that is a hinge between autumn and winter. The first time, Nain wept, and Robin, who saw the geese land, wept too. He knew then for certain that he was not wrong to protect this strange girl, and the nettles she wetted and stripped, wetted and combed with the thorns she broke off overgrown hawthorns, all mysterious to him, but done with such solemnity he knew that one day he would see something miraculous, so long as he held that net around her. When he saw the snow geese walk on orange webbed feet right to Nain's side, where she sat with the retted wet fibers in her lap, cursing at her clumsy hands, he went on his knees in a posture of prayer. A chill went down his spine.

When the geese came honking gently, black-edged wings folded, necks all snow, and pressed themselves to Nain's sides, and stayed that way all night, keeping her warm, grunting in their goose-sleep, Nain dreamt of tundras blooming purple with saxifrage and lupine and fireweed. She dreamt of eggs the color of milk in nests of white goose-down, and the feeling of them under her breast, which in the dream was white and feathered. She dreamt of a mate who flew beside her all the way south, and back again, and she dreamt of downy chicks and the terror of the quick fox, the beauty of the gentle velvet noses of caribou, sniffing. She dreamt of flying through clouds white as the eggs of geese, and those clouds were full of rain. She woke, weeping, and the geese were gone, leaving only feathers to prove they'd been there at all.

Each year when they visited, and Nain dreamt of northern tundras and being in a goose body, the geese dreamt of being in hers, a human woman with hands, with hips that grew and formed. For at the center of each snow goose was a newborn human who had never been a girl, nor yet a woman.

If they had not come, Nain might have given up. She might have lost her hope, or gone feral with loneliness. She might have joined the mountain lion who once and only once padded through the middle of her little camp, swished his black-tipped tail, looked at her with eyes the same as hers. Robin had almost revealed himself, then, thinking the lion was drought-crazed, hungry, but the cat walked away gently, swaying his haunches. Instead of hiding in fear, Nain filled his pawprints with the only hazel catkins to emerge that winter. She touched them every day until her fingerprints had replaced the pads of the cat's paws.

It is said that Nain fell in love with a hunter, but maybe it was a cat and not a man at all, for she was lonely, and spoke only to nettles, to alders, to songbirds, to the mountain lion she saw that once, but thought she heard from time to time, or felt watching her. She did not fear him, because he never harmed her, and sometimes left her pawprints to touch, and a golden hair. But maybe those eyes watching, those feet padding protectively, were also Robin, and maybe she loved both a hunting man and a hunting cat, because she felt something of both of them near her. The mountain lion was the only one of the two she ever saw, until the end, and he is so beautiful a creature, you cannot help but love him.

It was the snow geese who kept Nain with us, because they came back year by year, and Robin who brought food to her doorstep and asked for nothing in exchange. It was the snow geese who reminded Nain why she kept at the teasing and peeling of our stalks in her hands. The geese and the vision of the skirt of strings, which she etched and re-etched in the mud until one day, six years in, when she beat the dry stalks of my ancient grandmothers, and combed them with the haw-thorn needles fixed to her palms, the pieces did not snap, too short to be used, like they usually did. We fell into her lap, long and golden and clean. She spun our fibers immediately between her fingers, against her thigh, and wept again. It was such slow work; it would surely take a lifetime, but this year the creek was a single puddle and her throat always dry. She had not seen a deer in months, and no leaf buds pressed out at all at the tips of willows. This year, the land was starting to die.

She lay awake that night and watched the stars move. She saw the one she knew as the Hunter, rising. Her eyelids were full of the gold hairs of our fibers, spinning and spinning in her hands. She'd tried to tie us to a stone for weight, so she had something pulling us away from her to make a twist. For a moment, she saw the stars of the Hunter spinning, threaded, the fiber coming in at the top point, whirling around a shaft that ran from the bottom star to the top, the three parallel stars in the middle a weight to make it spin.

In the morning Nain drew that constellation in the sandy mud and laughed with delight. And so Nain came to make the first spindle in a thousand years, from the legbone of a fawn, from stone with a hole. Then she carved an alder stick into a forked tool, to loop all of her golden nettle fiber around to feed into her spinning, bit by bit, and that was the first distaff. Both took the shape of those winter stars.

Nain spun and she spun, and then, like the monarch who knows the wintergrove she has never seen, Nain's hands found the weaving naturally, using perfect strips of alder bark to thread her warps, to lift and lower the shed to bring the weft through.

Spin

You must remember that when you spin, the fibers drafted through your fingers have a life of their own. They will move for you like water or like clouds, drifting. Your hands are guides. They never grasp. They nudge and let the gold strands of the nettle looped around your distaff respond to the spin of the wheel. Its pull is a tide, each hair whorled and whirring, catching up its sister and brother fibers in that whir, in that coiling S-twist. Spinning is like breathing the nettle fiber *in out, in out*, through your fingers.

The wheel is made all of the supple branches and trunks of the yellow willows who grow beside the nettles. You may not build a wheel until you have spent your year as Sister of the Spin using only the spindle, just as you may not make the goose-carved clogs until you have spent your year as Sister of the Scutch, nor your bone knife until you have been a Sister of the Harvest. The distaff is made of the most slender of willow branches, shaped like the five fingers of the hand, come to a single point that gestures up toward the rainclouds, dancing, shaped like a closed seedpod in autumn, when all its flesh is gone and only its five fibrous strings remain. Up in the winter sky is a constellation once called Orion, the Hunter. Once you have spun, you will see why we call it Nain's Distaff, and the night sky itself the Wheel, as it spins through the seasons.

You must remember that the spinning, and not the weaving, is the nettle's dance, fibers twisting around each other, flying from distaff to fingers to bobbin, dancing just like the sky around us does through the year. From winter until the beginning of spring is the time of the Spin. When the weather is wet, spin at the wheel with your Sisters of Spin. Keep the fire lit. Tell the stories of Nain, spin out her yarn. Tell your story, too, spin it out in your heart, through your throat, into the air.

When the weather is fair, take your dancing-distaff, your

dancing-spindle, out to the meadow beyond the Convent walls where the grass is starting to turn green all over. Go to the places where the coyotes have been out dancing together their winter courtship, their paws making trails that thread in and out, over under, as they trot and frisk along the muddy banks, along the muddy footpaths you and your sisters use daily to travel down to the bay edge to gather the clams. The coyotes, too, like to nose the shorelines, dancing close at the heels, two trails plied, dreaming again of pups.

When the weather is fair, take your spindle and your distaff out, walk in the wake of the coyotes who are loving, and then dance so that the spindle sways, and the thread of nettle feels the wind. All the while your hands never stop their draft, their guide, their gentle motions, like dreaming, like clouds moving slow but sure. Your hands are the two sides of the sky, guiding clouds. They are the two sides of the creekbed, guiding the water to the bay, whirring the nimbus downward into columns of rain.

This is why you spin in the winter only. So the clouds don't forget again how to rain. So you may remember how to spin out your own yarns, plied with dreams, the nettle strings of your sorrows and your strengths. A life is a thread spun, from the distaff stars round the wheel of earth, your blood the spinning nettle thread, dancing footprints down the paths like the plied trails of coyotes, until it is done, and you're woven back in again where the nettles reach their roots down, and touch the bones of Nain.

Nain made seven skirts of nettle cord, of woven waist and thick, swaying fringe. Six for the geese, one for herself, because she could not take it off once it was on, making her hips round and sway as she walked. It whispered like the grass she had not seen in seven years. Robin could not breathe when he heard that sound, when he saw her, full grown, the string skirt at her waist and nothing else. He had to look away. She swayed now when she walked. She stayed up late into the moon-light, dancing. When Robin saw Nain dancing in her string skirt in the moonlight alone, it is said that he felt an earthquake, but it was only his bones, trembling with the passing of a world, making room for a new.

It is said that Robin left then, because he could see that the skirt was shield enough for her, because he found that he could not watch and protect her any longer, and not also reveal himself. It is said he went up into the trees and hardly ate with his longing for her until that winter day when the snow geese came again.

This time when the geese returned, Nain left the creekbed to meet them. She walked to the edge of the bay so she could see the moon on the water the color of those geese arriving. When they came skidding across the water, honking, she held out the skirts like flags, and one by one the geese paddled to shore. They shook themselves, making veils of water-drops and flash of white wings, black-tipped. They reached out their long necks, and Nain placed the skirts down around their shoulders.

The motion of their changing was as fluid as water, a creek swelling. Their white bodies grew taller, they became the forms of six women, their feathers falling in showers of white. They became six women whose hearts broke as they saw the skin and legs and arms and hair they had dreamt of, because they recognized the loss they could not have anticipated, as geese—the white-feathered mates they would never meet again, the dozens of downy chicks, the insides of clouds, the pale tundras, the opening of wings, which were gone from them now, forever.

But then the sister of Nain looked up from her skirt swaying, from her bare body in that skirt, into Nain's nettle-green eyes, and knew her not with the cloud-wise knowing of geese but with the keen, loud affection of women. Nain looked and saw in her sister herself, older, getting lined now at the eyes from the bright goose-summers of tundra. They went to each other, hugging, crying, the sister of Nain knowing no words but grunts and honks, and using her arms like wings. The other goose women began to ululate. They began to sway, to touch one another's arms, breasts, hips, marveling. They began to laugh.

For a night the seven women hooted and crooned, spinning in circles, clapping their hands for a beat, singing in wild goose voices to Nain's strange songs. They danced in spirals, and stomped their bare feet as geese do. They cried for what they had lost, reaching up to the clouds that were gathering, because they missed them, even as they loved the muscle and swing of their new bodies. Nain had only dreamed of the insides of clouds when the geese came, and could not understand their longing, but she reached up with them for the rain, and for her mother who was dead, and for her father who she would never see again, and for the gentleness of men and women to be restored to their hands.

By dawn, everyone inside of our stinging barricades, our ancient walls around this ancient city, had gathered at the far edge of the bayshore, at the mouth of the creek, led by Robin, who could stay away no longer. He built a fire in the mud and only when the smoke of that fire began to waft did the six goose-women and Nain turn. Fear went through them as it does through deer, fear at the sight of so many tangled, bearded, dirty faces, hair full of feathers and ancient plastic beads, eyes bright and a little bit lunatic with solitude, all welling up with tears. Robin held up his hands and lowered his

head, as he would have to any wild creature, looking
away. From behind his back, he produced a drum. He
sat down by his fire and began to beat it.

The women crept nearer to the heat, and to the
sound, and despite their fear of him—a man, when
the world of human men they had known, even for an
hour, had been cruel—the heavy edges of our fibers at
their knees, and the drumming, made them sway, made
them all roll their arms and their hips and dance again,
around that fire, this time illuminated by the sun as it
rose. Nain as she danced felt she knew this man, though
she had never seen him. There was a smell, and with
it the memory of a rabbit pelt, found at the edge of her
nettle-camp, a pile of bay nuts, that she recognized. But
she danced and for a time forgot.

The refugee men who lived inside our walls of nettle,
the men who had gathered as if to a church, picked up
stones and sticks, fumbling through their tears, through
the choking in their throats—for they had not seen a
woman, many of them, in decades, and a woman dancing as grass in a spring wind, as clouds before a rain,
never—and they began to click and clap out their own
rhythms. They wanted to be a piece of this too, this
single dancing sound. Soon their shy feet were moving
also. A hundred men, tattered by the world they had
known, wept and danced.

The dancing and the fire went on until dusk. The
clouds thickened and darkened through the day, and
as the women raised their arms at sunset like geese do,
hips swaying circles, strings moving like rain, the water
at last began to fall, and did not stop. Drop by drop, it
became a new rhythm that they danced to.

Weave

There are floor looms whose warps are weighted with smooth stones strung through their water-worn holes, where you will soon weave the robes of your sisters, the tablecloths and sheets. On the floor looms, in the spring and the summer, you will weave the bolts of fabric traded for in deer meat and rabbit-hide shoe, in polished beams of wood from the Robin-Bands who rove the oak and bay forests up the ridge. They are apostles of the man who loved Nain, who lived up in trees and unwound the old Camps where men had forgotten that to kill and not to love was a poison that one day ate you whole. You will build the cloths from nettle-thread, the cloths that have built again the sovereignty of women, string by string, in the way of little Nain.

But first, at spring's beginning, you will weave a skirt of string and cord, for the scutch dance, for the spindle dance, for the dance you feel underneath the ache of your moon blood cycle, for the dance you feel when you see the orange-bellied newts dancing down through the grass hills to the mud-creeks of their grandmothers and their grandfathers. You will weave a string skirt for the dance when the snow geese come landing on the bay, and when they leave again, when the clarkia blooms and Nain's Distaff leaves the sky, migrating too, returning again with the winter cold. You will weave a waistband to sit low around the widest part of your hips, and you will let the weft cords hang long and oiled by the touch of your hands.

You will weave a waistband, warped through thirteen weaving cards made from the hardened and smoothed nettle papers painted with Nain's Tarot. The spread you lay out before yourself will be your warp-cards, and a story for you to tell—six of Shuttles, two of Moons, Priestess of Feathers. The story of the cards is only a warp, and you alone can weave it true or change it. Under over under goes the heavy weft-cord of nettle, back and forth and back again, like the snow geese. As you turn the cards, as you open, close, open, the shed made between the strands, your warp holds your weft.

Let the weft-ends hang as long as the space from your hips to the tops of your knees on one side. You must weave the waist-band so long that it wraps around you twice. Cut the loops of nettle cord so each hangs free. Then twine them together at the end with one long and thin cord smoothed with the wax of bumblebees, like the Tying Up Cords, so that when you sway, the strings sway too, against a boundary, held in like water to its surface tension.

At the bottom edge, knot the fringe with polished metal beads forged from the city scraps of long ago. When you put the skirt on, feel the weight of that edge, its swing, its life, umbilical, a wind through nettle stalks, a breadth of movement not only your own, a sway that makes your hips swivel with the pleasure of it.

This is the skirt that Nain wore at the cusp between worlds, at the end of one and the beginning of another, a criss-cross of wefts as when two sisters weave one cloth, and trade shuttles in the center. Nain wove her seven nettle-string skirts right here, where you have offered and harvested, retted, stooked and scutched, carded, spun and woven.

Your hips are a moon that waxes and wanes. When you dance in your string skirt as the snow geese land, the cords swaying back and forth across your thighs are that moon, darkening and brightening, hiding and revealing, rounded at every edge. You will know, when you have swayed your hips in a skirt of nettle string, what it means to give birth to the world of the self, every autumn full of geese, every dark moon, every dawn. You will know the power of women, the thread spun between hips and earth which is the ground of all beginning.

The warps are latitudes, the wefts longitudes, and in your weaving you weave a world, a map, with lay lines the geese know how to follow, as do your wise old hands. Weaving is building, and one day you might take your nine years as apostle of Our Lady of Nettles, Saint Nain, and build a new place, far away across the bay and toward the ocean, or across the delta and toward the mountains, where women can learn again the miracles of their hands, where the men who have forgotten can remember again that a woman has the webs of making in her palm lines and her swaying hips. Or you might stay here, near the bones of Nain, and one day catch a glimpse of her yourself, Lady Nettle, walking in her skirt of string, just the way Nain saw her, and held her stinging hand.

SIX MEDITATIONS
OF TORREYA ITH

Laundry

You walk up the hill through the quince and apple trees, the laundry in a hazelwood basket on one hip to take to the washing-place. The quail, plump and bronze with autumn, are foraging under rosemary and in the rain's first grass. Speak gently, move slow, and you may one day manage to walk past them without scattering them all in a noisy wheel of wings. Dry the clothes on the line down in the lower garden, at the edge of the pines, on a good bright day when the pleasure of the smell of stiff, sunned linen will be worth all the work of washing it.

The Rabbit

At dusk, close the long-haired rabbit into his house so the coyotes don't take too much notice. A handful of dandelion greens, cilantro, plantain. In your lap he is lustrous, so soft he is his own cloud, warm as all furred creatures, and as all furred creatures glad of your warmth too. His coat is long, almost ready to be shorn and spun, but not today. Tomorrow maybe. Pet behind his ears, all along them and down his back, and he will click his teeth with pleasure. Warm furred rabbit in your lap, wood pigeons going to roost, last winter sun the color of cider on the witchpine tops, coming from the direction of the sea. You hear the first hoot of the great-horned owls, and say goodnight to the rabbit, and go down to your husband who is making soup.

Dishes

Wash the dishes—the chipped ceramic plates, silver, odd old colored glasses for wine, milk pitcher, iron pan—in a tin tub out where the well water comes. You boil the kettle, soap and warm, squatting wide-hipped, trying to remember the words to old folk songs. Wrentits are watching, making little calls, and the spotted towhees scratch at wet duff for bugs. Later, the gray fox will come to eat the porridge leavings you've scraped from the bottom of the oatmeal pot.

The Donkey

Once a week you look after the neighbor's donkey and goats while he is away over the ridge to set bones and doctor coughs. The donkey has decided, after a month shunning you for his own mysterious reasons, that he likes you again after all, and will eat the apple pieces out of your hand. It is a good day, after weeks of terrible fires in the north, when he comes to you without an apple and asks to be petted. Velvet nose, the smell of horse, warm hay and fur and dust. His gladness to lean against you heavily and have his neck and ears rubbed makes you glad. For a long time you stand still, leaning on each other, until you both feel better.

Baking

Harvest a sweet pumpkin from the garden to bake into the birthday cake. The smell when you cut it open and scoop out the seeds carries all other autumn seasons since you were a girl. It is hard to keep the cake from being too wet. Besides the pumpkin there is acorn flour, almond flour, creamed honey, chicken eggs, butter. In the end it is too wet in the middle despite your efforts. You share it with your family at your uncle's birthday across three ridges (it is a whole afternoon's journey with the cake in its dish in a basket) but nobody seems to mind. It is warm and sweet and tastes of pumpkin, the night is cold, and the wine is plentiful among good company.

Gathering Herbs

Go down the valley to the lagoon and the great dune beside the ocean to gather grindelia flowers. Your mother and your aunt go with you often there to harvest plants, the kinds that don't grow in the pinewood. It's only a half-hour's ride. The gummy, late-season blooms of the grindelia will make a good tincture for chest colds. At sunset flocks of cormorants wing one after the other from the ocean across the land toward the thin finger of the bay to the east. Their black wings make a great rushing sound, oiled and strong. You watch them, heading the way you will take to get back home when you are finished gathering. Most fly in big groups, a V. Some fly alone or in a pair. All fly the same route. The tide is changing, high to low. There are many more cormorants now in autumn than the rest of the year, come from far away to winter in the gentle waters here. In a little while, you fasten your baskets and ride the donkeys home again, talking together of far away, and who you know who has been there, and what the cormorants say to each other on such a long journey.

BURNING QUAIL WOMAN

Quail, the lady of bronze and smoke, she died midmorning. Neck snapped, not a mark. The little sparrowhawk with red eyes must have dropped her in the long grass.

Mother found her. I carried her limp and warm in my hands, stroked her feet and her beak, laid her with yellow tidytips, lupine, baby blue eyes, at the uproot of an old pine. Her eyelids closed, peace on the dust-blue lids, full of elsewhere now. A male called from the bough.

Once she danced for him, tail feathers swinging, a fan of desire:
charcoal copper dun.
The sway of her plump body
in the leafmold
in the amber duff
in the thrushsung dusk
was the sway of all abundance, the promise of worlds.

A man with brown feet and brown hands helped to skin her. One cut at the breast, the rest with fingertips, like taking off a coat. I gave her juniper smoke and roses. Cicadas clicked their wings in the dry oak hills, and called it summer.

Before Olympus there were the Titans. Big women and men of earth. Asteria daughter of Phoibe was mother of falling stars and dreams. She gave birth to Hekate. Her mother was the moon. When Zeus chased after her for sex she became a quail to escape him. She fled, leaping into the sea, and became the island Delos in the blue Aegean. It had no bottom. It floated, and the quail flocked there on their journeys south. Later when Zeus chased after her sister Leto, the island sheltered her.

Asteria was aunt of Artemis who loved the woodbirds and the wood, who loved the ones she hunted, who was the deer she ate. Artemis wore quail feathers at her waist and helped them birth their spotted eggs.

I placed the quail in the adobe brick kiln we built at dusk to fire earth-made pottery. Skinless, plump, wet, she smelled of sweet flesh and comfort, an offering to the clay to the fire to the night and stars, to her mother and her sisters Asteria, Artemis, Leto: women of the quail, of instinct, wilderness, and care

She burned with her tail feathers still on so she could take them up there with her, dancing. Her fat glazed the pots, her fat popped and sparked, her bones turned to white dust, delicate as crab shells by morning.

Up there in the stars, quail women are dancing.
They are dancing with her spirit they are singing in the smoke.
They are shaking their hips and lowering their blue-dusked lids to look upon their lovers.

I was so sad at first for her beauty, lost to death. Her body was perfect in my hands. I could not bear it. I thought of her mate, his loss. I did not want to erase his sorrow, the love that birds know. I felt so sorry for him, for her.

But she was far wiser than I, that quail, little woman. She showed me her death, she let me see it. How her beautiful feathers were only a skin; no less precious for it, but a skin nonetheless. That what was underneath was tender, that it could nourish me, a gift. The body is a gift, but more than that the body is an offering on the fire.

Borne on embers above the coiled pots she was transmuted.
She became smoke and heat and air.
She glowed, her bones molten.
She became starmade again, the first sacrament.

A woman offers a quail to the goddess, offers flesh to the earth and stars.In the face of what we perceive truly there is nothing else to be done. Learning to be fully human is learning to handle the dead this way. The old hunters say that animals offer themselves to the arrow because they want to come into the human camp to be sung, to be turned to fire, to be danced, to be part of that pathos, that beauty, that blaze.

I did not understand fully how to offer her, but she did. She went to my hands and the fire and taught me that we are not whole without this, without looking into the underworld, into the body of the quail, into the earth's hearth and there giving up what we know for the sweetness of a grief that is feathered, that is wise.

Down there quail woman is carrying an ember in her feathered hands. Through the underworld she is carrying it. Underground the dead are but sparks in the bellies of seeds. The spark does not go out, only leaves our view for a time.

Quail woman is dancing there.
Quail woman is dancing in the stars.
As above, so below, and the kiln in the center where all is transformed.

Back home I buried her bones, half dust, in the bishop pine wood where she was born. With rose petals, red wine and a pot sherd from her fire I buried them. At dawn, two quail called, flapped, sang, right outside our door, nearer than I'd ever heard them. All through the daybreak they carried on. Mating maybe. Mourning, maybe.

She lives everywhere now.

RHEA SILVIA

They call me the Mother of Rome as if I should be honored by the name. As if, after all that has been done, I should be glad of what it was my body began. They call me Mother of Rome now, but in the beginning I was Rhea Silvia, mostly just Rhea, a girl who loved the beechwood and who tended well the fire.

I was mortal then, but the love of the Tiber has since made me otherwise. And so I am in the river and the trees still, watching the city that long ago laid the roadways to the end of the world. All this, and it began when a woman's body was caught under the hands of War.

For so I was.

I had felt it in my uncle's gaze from the time I was a child. I felt the strain its absence made in my father Numitor, king of Alba Longa. He valued peace, which there was little of in the territories beyond Alba Longa. Still, it lived in him. Other men did not always like him, for he carried peace like a woman carries a child—out in the open in front of him, proudly, for all to see. I adored him and so did my mother, even though she was no ordinary Latin wife, but a woman of the forest. Silvia. She named me for herself. She of the wood, a daughter of trees.

It is no ordinary man who can coax one of the old people of the forest to be his wife, but my mother consented to be Numitor's. She came from the great wood that covered the Apennine mountains south and east of my father's land, the old oak and beech forests where in spring the woodland flowers made a blue and white froth, and sun through the new leaves was a numinous green. My mother took me there often in spring and in summer.

For weeks at a time we would go, just she and I, taking one mule along to carry our bedskins and baskets, one jug of fine wine to offer the trees and another for her family. My mother taught how to speak with the hare and the deer and the woodpecker. She taught me the name of every plant that grew there and their every use, and the way to talk to a beech, which was different than an oak or holly or hawthorn, a sycamore or a pine. She taught me to use a bow, how to skin a rabbit, how to make fire with two sticks, how to sing until a star fell through the night, how to calm an angry boar, how to earn the respect of wolves.

There was a spacious cave in the mountains where we slept on the fine lambskins we had brought. Wood violets grew outside under the beech shade. I loved the crunch of my feet through their bronze leaves. In all seasons they covered the ground, the new and old leaves together. My mother's people visited us there, bringing meat to share on the fire—bear sometimes, and deer, and a kind of wildwood wine made of honey and berries that was sometimes delicious and sometimes sour as vinegar. We never went to their village place because they moved with the seasons and because it was dangerous, in case we were followed by my uncle's men. They would have liked to see all the mountain people killed or brought as slaves into the cities of Latium, and the trees there claimed for timber. My father kept them from it, but barely.

My mother's folk were quiet, kind, gentle people. When I was very young I believed the stories I heard whispered about her among my father's servants and the people of the farms and fields of Alba Longa—that she was part tree herself, or part doe. A dryad, a nymph, a witch at least. *Does that make me part tree as well?* I would wonder, sitting by the Tiber with my feet in the current, examining my hands for green, for bark.

No, my mother assured me, the forest people weren't dryads, though they could surely speak with trees. They were the First People, she told me when I was old enough to also understand the word War. The last of the ones who had been here, living on the land of the place my father called Latium and they called an older, secret name, since the beginning of time. Our people, she told me, rocking me on her lap by the fire among them, her legs bare and sticking to my bare legs, they were here before even the great volcano first filled the sky with ash and turned the valleys to wastelands. Our people lived through that. Our people know how out of ash may one day grow the most beautiful gardens. Our people remember the time when great elephantine beasts walked here, and lions gold as wild barley, and the stars were people who walked among us too.

She taught me their language, which was much softer than the Latin of my father and the Greek I'd heard spoken by traders, and knew a few words of; closer to the Etruscan some of the servants spoke, and yet not that either, but stranger and softer still. Speaking my mother's language, I saw things differently. I forgot that I was separate from the wood, the wolf, the wind, the bronze leaves underfoot, the quail I skinned with my bare hands. I had known the gods and goddesses of my father's people all my life. I had dutifully performed the seasonal rites with the Vestal priestesses, learning from his mother, my grandmother, the way of hearth and earth and ancestors. But in my mother's language, among my mother's people, I *saw* them.

I remember the first time it happened. I was ten and spoke

my mother's way fluently by then, as wild and dark as any of my cousins, running free through the summer wood. That day I was alone with the clay jug down by the spring below the cave, gathering water. Across the stream a young stag raised his head and looked at me. He had two short antlers beginning to grow like the budding tips of fruit trees, all covered in velvet. They shone. He looked up at me, entirely, and in him I saw a god. He was a god. I made a sound. Swift as water, he was gone. But his look lingered behind him. Black-eyed, clear, his velvet antlers shining. A little god. His look had looked at me from an eternal place. All animals are little gods, I said to myself. I ran back to my mother with this revelation, the water half spilled by the time I reached her where she sat in the sun with her basket, separating hazelnuts from their husks.

She kissed my cheeks and scolded me over the water, but said, "Now you sound like one of us, my daughter. Today you have no Latin accent. Today you are of the wood. The god has shown his eyes to you, and I am proud."

PEOPLE TALKED, OF COURSE. How could the king allow his wife and only daughter to disappear unarmed into the mountain forests for weeks at a time? Surely the queen was a dryad. Did she sleep with wolves when she was away? Did her daughter too, the young whelp? But my father Numitor had worked hard to keep peace in his land, among his people, and they knew this. They felt it in the safety of their outer fields at night, and they too let their children run unarmed and unattended. They trusted him.

But the king, they whispered still, is he being made a cuckold? And does he not see his brother's treachery, waiting for the chance to spring? He should keep his wife and daughter near; you never know what might happen.

I heard all this from the servants, the kitchen women and the ones who helped my mother in the weaving room. I listened

when they thought I wasn't there. I had the quiet of mild creatures about me, and the cunning. I learned that from my mother.

She never did have much attention for the spindle or the
thread, and her weaving was penetrated by little inconsistencies
where she had stopped and gone to the windows to breathe an
autumn wind, or watch a gray dove fan out her tail as she flew, or
look to the mountains east and south and begin in her mind to
plan another journey there.

"After the first acorn fall," she said one day at the window. I
was fourteen, she thirty-seven, with a little silver at her temples,
but her eyes young as ever; young, I imagined, as the day my
father first saw her in the oakwood where he was hunting boar
with a few of his men.

She was already a full-grown woman then. Not, she told me
grinning once, a maid. Not close! Not nearly; your father's people are so strange, to value such a thing in brides. Your father was
glad of it too, come our wedding night. My mother always spoke
that way. I didn't know until I was starting to grow into a woman
myself that the other girl's mothers did not. I would speak of the
opening crocuses as little vulvas full of Earth's desire. I would
watch the stalking, well-hung tomcat mount a tabby, and ask
aloud if she felt pleasure. This made the other girls go scarlet,
and stammer, and their mothers call me names.

At the window the day I was fourteen, my mother looked at
the mountain and spoke of going there, lightly, as she always
did. We hadn't been since the first of spring six months past. But
since then it seemed to me that many things had changed. The
ground did not feel stable beneath my feet as it once had. Maybe
it was just the changes in my body, the feeling that I was growing
up. But also it was the rumors I heard, and my uncle's eyes on me
when he visited, not familial but frightening, too bright.

"My uncle," I said to her, softly. The other women always
liked to eavesdrop. "He stinks of war. He's stirring it up among
our allies. It isn't safe now, mother."

"You sound like your father," she replied, her eyes still far away, twisting at a bit of black wool that had broken off the spindle. I could see the cave and the beechwood in her eyes. The autumn fall of leaves, the smoke from fires under stars, her brothers' warm and laughing arms, welcoming her home again. A part of her was always going home, whenever she looked that way toward the mountains and the distant trees.

"But you heard it too mother. About the slaughter of the northern tribes. How they were raiding Sabine cattle, and uncle allied with their men to kill them all. Wild people, like yours. I've never seen father angrier. The men have the taste of war again, after sixteen years of peace. That's what he says, and the farmers, and the kitchen women too. Uncle hates you, and me. You know that. He hates where you came from."

"He is only one man," my mother spat, stamping one bare foot on the stone floor the way she did when she was angry, when she wanted to feel the power of Earth inside her. But I saw fear hiding in her eye too. A heron flew past the window just then, up from the marsh at the river's edge, winging toward the land across the river, toward those seven distant hills. His wingbeats were slow and grey, and he called out once in a harsh voice. Dread leapt through me at the sound.

Over dinner that night my mother mentioned the autumn journey to my father.

"For acorns, Numitor," she said in a low voice, her eyelashes the color of dusk, and her hair too. A dark woodland dusk. I could almost smell it. I knew my father could. Sometimes I was certain of my mother's magic. Other times I thought she was only a woman who knew the forest's ways, and so was powerful and different from others I knew. Perhaps they are one and the same thing.

"I will make your favorite spiced nut wine, in time for Saturnalia," she went on. "It's been long. My brothers will fear Alba Longa has forsaken them. They must be afraid, hearing news from the north about Amulius and his alliance with the Sabines. I could assure them of their protection."

"Your going now might well be the greatest risk to their safety, my love," Numitor replied, taking up the hand that touched his hand and turning it over to kiss the dark palm. I saw the shiver run up my mother's neck. I knew my mother's perfume, rose oil and musk and dry leaves. My father knew it better. He breathed deep from her wrist before lifting his head and taking a swallow of wine. "I fear Amulius would follow you. I do not know how I could prevent it. He's restless, prowling for a fight. Like a caged wolf. Farming never satisfied him, and peace makes him restless. Perhaps I've been a fool. He stirs it in the others. This business with the Sabines, I fear it's only a beginning. He undermines me, and yet to retaliate is to break what is most sacred in me." He sighed, and drained his cup. It rattled when he set it down. The bronze caught the fire's glow.

I saw my face in it, long and dark and solemn, like my mother's. But I saw I had my father's nose, his chin and curving hairline, and this made me glad. He was a striking man, my father. Only a little older than my mother, perhaps by five years, but with much more silver, and lines all around his eyes and forehead. The cost of carrying peace inside him when the world seemed always hungry for war. The cost of holding a kingdom together by gentleness, integrity, intelligence and trust, and not by fear. It took all of him, and lined him young. I saw this clearly in that moment, and saw why my mother would have left her people to be his queen.

"You know I am quiet as a doe, and take the forest paths," my mother replied. "No one sees us. Amulius has tried to follow before. I did not tell you, I did not want to worry you, but he is no match for me. I am a wolf when I must be, Numitor. I leave no trace, the trees look after me. You know how it will go with me if I do not go home soon. I must be watered, I must." Her voice had a desperate edge. It alarmed both me and him. His eyes were dark, but my father sighed and kissed her, and I knew she had won.

The next morning my first bleeding came. This, I thought, must have been the cause for my anxiety, my presentiments of doom. It delayed our journey a little, but my mother was delighted. She took me down to the Tiber and bathed me in the way of her people, singing old songs to the water, singing of my beauty as a growing living thing, singing of me as an oak, a nut, a flower, a quail. I wept, feeling sore and afraid and glad all at once. Other women came. They burned laurel smoke around me and fed me honeycomb and saffron, and crowned me with purple crocus petals. The river up to my waist felt cool and soft. I saw myself rippled in the light green water, shifting. It seemed for a moment I could see myself growing and changing. I reached out underwater and clasped my hands together with the exhilaration of that feeling. For a moment it seemed I held the hand of some other being. The river himself. It was a strong, big hand. Then it was gone, and a younger woman was teasing me.

"Open up your legs, the river will teach you of your own body with his current, of where the pleasure lies."

"So is that what you're up to when you're late to the weaving?" my mother teased back, her breasts shining copper above the water.

We were all naked in a shaded part of the river under sycamore trees. No man would have dared disturb our rituals today, but even so mother had stationed several of her women to guard the river bend where it opened on the town. I blushed, though I had thought before that these matters didn't embarrass me. But it was true. The water felt nice there, different than it had on any other day. Alive.

The feeling didn't go away when I left the river. It stayed with me all the while traveling into the mountain with my mother. My bleeding was light, but I was tired after it was over and my mother let me ride the mule instead of walking. That seemed to make the feeling stranger. There was a warmth at the very quick of me, right between my legs. I had never known that before. Vestal, like the beginning of a fire. The women said your first bleeding was the beginning of being grown, a ripening so that you in turn might make new life. They had not said how it made you also a fire. I wondered if maybe it was like the one we kept for Vesta at the sacred hearth. Something that would never go out. These things I thought and felt as we went along, distracted and flushed. My mother took a circuitous way to get there, just in case my uncle followed us, but what she had told my father was true. She was quiet and clever as the deer, as the wolf. We left hardly a trace. We followed animal paths through the beechwood, through meadows up to the valley beyond which her people lived, under the snow-topped peak of their mother mountain.

IT WAS A VERY GOOD TIME, that autumn visit when I was fourteen. Perhaps because of what had awakened in my body, I remember it with particular vividness. Perhaps because we went only once more after that, but that time ended in a darkness too complete for me to speak of before I first tell you of this time, the penultimate, so I have it to hold as a crocus flower, a bright thing. The time I was fourteen holds all the other times since I was a girl, caught in amber, in my memory.

My mother, smiling to herself, seemed to understand just what was behind my flush. The first night back among her people, as we ate and sang around a great fire, she sat me beside the three sons of her childhood friend Thisbi, who I called aunt. Everyone hooted then. The men whistled in praise, for my mother doing so showed them all that I was a woman now, and could sit among men as I pleased. I was terribly red all over. I felt hot. I felt the ember of myself and it frightened me, so I had a good swallow of my mother's wine, which I didn't much like, and tried to speak to the brother nearest my age.

I cannot recall his name now. For it was the young singer who regaled us with songs of the trees, the deaths of brave warriors and mothers, the love story of the hunter and deer woman, who watched me, and who I watched too. All the night long we watched each other. As he sang the tales he watched me, and for the first time in my life I relished the feeling of a man's gaze.

There was dancing. My mother gave me her own fringed skirt and I, a little dizzy with wine, danced with the grown women, swinging my hips as they did, feeling now why they did. Because it was as a bellows on a fire, on a power. We were alight. The younger girls watched me in awe, as I had watched others before me don their mother's skirts. Nobody made a great fuss but all noticed me that night, and most of all I noticed what was in my body that I had never known.

When the waning moon rose at last and the fire was low, all sought their beds but the young singer and me. He found me at the wood's edge watching the moon, too alive to sleep. It rose the color of an ember over the eastern ridge, through oaks. I did not seem able to catch my breath. I turned to him like a flame in wind, and I kissed him. His name was Vare. All through the night we kissed. He was very gentle, very kind, never pushing, only kissing and caressing me until I was liquid. We slept in the beech leaves under his fox coat, and woke in the morning besotted.

Later in the day down by the creek, washing our road-worn things, my mother teased me. I could not reply, for what had happened in me set me adrift in myself, a whole sea where a mother cannot go. She knew this, and stopped teasing. Instead she solemnly tucked a late wood violet into my wet black hair as we laid our clothing to dry on stones and said, "Now you know the secret that all women know. People will make a fuss about their gods and what is holy and what is not. They will call this and that a mystery, and tiptoe round the fire in the temple. But today daughter you know the mystery behind their mysteries. That all of the world is suffused with that pleasure. That what you feel stir in you is the light that is all of life. You know now the pleasure of myrtle flowers and quince fruit and oak leaves opening. But remember, at the root of the fruit you have picked dwell the dead. At the beginning and end of all Earth's pleasure, the dead. This is what we dance for, what we love for. The eternal return. Gods is it terrible, is it sweet."

I HAVE NEVER FORGOTTEN THOSE WORDS. In my memory that autumn stay among her people is suffused with them. I was, like she said, the pleasure of the ripe earth. The acorns sleek and plump and shining. I thought for those brief days I understood everything. The language of every tree and stream and stone and rutting stag. Even the language of the dead. My mother often sent me and the young singer off with an acorn basket, bemused, not confident that we would be very diligent, and so gathering enough of her own too. She was right to. We came back with spined oak leaves in our hair.

When we left I wept as if I were dying. Though it was a small thing, compared with what I have known and wept for since, I do not belittle her yet, my girlish self, for to my young heart leaving the singer was the sorest ache I had ever known. What I had felt was all pure and wild as new fawnskin, as the softest berries, for all my mother's words of death. Now I understood just a little of it, the danger of feeling so strongly, of love. She let me weep. She held my hand and picked me autumn hawthorn berries and strung them on a thread.

Oh, to have lost only that. An autumn crush, the first young taste of love. That is a gentle fruit, a quince eased pink over embers. I have since been bared, been stripped, been cut to earth and trampled. Only I know still my mother's truth. But now I know it better than I ever wanted to, better than any woman should, for I am not just a woman any more. I know it like the river knows it now, like the roots of trees that once grew beneath the city of Rome, and will again.

NOT LONG AFTER WE RETURNED, my mother found she was carrying a child. She had tried so many years to bear my father a son but none of her pregnancies since me had held. A son to be king when he was gone—this my mother had wanted as much as my father did, for she had a dread of Amulius ascending the throne of Alba Longa one day. So for the next four years we did not go to the wooded mountain of her people, though we sent word of her pregnancy to her brothers, and the day of the boy's birth in early summer. She doted on him, her late, miraculous boy. She would not leave his side. Much to the scandal of the women she refused a wet nurse or even a maid to help her. Only I was allowed near enough to change him or dress him, the little prince of Alba Longa.

I had never seen her so happy, not even among her people making acorn cakes with a niece or gathering elderflowers with an old aunt. She nursed my brother in the courtyard in the sun, where my father long ago had planted orange trees for her, traded from the Greeks because she loved the smell of their blossoms. When my brother was born the last blossoms were falling. The people of Alba Longa, who loved my mother and my father equally, left votives at the gate—rough figurines of women, handfuls of crocus or chamomile—that she might bless them, she who had borne a son so late.

My father refused that his son should go to the mountain to meet her people and for once my mother, docile as a milk cow, agreed, her big dark eyes bright on their son. And so I did not see the young singer called Vare for many years. But that ache, a small thing really, passed by the first winter as I helped my mother with her tasks while her belly swelled. Spinning and weaving; shaping clay votives for the sanctuaries; preparing offerings for our ancestors, for the wood genii, the local gods, the river and wild birds; feeding, stoking and banking the Vestal fire at the center of the palace. I was busy, and forgot him soon.

It was a good time, the time of my brother's birth and those first three-odd years of his life. A window of peace, impossibly still and calm. Like a high summer noon when nothing stirs but the welling songs of the bronze-winged cicadas. Now I see it as the stillness before a storm. I could not see it then. I was young and blooming still. I was only aware of my own blossoming. I often ran off to the river with or without the washing, with or without my handmaids. I had a hidden place I liked to swim where the water pooled under ancient sycamores and the banks were broad. Sometimes I thought the river watched me. I daydreamed of him, splashing in the clear water between lime banks, imagining what kind of man he would be, that river with a thousand hands.

In my mother's language the river and the tree and the woodpecker all looked back with their intelligence at me. The Tiber seemed to hold me gently, enjoying the words I spoke to him in her tongue. Sometimes I brought my little elderflute and danced naked on the warm rocks, thinking I might conjure him. Some days he looked like Vare, who I longed for fervently for a little while. Later he was more grown, a man like the farmers I saw working strong-backed in the fields with their shirts off in the heat, muscled and big-armed. I dallied. I was a girl of fourteen, of fifteen, of sixteen, naïve and lusting after wild irises, honeycomb, rainstorms, the touch of men, music and dance. I was a giddy, feral thing. I do not know that I was beautiful the way men sought, but I had more life force in me than a young doe, than a grape vine, than any other girl of Alba Longa, and I could feel the eyes of boys and men and women too, and trees and rocks and birds and the river god, and savored them all. I must have been such a painfully innocent sight back then. It makes me sorrow to remember.

When my little brother turned four, everything changed. My uncle Amulius had been quiet those years. We took his seeming meekness for acquiescence, even fondness for his nephew. A son had been born. His hopes for the throne were lost. And he played the part of a good uncle, even a doting one. He brought wooden toys from his travels north for horses—a miniature cart, a carved red stallion, a duck with wheels. He was gone often on such trips in those years. We hoped he was looking further north for some bit of country to seize for his own. We should have suspected something worse. Perhaps my father did, but could not see what else to do but trust his younger brother, who he loved, and continue to raise his son, to husband his flocks and herds, to carry out the rites that kept the land fertile, the river's flood regular, the harvest rich.

But not long after my brother's fourth birthday, when I and my maids were up ladders barefoot in the walnut trees, gathering green-husked nuts to make our yearly spiced wine, my uncle rode through Alba Longa right into the courtyard of my father's great house with an army at his back. I saw this all from the top branches of a walnut down in my father's orchards just outside the palace walls. Men streaming through the peaceful city, armed and armored, shining like a hundred cicadas, their horses' hooves loud on the stone streets. People hid inside. I could see some running at the sound of armed men. In the fields, farmers and their wives and children hid, watching from behind wagons or the stands of barley.

From up the tree the red of the summer poppies that bloomed in the fields looked to me for a terrible moment like a seep of blood. I bade my maids be silent and those nearer the ground to run, and quickly, somewhere hidden. I knew my uncle's colors from a distance. I understood the language of their armor. They did not come in peace or in negotiation. My father's standing army was loyal and fierce, but a fraction of this one. I heard fighting already from the courtyard. I could see my hill city gleaming white in the hot sun all across the rising land. I could see the Tiber flowing pale green between farmland, past the orchard, and on for several miles toward the sea. Everything that had been held for my lifetime in peace still looked peaceful, still carried peace. Only the sound of bronze on bronze, and men's screaming, proved that it had been broken.

My father surrendered Alba Longa without much of a fight. He ordered his men lay to down their arms, for he saw that this would be a massacre if they did not. Already all those at the gates had been cut down. So my mother told me later. Numitor negotiated with his younger brother. He agreed to live in exile among his wife's people in the mountains, if Amulius would spare his men, would not cause his beloved farmers to take up weapons and be killed.

"You do not make the terms, brother," my uncle spat. "It is I who make them now, for I could kill you with stroke if I chose, and your son."

But he did not. My mother thought it was lost love that stayed his hand. In the final moment, she said, he could not, after all kill, his own brother. He was being merciful, she said as we rode out in the dusk in plain clothing.

We rode shaggy work horses through the moonlit fields. We did not want our people to know and follow us—their king and queen in exile, in shame, running away like dogs. But my mother and my father both would have done anything to keep their children their people safe. The barley and the wheat brushed our feet. The climbing beans looked so eager in the moonlight, little green hands and tendrils. I don't know why I remember them still, and the quiet. No dogs barked as we passed. My mother was knotting and re-knotting a piece of red wool in her fingers. A charm for protection, tying up the voices of the dogs. My little brother rode in front of me on my mount. His hair and head leaned on my chest. He was half asleep after a short time, though at first he had been entirely thrilled to be on the run, not under-standing why.

"To mother's people?" he had cried as I saddled the horse. "Will I learn to skin a rabbit as fast as you, Rhea? Will I learn to talk to trees like mother?" His excitement made me want to

weep. He did not know it was his head as much as my father's
that my uncle sought. The boy might grow up to lead an uprising
and depose him; he could not be let to live. I did not know this
then, but I sensed it I think. I sensed the doom around him, my
young brother with his skinny dark neck craning eagerly as a
little bird's as I hoisted him up into the saddle and followed my
parents out of the sweet-smelling stable where the field horses
were kept, out through the back lanes, toward the mountain.

We rode all night. I wondered at my uncle's clemency more
and more as we went. It seemed too generous that he would let
us flee this way, choosing our own exile. And yet, I reasoned,
trying to quell my dread, he was our uncle. He had sat me on his
knee when I was a girl and sung old rhyming songs, and once had
given me a blue ribbon and a copper bell from Scythia, where he
had gone to trade for fine metalwork and horses. In truth there
was only once or twice that I recalled when he actually had the
patience to sit and sing to me and give me gifts, and then probably after a long dinner and several cups of father's finest vintage,
but still, he did not want us dead, surely not. So I soothed myself.

The moon moved over us, and faintly the constellation called
the Scorpion wheeled in the south, her navel glinting red. Now
and then an owl screamed. My brother's head lolled, smelling
of yesterday's sun and wheat and a last sweet hint of babyhood,
when he had smelled entirely of rising bread and honey. I kissed
the top. We ascended into darkness, beyond the river valley,
into the foothills. My mother knew the way in the dark. Once
or twice I thought I heard something behind us, but faintly; animal noises only, I told myself. My mother and father didn't speak
at all except to bid me hurry, or slow, or go more quietly. Once
when my father turned his face back for me I saw it glint under
the setting moon with tears. All the lines around his eyes looked
deeper, like wounds.

The air was damp and cold as we went higher between stones
and twisted oaks. My mother took us a circuitous way. She too

had heard noises, and didn't trust my uncle. But it seemed too elaborate, too cruel, to send a brother into exile only to follow and kill him. It would have been much easier to kill us all right there in our great hall in Alba Longa. So we were not overcautious, and reached the cave by dawn, where we slept all day in a kind of heartsick daze. My father would not eat or drink. He shook, not from fear but from loss, and from anger at himself for his own stubborn pact with peace. In his face flashed the desire to kill.

At sunset my mother went to the ridge above the cave and called out in the voices of the cuckoo and the tawny owl, as she always did, to tell her people we had come. They arrived a short time later as silent as deer, suddenly all around us, weeping with happiness to see my mother and me after so many years. They were wary of my father, until my mother explained. I was passed between arms and kissed on both cheeks by aunts and uncles and grandparents and cousins, in a great ululation of grief and gladness both—that we were in exile, that we were home. Vare was there, but we seemed a little distant, and embarrassed. I will never forget the look of terror and delight on my brother's face when he first saw our mother's people, brown as the trees and dressed in soft deerskins that clicked with amber beads and coral.

"Are they spirits?" he whispered to me when we laid down that night to sleep, well-fed and warm by their fire. "Is mother a dryad like people say?"

At this I laughed. "I don't think so," I replied, stroking his dark hair. "But I wonder too sometimes."

We fell asleep that way, my hand on my brother's hair, there among the old beech trees on the mountain where the first people still lived, thinking of our mother.

WE WOKE IN HELL.

We woke to betrayal and slaughter, to the war god Mars

stalking through our hidden camp in the form of my uncle and two dozen of his armed and mounted men. And yet in the haze of kicked embers and smoke and terror, I saw not many men but one, larger than all of them, the bloodlust that moves through men in battle animated into a single awful looming figure. War Himself, with a hundred arms and legs, a hundred bows and knives, a hundred hooves, a body hard as bronze and hungry for what lived. I saw him very clearly for a moment as I woke to a scream and the ring of metal. Then he broke apart into men. Silent, expert men who slit the throats of my mother's people where they slept.

My brother and I had chosen a place to sleep a little ways off from the fire, among a patch of woodviolets. It took them longer to find us. By then those still alive had woken and fought back with their own hunting bows and knives, with rocks and teeth and fists. My mother's people did not in that clamor seem wholly human either. In my memory stags and sows and bears and beech trees fought inside the wild smoke and ash between the men and women I loved. The forest fought, but Mars and his men of war won.

My brother and I kept very still among the violets and beech leaves, bellies down. He whimpered but I put my hand on his mouth and held him. Until I die I will keep him there in my heart, warm and sweet smelling, still half the baby he had been, a boy of four who believed me wholly when I whispered to him *we will be alright, don't worry my sweetheart, I will keep you safe, we will escape, a wolf will save us, I will save us, we are the forest's children, she will keep us safe. I love you I love you I love you.*

I said those words into his hair. I put my hands over his ears but I know he still heard the screaming, because he shook in my arms. I tried to shift us further into the forest, into the dark, into some deep fathomless bush, but every movement made the leaves crackle, and fear made me clumsy. I could feel my heart clamoring against my bones, thudding against my brother's back where I held him.

After a time there was no more screaming, only the sound of a new fire crackling, and men in metal armor moving about, gloating over the bodies of the dead, stripping them for trinkets and rings. Then I held absolutely still, and told my brother to be quieter than any mouse. But the fear was too great, building and building in him, and he let out a helpless whimper when he saw a man shoving through the piles of the dead, searching for something or someone. For us.

It was my uncle who found us in the end. I should have known he would not leave until he had found my brother, heir to Numitor's throne and a future threat to his sovereignty. He came toward us from the fire, backlit by those terrible bright shadows and a rush of smoke. He was not my uncle but the god of War. War was in him. He was covered in other men's blood. He saw us clearly, as a hunter does, not for who we were but for what he wanted from us. I struggled up and tried to lift my brother so we might run, but he was too heavy to carry and too terrified to move, and my uncle killed him with one blow. Then all my fear turned to rage and I whirled on Amulius, screaming as the owl screams, as the wolf screams, as the mountains. I threw myself nails and teeth at his neck, trying to choke him with my bare hands. I saw as if through a veil or from a distance; my uncle was and was not my uncle. Another man stood in him, as big and awful as death, helmeted of stars and far more terrible than Amulius. Both would have killed me. Both were on the verge of killing me. But violence is its own kind of lust, and so my uncle and the War in him, and then all of his men after him, did to me what at the time seemed worse than death.

AFTER THAT I FELT NOTHING. When they bound and gagged me and set me on a horse behind my uncle, I looked back at our encampment with unfeeling eyes. I had been broken from my people and my family. I was entirely alone now. I could not weep. I was stone. I had made myself stone the moment War decided not to kill me and took me instead. I felt nothing as I looked, trying not to see in the bodies the body of my father, my mother. In death there was a terrible sameness.

In the last moment as I craned to see what remained of my people, my eyes the only witness or last rite I could give, I saw a flash of red and black. A woodpecker, alighting. Old Picus, god of the wood and the autumn rain. And there among the beech trunks a long-legged wolf whose head was bent toward the earth. There was a man below her. She licked the wound on his neck. The woodpecker cried, calling out his rattle calls. It was my father. I made a sound in my gag. Under the wolf's tongue I saw him stir.

Then we were galloping, and that place and my mother, my father, my brother, my people, were gone from me forever.

When we returned to Alba Longa and my uncle's men were sober again, feeling their wounds and the black pall that killing brings, Amulius looked on me as if he could not remember why I was there. My city was no longer my city. The fine farmer's huts looked hunched and dark. My father's palace was like a pulled tooth, a terrible white molar. It had never seemed so to me before, but I was not the Rhea who had left it.

Only the Tiber was the same, pale green and gleaming, a broad muscled arm dancing to the sea. For a moment I saw a man standing in it, the water at his hips, bare-chested. He was dark and muscled as the farmers who worked the fields, and slouched the way men slouch who know their own strength and are at ease. A farmer, bathing, I thought, very distant from myself and full of a terrible sadness that touched everything with loss. My father's farmer. The man looked up and I flinched, surprised. His eyes were the Tiber's eyes, pale green and startling as his face was—wide-nosed, fierce, a warrior's face but with none of the violence. A strange thought, a strange sight. He dove straight into the current. I watched for many minutes in the saddle behind my uncle as we crossed the bridge into the city, but the man did not emerge again.

I forgot him. I did not wonder where he might have gone. I did not wonder at anything, because wondering at all about anything save the next step and the next breath, the next bite, was too much for me to bear. I did not think I could survive the horror of what I remembered, and so I was as a shade to myself, and to my uncle, to all men and women, watching as a shadow does.

From that dispassionate place I understood why my uncle had not killed me, why he had stayed his hand at the last and brought me back. He knew my father's people would be more amenable to his rule with me as a figurehead, their eternal daughter, keeper of the fire. This I became, and the business of Vesta, the sacred hearth, became a different thing than it had been under my father's rule. More public, more harshly moralistic. More my uncle's. He got rid of the old matron who had been in charge of the central fire-temple in the palace since I was a girl— my father's nursemaid and grandmother to dozens—and put me in charge, and three witless girls under me to do my bidding. So he said, but I knew he also set them to spy on me, to make sure I inspired no rebellions nor met in secret with men who might have challenged him. The health of the city was tied to the health of the fire, he said. If it went out, I would be beaten. I was the city's daughter now and could marry no man, but must tend the fire, carry the spring water, grind the holly emmer flour for offerings, until I was old, entirely chaste unto death. This was a new Vestal service, different from what I had known as a girl, in service to my uncle's rule.

I did it all at a great distance from myself. I hardly remember the details of those months save the cold clarity of my hatred. I plotted to kill my uncle I think, though not with very much foresight. I would stab him with the firepoker; I would gather hemlock seeds from the fields and offer him a Vestal cup. So I planned, so I dreamed, but the life was so thin in me those days that mostly I went through the motions of wood-gathering and the baking of offerings as if in a dream, and wept cold, un-relieving tears on my pallet until I slept.

But despite my distance, the people of Alba Longa flocked to me. My uncle had been clever, knowing that my presence would distract them, appease them. Hands touched my white dress in the street when I passed, coming or going on an errand for the sanctuary. On such errands I was followed at a little distance by my uncle's guard, but this did not perturb the people in the least. They pressed gifts upon me as if I were an idol carried from the temple, as if they were making wishes on my body. Apples, walnuts, quince, a lucky bit of amber, a red scrap of cloth.

In truth I think that those loving touches and small offerings helped to keep me living. In their hands they told me that they did not care so much about the hearth as they did about me, the daughter of their lost king, daughter of peace, daughter of fearlessness, of that time when young women still ran free and safe in the lanes, and their sons were not imminently to be mustered for a new war. They knew some treachery had occurred and were desperate, I think, to ask me of it, but I rarely spoke in that time, and anyway it was too dangerous. So the fruits, the nuts, the ribbons, the charms, were give instead of words, a language of hope over me—*do not, oh gods, take her from us too. See, it is all right, it must be, she is still here.*

I might have run away if I had been less listless, but the damage done me in body and in mind was a terrible kind of chain for the first months. It would have been a gamble anyway, for my mother's people had been the last of the old tribes and I did not know where I might go to be assured protection and not yet more ill use by men. But everything changed in the second month of my uncle's rule when my bleeding did not come and I found that I was pregnant.

It was impossible for me to say who the father was among the many who had killed my family, though sometimes in a sick malaise I feared it was my uncle. But I could not know. I never will. War was their father. This is what I tell myself now, and it is true. What War did to men—He was the unwanted father of my sons, and yet I pitied the babies who grew in me after hating them at first and trying to rid myself of the pregnancy using the herbal knowledge my mother had carefully taught me. My sons were little fighters even then. I bled dangerously and the old nursemaid who had once tended the Vestal fire helped me not to die, so that I kept both my life and my fierce twins.

It was she who first told me I carried twins, though I had felt in my fatigue their twoness, and in my daily sickness which I struggled to hide from my handmaids. Out of sheer desperation I managed to do so by going down at dawn to the river, to the spring where I gathered the Vestal water. There I would be sick in the deep shade of the sycamore trees where once I had played a little elder flute to Tiber and danced naked on a rock. A woman's place, that pool, the spring under a limestone rock, the shapely tree. Only the cold, clear water from that spring could soothe me on those mornings. I'd drink with my mouth right in the current, lapping with my tongue.

Once or twice I saw a man's face down near the clear bottom, where the white stones were round and the floating bronze leaves cast their shadows. I didn't pay it much heed, for my closed eyelids were so often full of the faces of my uncle's men. I did not want to look very closely, neither at the memory of them, nor the memory of my father and brother. I drank the cold water and it always settled my stomach enough that I could sit quietly for a time before I thought I would missed, and watch the leaves float, the small fly-catching birds flit and dart, and listen to the Tiber's low, sweet sound.

I brought some of the gifts the people pressed upon me to the river, to that water which had never deceived or betrayed me, and by whose side I had always been safe. Coppers, quince, red ribbons, walnut shells full of tallow and a wick. There by the water under the sycamore I came to love my unborn sons. I felt their tiny knees and elbows, shifting like the flutter of birds. A woodpecker often came to the tree and tapped while I sat, half-dreaming, hands to my belly. They were innocent. This I saw and knew when I sat there—innocent as I was, unspoiled though not unstained.

In my uncle's presence I still hated them sometimes, and thought of them like two leeches draining me, taking from me, put inside me when I had not wanted them, and yet my body cared for them with the absolution of Earth for all her creatures, making them beautiful, making them forgiven. After a time, thanks to the river and the tree, I loved them even in the face of my uncle, in defiance of him, of his men, of his wars. I thought if I loved them well enough I could protect them, I could will them to be other than what had brought them to me. But it wasn't enough. A mother's love for the sons nine months in her womb is not enough to keep them from the wars and deeds of the world of men, without her the other eighteen years until they are grown.

I managed by some miracle to hide the pregnancy from my women until it was seven months along. The robes we wore were loose, and I kept myself private from them when I changed, and I had always been small. But twins do not hide well, and when the cleverest of them, a girl called Mia, found me out at last, my suspicions of their daily treacheries to my uncle were confirmed. She had ambitions for my position as head Vestal, or perhaps aspired to be queen. In any case, when I saw her eyes on my belly in the sanctuary one day as a betraying wind blew my robes taut against my body so that the outline of my sons could not be hidden, I expected the worst. My uncle had proclaimed loudly to us, and to all in the city, that his Vestals were virgin, chaste, the city's pure vessels, a sign of the divinity of his ascension. Pregnancy was therefore punishable by instant death—drowning or burning outside the city wall.

Two days later I was seized and thrown into the dungeon. I still do not know what my uncle recalled, or suspected, or knew, whether he believed it when he called me slut and whore and accused me of intimacy with one of the guards, some seduction right in the Vestal sanctuary. When I said, to defy him, that the god of War had done it, he spat at my feet. Sometimes I think he really didn't remember; that he and his men had been too drunk on the violence they had done, so that everything around them that night was of the same matter, indistinguishable, I no more to any of them than the bodies they had slain. I don't know which is worse. That he did not remember, or that he did and still treated me thus.

What Amulis didn't reckon was the fury of the people of Alba Longa at my imprisonment, who by the following morning were gathered around the palace walls, chanting for my release. My uncle had not reckoned the law of the matriline among the ancient laws of our people. That the children of a daughter of Numitor had more right to the throne than his brother. I was a daughter of Alba Longa, Vestal priestess and, thanks to my uncle's rhetoric, not a whore in their eyes but a miracle, a virgin conception, the lover of a god, and therefore the mother of gods, or at least great heroes. Amulius, seeing the sticky place he found himself and the very real danger of revolt—and not wanting the blood of an entire city on his hands, not when he needed my father's farmers to take up arms for him come summer to conquer the neighboring Sabines, to bring more and more wealth to Alba Longa—did another clever, cruel thing in order to get what he wanted. Of course, it seemed benevolent to the people of Alba Longa, which was exactly what he intended. He released me from the dungeon and kept me on house arrest for the final two months, saying to the people that he was giving me the finest treatment as mother of a deity's child.

He allowed me once or twice a month to walk, heavily guarded, to the city center and back, just enough to appease the people that I was alive and well. On those days he dressed me in finery and had my maids apply lip paint to my mouth and kohl to my eyes, so that I appeared just as the people longed to see me—a beautiful auspicious thing, a quince tree bearing golden fruit, a nymph who might bless them if they only touched her round belly.

I bore it in numbness. Those final months were the worst of all. Hate alternately burned and numbed me. I remember mostly just the haze of it, like what's left behind after a fire. I hated the people of Alba Longa as much as my uncle by the end, for prolonging my humiliation. *Let me die, oh let me my sons when you are born.* I prayed this way, terrible prayers. I prayed pestilence and fire, earthquake, volcanic eruption, plague, all upon Alba Longa.

But at night I dreamt only of the Tiber and the cool spring water in my mouth. I dreamt I was swimming in the river, the water carrying my body, holding me, my round belly a buoy, a boat. I dreamt the eye of the river, as pale green as the water with its limestone banks, seeing through me, watching me tenderly.

I thought these were dreams of my death but they were not. They were dreams of something far stranger. They were dreams of what was to come.

Plague indeed struck, a terrible smallpox that took many of Alba Longa's children and left mothers and fathers desperate for someone to blame. My uncle was only too happy to supply that someone before they thought to blame him as the true cause, to blame the squalor his rule had created thanks to the taxes levied to support his many invasions. I became the blame, the source. The unclean daughter of Alba Longa, a whore after all. I had invited ruin on the city, just as he'd warned. I became scapegoat, spectacle, sorceress, no longer goddess.

He took my sons from me the moment their cords were cut and gave them to a solider to drown. I was bound and gagged and weighted down with stones inside my dress, my breasts searing with milk ungiven, blood still on my legs from the birth, and thrown in the river. A public spectacle, a sacrifice, an offering.

If she floats, she is divine, pure after all, and she will save us all. If she sinks, she is a curse, the cause, and it is I who have saved you. So my uncle said before the gathered crowd.

Needless to say, with so many stones in my dress and my limbs bound, I sank. Also I did not fill my lungs enough to even attempt to float. I sank to the very bottom of the deepest bend in the river where I had been thrown, a mile outside the city so as not to bring ill luck too near. The people of Alba Longa threw flour and coins in the water after me to appease the evil I carried. I saw this as I thrashed and sank. Then I hit the smooth river bottom, and it was a relief. Darkness filled my eyes, and I remembered my mother by the fire in the beechwood and how she danced. I saw the young singer I had loved for a season, and my brother running until his dark hair flew among the rows of wheat and red poppies.

After that, I knew no more except arms carrying me, warm and strong. The Tiber bore me out of time and into darkness, into a place of rich and woven shadows, a place of roots. The arms carried me into the river's unending time.

I drifted without name, without fixed form. I was a wolf, fur of sky-gray, suckling the sons I had lost. I was a woodpecker, red-capped, knocking at the trees for word of my children. I was the wife of a shepherd in a humble clay house on a mountain, raising foundling boys as fierce as wolf-pups. I was a sycamore tree with my wide roots in the river and my trunk curved as a woman's body, my leaves filling and filling with sun. I was the beech forest of my childhood, and the oak, and the mountain's white stone.

IT WAS ONLY WHEN, much to my surprise, I actually woke up still Rhea, though entirely naked, that I realized those arms had been real and not the arms of death. They were familiar arms, belonging to the man by the fire. I had seen them before. This I thought vaguely as I woke in a deep holt in the riverbank among the smooth roots of a tree. A place like an otter's home, only bigger, drier, polished with light.

I lay warm under a nest of carefully braided rabbit skins, on top of a dense ram-skin and a bed of dry reeds. Light came from the fire in a hearth, and from the man who sat, somewhat hunched and big-shouldered, at the far corner, mending something green as beech leaves in his lap. A light came from him that was not the fire's glance, but something deeper, veined, green as the Tiber in sun.

I remembered him then.

He was the man I had seen the day my uncle brought me as a captive back into my own city, who dove into the river and did not emerge. He felt my eyes and looked up from the needle and cloth in his lap. How can such a large hand thread such a small needle? I thought, still vague. I knew his face too. Wide-nosed, eyes pale as river water and deep-set, hair short and dark as an otter's. He smiled when he saw me wake, a smile that turned all that was harsh in his features to something gentle. It was the face I'd seen in the Tiber's pool when I drank from it to ease the sickness my sons had brought me.

My sons.

I don't know if the words came out of me or stayed in, but the one who sat green-eyed by the fire spoke to me as if I had said them aloud.

"Your sons lived. I made sure of it." His voice was as smooth as the river that had carried me, and as deep. "I am sorry I could not bring you to them. I am sorry I could not carry you all elsewhere, to another land. But to keep you from death I had to take you far away, and it took many turnings of the world before you would come back to yourself." He stood, holding the green cloth out, and came toward me, moving as a muscle of water and yet steadily, so as not to frighten me. But I was frightened still, for he was a man, the river's god, and some of the memory of before was in my body still, though not as much as there had been. I flinched, and he stopped halfway to me from the fire, holding out what I saw was a green dress. His face hardened, but not at me.

"I have yet to forgive what was done to you, daughter of the wood. Know that I drowned as many of your uncle's men as I could manage, though not your uncle himself. Another who hated him just as well got there before me."

"You've—what?" I think this was the first thing I actually spoke aloud, and my voice was hoarse with disuse. "Why have you done these things for me? And—who are you?" I knew the answer to that part already, but I wanted to hear it spoken just to be certain.

"Surely you know me. I am the Tiber, and I have watched over you since you were young. You who never failed to bring me honey and milk and wine. You who sang my secret names, and danced on the stone."

"Did I?" I said faintly, trying to remember what it had felt like to be a girl carrying jugs of milk to the riverbank, and singing to the current.

"You did," he replied, low, still smiling, still perfectly motionless in the middle of the room with the green dress in his hands.

"Very well," I said. "But I do not remember your secret names now. Tell me, Tiber River, why it is you speak of my sons in the past, and my uncle? Tell me, where are we, and how long have I been... not myself?"

Keeping one eye on me like one might a frightened deer, he stepped nearer once more, and again, and sat down on a smooth seat, not too close but close enough to lay the green dress quietly on the bed.

Then he told me the story of Romulus and Remus, my sons.

As he spoke in his low, riverstone voice I remembered the dark, formless time that had seemed like death. I felt the many seasons that some part of me had passed through, not my body but some other piece of me, while the Tiber held me in the bank, keeping me warm, keeping me safe.

He told me how the soldier had not killed my sons as my uncle had ordered but, taking pity on the tiny newborn things, set them in a covered basket given him by his wife and put them in the river, where Tiber carried them in his arms just as gently and effortlessly as he had carried me. He brought them to a deep bank of reeds where a wolf whose cubs had been killed by hunters found them and loved them at once, and took them back to her cave. There they were all three watched over by a red-capped woodpecker. One day a woman named Acca followed that woodpecker because she had dreamed of him, and found my infant boys in the wolf's cave, wild as cubs and covered in sticks and leaves. She took them when the wolf mother was hunting, and she and her husband raised them as shepherd boys who knew no violence save the necessary slaughter of sheep, and much happiness among the seven hills of that valley where the Tiber ran most beautifully toward my mother's mountain.

It is a story well known, the story of Romulus and Remus and the founding of Rome. How my father, the old king Numitor, having survived the slaughter, returned from a long time hiding in the mountains to find a contingent of young angry men eager to avenge the murder of his family. In his loss he had become honed for vengeance too. How my boys, full grown by then, became leaders of that pack of youths who were hungry for justice, for freedom from Amulius' harsh reign, but mostly hungry to be heroes. How Remus was captured at Alba Longa and Romulus led the men in his rescue. How Numitor and Amulius both recognized their own faces in the faces of my sons. How Amulius was killed, and Numitor restored to the throne of Alba Longa, and the boys, my boys, my young sons, went home to the place of seven hills where they had been suckled by the wolf and raised by the good shepherds, full of their own virility, their own power, and the blessing of support and resources from their grandfather. How they decided with the exuberance of youth to found their own city, the greatest city in the world.

They had many followers, Romulus the most, being the bigger and stronger and more daring of the two. Remus had become troubled after his stay in his great-uncle's dungeon. I do not like to wonder what befell him there. He cowered at the sound of metal brushing metal, and liked to be alone. Wolves came to him and treated him as brother when they had long since abandoned Romulus.

The Tiber told me my sons quarreled about where their city should be founded, which of the seven hills in the great valley should be its center. Remus preferred a wilder hill, the one where they had roamed as shepherd boys, while his twin favored a hill more gently sloped, more open. It was a stupid quarrel. They sought auguries, watching for birds, so that the gods might show them who was right. Romulus had become a little cruel in his arrogance, and Remus a little cruel in his pain. Killing did not sit easily on the latter, and all to easily on the former. Still, I do not believe that it was Romulus's hand that struck the killing blow in the end, but rather one of his followers, eager to put Remus in his place when he tried to argue against his brother's vision for the city and how they would begin. They'd need women, being a lone band of men, Romulus had reasoned. Why shouldn't they just steal some from the Sabines? This was met with hilarity and excitement both, save from Remus, who hit his brother square on the jaw at the idea. Young men and drink and bloodlust and knives, alone among seven hills, dreaming of cities and glory.

It ended with Remus dead. His grieving twin buried him in the hill he had preferred, the Aventine. Wolves sang that night in mourning, and never showed their eyes to Romulus again.

"BRING ME TO THEM, BRING ME TO THIS CITY called Rome," I said to the Tiber when he was finished. I spoke through tears that were many, so many they had begun, without my realizing it, to carry off the stains of before.

"We are in it Rhea, daughter of the wood," he replied, saying my name softly. "But this was long ago, these stories I tell you about the lives of your sons. A hundred years, a thousand, I do not count in human time. I only kept track for your sake, to carry the story to you when it was too late to carry you to your sons."

"But—why is it too late? Why did you take me away from them?" I said with a wolf's ferocity, almost snarling. He did not flinch.

"You were so near to death, I had to take you out of time. I had to make you other than time, or woman, in order to save your life. You may be what you choose now, but you, like me, will never walk within time among human beings again. You may walk beside them but you will be apart and only some will believe in you enough to see you, like you have always seen me." His pale eyes held mine, and he let fall his long arms to his sides. "I am sorry."

"Why was my life so worth the saving to you?" I whispered. "When it was not even to me? When I would gladly have died, rather than know what sorrow met my sons?"

"Because," said the Tiber, and he looked at me with a look no man had ever given me. A look that saw me not as Rhea Silvia, not even as a woman, but as a mystery equal to the night. A vast brightness within a skin. Something that was only temporarily held by banks. Something immensely beautiful, and precious. "Because," he said again, lower yet, with a twitch of muscle in his jaw.

And I saw for an instant what he too was without the shouldered strength of riverbanks. How I, as a young woman, had danced right at the edge of him, without fear, and recognized all of him then.

But he said no more. A great ripple seemed to move through him under his skin. Of longing, of sorrow, of patience. He turned away and went out of the holt into the daylight, leaving me there alone.

After a moment, watching him go, I reached for the green dress he had laid on the bed, the dress he had been stitching. It fit me like a wolf fits her skin. It was made of no material I knew, not wool or linen or leather, more akin to beech leaves than to any of these. Dressed in it I stood up, a little tentative. But when I felt the weight of my body, my bare feet, my hips and breasts, I felt the life of me rise up from the roots below the riverbank and return to me, to the center of me, where nothing had stirred or lit for what seemed an eon. I stood alone and felt how I had been wolf and woodpecker, shepherd's wife and tree, as well as Rhea daughter of Silvia, princess of Alba Longa, mother of twins.

I went slowly to the fire and placed one hand on the seat where the god of the Tiber had sat sewing. It was warm still where he had been, and I smiled to myself. It had been many seasons, I think, since I had smiled that way. I set a log in the flames and felt the last pieces of humiliation and shame and pain in me settle into the fire with it, on their way to becoming ashes as all the ones I had known or borne or loved were ashes now. Save one.

Then I went to the mouth of the holt and looked out across the Tiber's pale water upon the city of Rome.

THEY CALL ME MOTHER OF ROME, and though it is true that the boys who began it were of my body, they were equally of the body of War. If I had been their mother after the first second of their breathing, if I had been their mother and brought them to the mountain and showed them the ways of my mother's people, and the peace that their grandfather once carried, I wonder, what of Rome? Would other men have made it, or none? Would Remus have lived to watch his own granddaughters come running down the hill, hands full of crocus and chestnut? We will never know.

But this I do know, as I knew that morning when I first looked out the Tiber's holt and saw it—I am not mother of Rome the city, Rome the empire, Rome the conqueror whose way is still eating up the world. But I have become mother the trees that men cut, and I have become mother of the stones men hew. I am mother of Rome the soil, Rome the seven hills, the wolf cave, the fertile valley beneath, mother of the sacred fire women held for a thousand generations back to the first, back to the stag in the beechwood and my mother's dryad hands. And I am no longer mortal but the wife of the Tiber that runs through it all, from a spring in a mountain to the mouth of the sea.

These days, my Tiber aches in his stone canals, ugly with the iridescence of petroleum, the plastic wrappings of despair. But I still know him as he knew me that day when he looked into me and saw the night. We have held each other long now, tree-root twined through river-bend. And we will be here still when the buildings have all fallen and are a crumbled skin of metal and marble at the feet of the seven hills. When the cities of humankind are ruins and the shepherds graze their goats on hills once made of trash, and the Tiber's flood at last breaks down every levy that has held him.

Then, no woman will ever be held down under the hands of War, and no man turned into them, again.

THE DARK COUNTRY

Once she wakes, everything—star womb hand hoof cave thread boat tide bat prince lace—is her matter. Women especially should take care, if they do not want their hands to do her bidding. Hers which is ruthless, beautiful beyond word, and just. Her justice the circle that knows no end.

-*Of Earth*, in the Old Language

The day the men from Tar brought the bandit girl Lillet back to the newly conquered acropolis at Kranea, a small earthquake shook the island of Kefthyra. It wasn't strong enough to dislodge anything more than a few loose stones from low walls, and startle the goats. But what the earthquake shifted below the ground could not be seen, and in all the city only the old charwoman Arete had the vaguest idea.

Lillet was just one of a cartload, the latest prisoners brought in from the Tarish conquests along the southern coast. She sat apart, very straight and alone in the back corner against the wood, her knees to her chest and her arms around them. Like the other women in the cart, there were bruises across her body. But unlike the others in their torn yellow shifts and linens, she wore tanned goatskins, bloody now, and no shoes. She didn't weep or moan or prattle. She didn't move at all, and hardly blinked. The black intensity of her eyes, staring at nothing, made her look feral. It frightened the other women, though she was the youngest among them, a girl of just thirteen. When the earth shook and the carthorses bolted, she did not make a noise or stir in fright. She kept as still as before, staring at her long thin hands, like a girl made not of flesh but of stone.

THAT MORNING THE CITY OF KRANEA smelled of rain. Small purple crocuses pressed through the red earth. Pomegranates, near ripe, hung russet and beaded with silver. Thunder had filled the night, and bolts of violet. At dawn, hearth-fires from the houses of the common people, both in the city and on the plain around it, sent smoke up to the clouds, full of offered meat and prayers to the One Who Brought Thunder, beseeching that their homes be spared lighting, thanking Him for rain. Many houses bore olive branches over the lintels for protection, or the dried bodies of kingfishers hung at the hearth, iridescent blue.

By his bedroom window, naked, the Prince of Tar snorted at the sight of all that smoke. Nonsense and superstition, he thought dismissively, pushing his wooden shutters open wider and looking out across his city. *His city.* The thought thrilled and satisfied him. Limestone walls and red clay roofs gleamed fresh under the hands of dawn. The thunderheads were sailing south, out over the bay. Not god sent as all these simple islanders believed, only weather. He had already enacted the rule of Tar across the land to eradicate any such notion of a higher power beyond himself, sending his men to destroy every temple and place of worship they could find. There were no gods in Tar, only winds, and stones, and storms. Not fate, only might. Gods did not win you cities, nor wreck your ship upon the rocks; only might, and chance, and luck. Might was generally the best of the three.

It was the prince's father who had declared it so in Tar some thirty years past—that there were no gods, only he, a god of men and land. The prince knew even this for the posturing it was, useful but empty. A god was only a man who got his way. Nothing and no one was holy. One's own death could not be controlled, which did not make it sacred, but simply a nuisance. Other men's deaths were more easily arranged. If there were gods of thunder, then surely he and his father would have both been struck by lightning long ago, for declaring the gods a lie and man the only power. Well, they hadn't been. They were alive and well. The prince ran his hands down his bare chest, muscled from war. That was proof enough.

THE PRINCE OF TAR, LATEST IN THE LINE of Kefthyra's conquerors, had subdued the acropolis at Kranea with little trouble, his forces far outnumbering the city's guards. Tar itself lay to the west, on a long thin peninsula that jutted out from the mainland, but its empire was rapidly growing north into the mountains and east across the islands of the White Sea. Kefthyra's previous ruler, a man not native to Kefthyra but from the desert kingdom called Aget that sat along the White Sea's southern reach, had been easily disposed of; for years Aget's forces had been stretched thin due to a drought at home.

Kefthyra was a jewel, and so it had been passed between conquering hands for generations. Its biggest harbors were the color of purified lapis. Everything that was scarce in Aget and in Tar grew in abundance there—olives and pomegranates and quince, figs and pistachios and the oak tree called kermes, for the little insects who fed on its sap and produced a red dye under their shining carapaces. The island's central mountain, Mt. Enos, was a rarity for its pine-dark slopes. Thunderheads sat on the mountain as queens upon a throne, and more rain fell against its verdant slopes than anywhere else across all the White Sea. It was mainly that dark, unbroken pine forest for which Kefthyra was invaded; that and its position as an outpost between enemies. Tar had long since deforested most of its native mountains and hills for timber, and Aget, being a desert land, never had any to begin with, which made the acquisition of a forested island all the more appealing.

For close to three hundred years, Kefthyra had been Aget's furthest colonial outpost. Mostly, their reign had been an economic one, trade-based and little concerned with day-to-day life. Fishermen and traders learned the Aget words for the things of their crafts, and otherwise carried on as they always had. The Aget court at Kranea was lavish but insular, and little affected the common folk, save in the way of religious decrees. Always, conquerors brought with them their gods.

But now, a Tarish prince sat on the Kefthyran throne. The youngest son of the King of Tar. Kefthyra had been his first conquest, led alone and without the shadow of father or brothers. He was impatient now, though it had only been a month since his decisive victory, to turn the court at Kranea into a place of unrivalled splendor. Already his men were busy looting the coastline. He wanted silks and carpets, robes and cloaks and wall hangings all spun and woven new for his court, so that he might welcome his brothers and his father into a kind of opulence they would never have expected he could achieve so quickly. He wanted to exceed them in all things. Already he could see new gashes along the slopes of Mt. Enos, where his men were harvesting lumber. Their bare, widening swaths gave him pleasure.

He wanted a court of red. The finest crimson. Trade in purple was on the wane across the White Sea; the little whorl-shelled creatures from which it came were all but extinct from the hunger of princes and kings for robes the color of storms. But red! This was a better color even than purple, and Kefthyra was known for its kermes, its vats of vermillion. He would make red the color of kings.

Only a fortnight past, he had sent his men to seize a woman, one of the dyers of the north coast renowned there for her red, so they might have the best crimson made right inside the city walls. His own red. No one but he would be privy to it. Slave-women had been set to work spinning and weaving cloth for her to dye. The latest cartload of female prisoners promised more hands for the weaving, and more maids for the kitchen and hearth too, as they had the unfortunate habit of getting with child. The prince's bastards, and his soldier's.

Besides the prince's desire for a red court, the soldiers from Tar were short on clothing of every kind, having ransacked half the island and unthinkingly burned most of its looms. Where villages remained intact—up the steep, rocky flanks of far Mt. Calo, hidden in oak valleys out of sight of the sea—the women were not forthcoming with their linen or their wool. The island had known been conquered many times before, and the people knew it was best to remain as quiet and uninteresting as possible, like the sheep they tended, and hope the threat would pass, and life return to some semblance of what it had been before.

But the men of Tar were different than the men of Aget whom they had taken the island from, and the eastern steppe-riders before them both. They saw no reason not to seize a village just for the sport of it, killing the men and taking the women back by the cartload to the capital. They struck at random, like boys at play, gluttonous and cruel.

Some villagers responded by hiding in the forest. Others with defiance. Far up Mt. Enos one village refused to be taken, though they were far outnumbered. Old men fought with rakes and axes. When the women saw that they were surrounded, and that they would be seized, they joined hands with their children and danced the harvest dance in a circle at the farthest cliff's edge. One by one they stepped over the side, all the while singing, until only an old woman was left singing the song of the barley alone. At last she leapt too, with a curse on her tongue.

Seven hundred years before Aget, Kefthyra had been invaded by the nomads of Helladia, who sought land to pasture their livestock and grow their strange ryes and barleys. Before the men of Helladia, Kefthyra had known no conquest. Back then, Earth kept her own justice. When someone wronged her in any significant way, she swallowed him and left a mountain in his place. Not the pettier wrongs that humans so often fight over—my pasture, my silver, my wife—but wrongs that bent the boundaries of a wider wholeness. Wrongs that harmed the health of woodlands, of streambeds, of seas.

In those days, humans could still understand the language of animals, and followed their laws of balance and restraint. Cycles of abundance followed cycles of lack, and worship was made with dance and song in a tongue the oaks and birds and bears all gathered near to hear. But when the horseriders from Helladia first came across the mainland and colonized the islands of the White Sea, they killed the bears without ceremony. They cut the trees without prayer. They slaughtered men and took their women and looked up to the sky, not down to the ground, for their gods. They set their cattle loose everywhere. Powers too powerful for names became nymphs that gods chased to the last, turning into every kind of bud and beast until they were seized, and bedded on cold ground which did not, no matter their screams, swallow them whole. And because Earth no longer seemed to exact her justice, the people believed that maybe the new rule was her will, the will of unseen forces. For would she not have buried these men and their horses under a mountain long ago, if it had been otherwise?

But they did not reckon the Earth's own sorrow. How her darkness was her power. How she could not swallow when humans had lost the words of the dark country below their feet, the words that animals know, and stones, and stars. For her justice had been theirs. The dark country works too slowly for human knowing, when words are lost.

Slow, said the stories that women remembered down the generations of war. A piece here, a piece there, none of it entire. A human life is a day in her time, not even yet the night. *Slow*, in the old words for stone, and sea. *Slow*, until words were whole again, and made of fat and darkness. After a time, no woman could remember what the stories meant, or how anything could ever be changed. Only the words and their pieces remained, surfacing in dreams when they had been all but forgotten, from some great and bottomless depth.

THE DOOR OPENED BEHIND THE PRINCE OF TAR as he stood at the window. He hoped it was the pretty serving girl with his breakfast tray and her body on the offer too. He turned, hot with the thought. But it was only the old charwoman Arete, lined as a horseman's boot and just as dark, come to stoke the fire. It was early. Normally he slept past dawn, and didn't stir when she entered. But the thunder had woken him today.

Arete was startled to see the prince at the window, unclothed. She began to back away.

"Get on with it then," he snapped, turning, irritated by her age and her body, lumpy as a quince in the doorframe. He was disturbed by the way her dark eyes lingered on his half-risen cock, not with the blush of the serving maid but with a cold, almost clinical disdain. "Unless you feel like a fuck," he added savagely, more irritated still that she would not turn her eyes from him.

There were a lot of things Arete felt like saying in reply, coarse, nasty things and perhaps a handful of hemlock tossed in his fire along with them. But she valued her life; free or enslaved she loved without fail the blooming things, the smell of the sea, the bluegreen olive trees, the sun. For why else had she not thrown herself off the walls at midnight long before? Besides, there was that nagging feeling she had more and more of late, of something she could not quite remember that nevertheless needed to be done. So she allowed herself only a dry little chuckle and a single knot untied from the bit of lace in her apron. It was a strange, girlish sound, and it sent a flick of dread down the prince's spine.

She built a sturdy eager fire of olive wood and did not look at him again. The fire was smokeless and hot. She dusted the ash from the hearthstones with the boar bristle brush that hung at her waist and tossed a handful of rosemary into the blaze.

Just as the sprigs caught flame, the stone walls made a low jolting noise, shuddering dust. The fire leapt and one of the logs fell out onto the floor. Outside, the horses pulling the cartload of women through the city's gates bolted. There was a clatter of hooves and the sound of one wheel breaking out in the entry court. Calmly, Arete rolled the log back into the hearth with the iron poker and said a prayer for stillness out of habit. Small earthquakes were so common on the island of Kefthyra that the people grew uneasy without them. Already the earth had quieted again. But the prince's hand had gone very white where it held the bed's oak post. Arete wanted to laugh. Outsiders were always uneasy when the ground shook. Instead she bit her tongue and watched the fire until the flames had grown orange around the log once more.

Another, much smaller earthquake quivered far underground, but the prince didn't notice. The serving girl had come in with the breakfast tray. Arete could hear her little laughing sighs. Disgusted, she stood. It was then she saw the shapes of snakes flickering across the olive wood in the hearth. The lace in her apron pocket, which she worked on daily between tasks, felt hot against her thigh. Alive. She stepped back from the fire and the lace stilled again in her pocket.

"Oh," said Arete, eyeing the flames. The snakes were still there, seething, shadowed inside the heat. The old word for Snake came to her: a thick, smooth word that curled on her tongue. She didn't speak it. She wasn't sure she had ever heard it spoken, or how she knew it now. Only that with its knowing, she knew other things, brief but vivid, and the lace in her pocket seemed to be of their shape. As if she could see all the threads of the world, each thing hooked to the next and all of it pulsing and alive. That was what the old language spoke. She knew this without ever having been told it as she looked into the fire whose shadows were snakes. And she knew that what made her a woman, and had since she was young, carried this shape of power. That the knowings she had dismissed her whole life long were in fact nothing less than this: her own power.

"Old woman," came the prince's voice from the bed, muffled. A giggle beside him. Arete didn't turn. She barely even heard him, so full was she with her own selfhood. "Old woman," he repeated, with more disgust now. "She must be demented. Leave this room, old woman, you're spoiling my mood."

THAT EVENING ARETE'S EYES ROVED the slavewomen's weaving quarters for signs of snakes and found them everywhere. The way a ball of red wool fell, serpentine. The way a hank of yellow fleece at a spindle-tip danced its vortex. She saw that all of it spoke, but she didn't know what it said. Talk was low among the women. The prince's new dye woman Zola sang a kermes-gathering song from Ateras, a valley up the northwest coast. A matron, but firm and slim despite, with long breasts and fine wide hips. Her black hair was braided in a heavy hank straight and thick to her waist, as streaked with silver as a moonless night. She sang in a deep voice, a low dark river of wine run through with sorrow.

Arete hadn't paid her much heed before tonight—she was just another woman with sadness in her eyes, with a burnt village and a slaughtered husband crouched there like silent screams in her heart. So much loss had made Arete distant, and hard. But tonight, she watched the woman from Ateras and saw the red snaking at her hands as she dipped and tested her crimson skeins.

A new girl, Lillet, whose name was the only word she had uttered since she arrived, sat in a dark corner, trying to spin flax well away from the others. She was making a mess of it. Her skinny hands shook in the torchlight, and she pricked one finger on the distaff beside the heap of sun-burnished flax. The pain of the prick, though light, broke her. There was so much in her ready to break. She stifled a sob. Arete looked up at the sound. It was its own thread, and it pulled her to her feet, seeking the source.

Arete hadn't been there earlier when the latest cartload of women arrived. She'd been in the prince's room, building up the fire. Whenever she could she tried to be in the slavewomen's quarters when the new ones arrived, to help bathe them and clothe them in fresh linen, to comb out their hair and braid it back, sponge compresses of rosemary and thyme on bruises and wounds. As for the unseen wounds, the sons or husbands or fathers whose deaths they had witnessed, the damage often done to virginity and self-respect, Arete burned a bit of the resin of the poppy to let them sleep that first night in oblivion. She was the only one of the women to administer such occult mercies. Others looked at her with fear, or sidelong, knowing the danger in the practice of old ways, especially now.

Clearly the poor child in the corner had received no such attention. A bath, yes, for her hair shone wet in its tight new braids, and she wore a clean belted shift with a plain black shawl. Maybe it had been hard-eyed Vela on hand when the cart came, a youngish woman from the southern coast whose grief made her mean. She especially scorned the ones who had been raped, as her husband had been killed protecting her from such a fate. She would rather he were alive and her body defiled, than to have lost him thus, and so hated those who had been with a kind of convoluted, irrational rage. Vela was watching Arete now from over her spindle, where a skein of fine wool grew. Her eyes were hard, perceptive.

Arete tucked the lace into her apron as she made her way toward Lillet. A few others glanced up, then away. Sorrow lay close to the skin. Someone sighed, but didn't stir. Zola was the only other woman to rise and go to the girl. She didn't stop her low singing as she moved, but Arete could see that the red snakes were still at her hands, though she'd set her skeins aside. When she blinked they were gone, coiling into the fire's shadows, which leapt across the room where the girl sat sucking her pricked finger. Arete and Zola reached her at once, meeting one another's eyes only then.

A strange recognition moved through them and through the limestone floor, through the worn goat hair carpets and their fading patterns of cross and line. Zola felt what she had felt only one other time before, in the oak grove when the men of Tar seized her, and the red of the kermes had risen through her body to protect her. Arete felt the same power she had been watching all day, and all her life without knowing.

Filaments, moving.

"Child," said Zola to the girl, offering her hand. "Spin no more tonight. We will finish the work."

Before ever and any
The stones dreamed
The limestone
The granite
The flint

When stones walked
The world dreamed
In the dream
Stars came down
To crouch in stones
And tell them words

Stones could go anywhere
Back then
Time had not yet begun

Kefthyra walked everywhere
Moonwhite her limestone

Where she went
And what she saw
Those are a Greater Mystery

The word that rang in her
When the world
Was stone and dreaming

That is the word
The snake swallowed
And swallows still

The Firstmade
Told by Moon

- *Of Stone*, from the Old Language

L illet never intended to become a bandit. Neither did the three shepherd brothers who saved her life. But loss necessitates many unlikely things. She never intended to become anything other than a small version of her mother: a fisherman's wife who mended pine-dyed nets by candlelight, who could gut a fish without looking and knew all the lore, prayers, songs and secrets of the Moon that a woman could know in those times, given what had been lost. But the soldiers from Tar wanted the eastern port called Pore where Lillet and her parents lived, and to secure it at the end of the first month of their rule they took possession of every last residence, killing anyone who didn't flee. Lillet's father wouldn't leave, and her mother stayed by his side.

My blood is this sea; my soul is a fish, he said. He armed himself with net and fish knife and an anchor for a club. Her mother did the same. *Hide, my little goose, my dove,* she said to Lillet, and tucked her, gangly-legged, into the burl of an old olive tree behind their small stone house, a hollow where Lillet had often played. It was beginning to feel too small for a thirteen-year-old girl, but still she managed to tuck her knees out of sight, fist tears back down her throat, and wait. *Run, my heart,* her mother said, *run in the night when you smell their cook fires. Run to the cave and wait for help. And do not be afraid for us. We are ever in the hands of the Moon. Look to her, and I am there.*

Lillet didn't understand then why this sounded like goodbye.

She was too afraid to understand anything. Later, huddled in the olive tree, she heard the screams and saw the men from Tar with their plumed helmets, their bright breastplates and their warhorses in the streets of Pore. Then, she knew. She knew that the screams from her house were her mother and father, going. She wanted to run right then. But she held her mother's words close like white sea stones, like pieces of moon, and waited until the evening star had risen.

All was quiet then, save a blaze of cook fires in the streets of Pore, and the voices of blood-drunk men, singing and shouting and laughing. They didn't sound like men to Lillet. Their language was rough and spined. It was angled in their throats. They sounded like demons. She uncrooked herself from the olive burl and saw then that her mother had stuffed a bundle of shawl and dried fish and bread beside her. With this in hand she ran.

The night smelled of smoke and a cold wind off the sea. It smelled of metal and of blood, but that was the smell of fear in Lillet's nostrils, its taste in her mouth, which she forced closed to keep herself from screaming. She knew the way to the cave by full moonlight, but tonight there was no moon, only the stars, thick in their brightness. Milk from the breast of the moon, her mother called that snaking way. Tonight, Lillet only saw blood. Still she found her way in the dark. Her feet knew it, bare for silence. She made no more sound than a bird. Just the small hush of her feet, the feathered rustle of her skirt, her bundled food, following the riverbed into the gorge. Soles on smooth white limestone, the summerfall of sycamore leaves. Where the river bent left at the sideways scrub oaks there was a moonwise path, steep as a goat track up the gorge wall. It was best not to look down.

When Lillet was younger, and her mother first brought her to the cave called Drakaina to leave offerings for the Moon, she had frozen halfway up from the fear in her legs. But her mother had shown her how to breathe away fear. That fear was a priestess whose lessons were hard, but vital. Now she remembered her mother's words, not for fear of heights but for fear of what she had seen and what she had not seen of the men of Tar. Her hands were clammy with it on the helping boughs of the scrub oaks. Her knees shook with it on the stone ledges where soft sages grew. What it had been like, when her parents died. If the Moon had folded them into her light, into the curve of eternity, into her coves of salt. And had the men of Tar seen the Moon do so, bone-white? Surely not. Surely they could not, or they would not do the things they did.

Tonight the climb was endless. Lillet was walking into the dark and into the stars. Right up into the constellation they called the Moon's Crown, that northern circlet led by a bright and distant planet. Her breath and her knees made her dizzy. Her mouth was dry but she said the words her mother taught her, the prayers so old they were in another language, passed on from mother to daughter since before the time of kings. Words for the moon, for the stone, for the water. For the life inside the dark's seed. She stepped on thyme and furred sage and smelled their night scents. At last, bruising her nails, she pulled herself up the last stone ledges and reached the cave.

Its darkness was complete. She lit the candle from her mother's bundle with a flint. The cave shuddered and loomed, but its ledges and ribbons of stalactite drip, its floor stones and small fire circle and far recesses, were all familiar. She lay a crust of her bread on the offering ledge, clambered into the deepest, darkest corner, far back in the cold where it smelled only of earth and nothing human. There, exhausted by fear and grief, she slept without moving and without dreams.

Wait there for help. Others will come, her mother had said. *Never forget whose hands your life belongs to.* So Lillet waited for four days and four nights, eating the salted fish and the crust of bread, leaving a small portion of each as an offering though she starved. She lit no fire, fearing the smoke's giveaway. She only ventured as far as the mouth to relieve herself. By the fourth day, she was in danger of dying from thirst. By then, she was too weak to move, and too sorrowful. *No one is coming, mother,* she rasped into the dark. Her lips bled.

Only a handful of other women and their daughters and granddaughters still came to the cave as Lillet and her mother did. It had been many hundreds of years since women had gone openly to worship in the island's dark, to listen for what it said. Five hundred years at least since there had been schools for women to study the mysteries found only in that slick, chthonic quiet, bearing snakes in clay vessels. Lillet's mother whispered some of those stories at night, and on their way up to Drakaina. Some of the words were in that older tongue, a language that hissed and waned and lapped. Now they waxed dizzily through Lillet's weakness as she lay in the cave dark, smelling chthonic depths and old fire ash. Strange dreams visited her. The dark wet warmth of being born. The suffocation, the sudden, screaming light. Snakes hiding by the hundred in the earth. The little broad-hipped, snake-faced figurines and votives on the ledges came to life, dancing, calling out her name until her name meant nothing and she was nothing and the cave was her mother and she was only a little stone that had been around as long as stars, to whom death meant nothing.

At last she dreamed that she was cocooned in spidersilk like lace, and knew that she was dying. That all the other women had been killed. That no one would come for her. Was she the last who knew the old words? She rasped them, a stone's song, to the darkest part of the cave, into the cleft, into the underworld: *stone, snake, bear, salt, water, moon, red.*

That's how the bandits found her. Curled up like a near-dead lamb in the furthest dark, her lips to the wall. There was a little moisture there, which she had licked.

"A dying nymph, a husk, a child!" called Alzance, the oldest and the one who saw her first. He kicked back the goats and the black dog at his heels. He held a torch of olive wood dipped in oil, and the light blazed through Lillet's darkness, waking her enough to croak.

"Water!" cried Alzance.

A giant, Lillet thought. A beard of wild black wool, and hair the same, and skin as thick and dark as acorn shells. Knives all along his belt, and silent kidskin boots, and four goats with horns and no bells. Just enough for milk, and meat. A shaggy black dog, silent as earth and with a white star on his chest, watched her.

The cave was suddenly full of men. Three only, but they seemed dozens to Lillet. The first one, the biggest, scooped her up as if she were no more than a newborn and laid her on a goatskin. He fed her the water from a squeezed bit of leather so she didn't choke on her own thirst. A smaller man, but still of wooly beard and wild dark eyes, built a smokeless fire. The dog lay down beside Lillet and put his head on his paws, whining. His eyes were amber. She slept again.

The three were brothers, and only bandits of late, spurred thus by desperation when they lost their home and flocks to the men of Tar. The youngest was fifteen, the oldest twice that and a widower. Alzance, Spiros and Vris they were called, and even Vris, the youngest, had a thick and early beard. It would be as wooly as his brothers' soon.

"Do you worship the old gods too?" Lillet said when she was awake again that evening and had swallowed down a whole horn of water. "The goat-hoofed one, the piper? Are you his? Am... am I dead?" This thought alarmed her more than a little, and she sat up all the way, propped on skins by their hot and smokeless fire. Meat cooked there in a soup pot. All three laughed at this, enjoying the laughter, for there was little enough to laugh at these days. The goats grazing sage at the cave mouth looked up.

"No, little lady," said Alzance. His broad, furred face seamed gently when he smiled. "We aren't wood folk, though we do honor the name of the Hoofed One, especially of late." He put a hand on the cool, mineral-lined wall. "Is it a holy cave? We are far from home, and sought it for the shelter. The goats seemed to know the way."

"It is." Lillet swallowed. Her mother. The old words. The Moon. Tears sat close behind her eyes, and though he meant it kindly, they began to fall when Spiros, the middle brother, stood and bowed to the ledge of figurines and vessels, making a sign of honor with his hand. Not everyone still remembered or made that sign. He was a little clumsy, but the low murmur of his prayer, asking forgiveness and protection from the cave's mother, warmed Lillet behind her tears.

"Did they burn your home, too?" said Vris, eyes big and bright on Lillet, like the dog's. He got a heel in the side from Alzance.

"Little brother, that is no way to soothe a child."

"I'm no child," Lillet said. "Not anymore. I'm all alone, so I must be a woman now." She shot them all a fierce look, tilting up her sharp chin. She supposed, belatedly, that she should be wary of strange men. But these men did not frighten her, despite their shagginess, their size, their many knives. She felt herself in the company of bears, like in an old story. Her look quieted them. It was gaunt and angled in the firelight, her brown eyes hollow, her black hair matted and wild, her nose sharp like her chin. A witchgirl she looked, a nymph. Childish, yes—for she was yet a gangly, flat-chested little thing. But there was a glint of the fierce woman she would become. A woman that four days past, she never dreamt was in her.

Vris blushed. The others lowered their eyes before the hurt in her, and the power.

"You'd make a good bandit, with a glare like that," Vris blurted, breaking the silence. This time it was Spiros who heeled him. Alzance only laughed.

"Little brother, being a bandit has done nothing for your manners," he said. But in his eyes was the darkness of what he had seen. Still, it made Lillet laugh too. The sharp points of her face softened. Spiros handed her a small bowl of broth, cautioning her to eat slowly.

Outside, dark fell. The horned moon rose over the sea, her path netted with hunting bats.

THE BROTHERS FASHIONED A SHEATH of goat leather for Lillet that night, and Vris gave her his lightest dagger. In the coming days, they made her a small bow from willow growing along a seep, and arrows of oak. In the forest above the cave, they taught Lillet to shoot her arrows straight, which she managed well enough. And so she became one of them, a bandit and an outlaw, living in the cave called Drakaina and making small mischiefs among the camps of the men of Tar.

They knew they were not numerous enough to withstand even a single sighting, so they made like ghosts, so silent and cunning on their feet that they could lift a handful of barley from a sack of horse grain in the heart of an armed camp. Dusk was their favorite time. The hour the bats came out. Little Bat, they called Lillet, for she was just as swift and small and clever. And because she loved the bats who slept in their cave. She said prayers for them at sundown when they flew out for their supper, and watched the tiny mothers suckle their bat pups upside down in the shelter of shadow.

Together, Lillet and the bandits haunted the men of Tar. It was the only form of vengeance available to them, short of a suicide mission, and maybe, miraculously, their mischief would spook the soldiers into retreat. It was Lillet's idea, the haunting. To cast terrible, brief shadows in the night outside their tents using sticks and cloth and bones and a lantern held aloft; to cry out in unearthly voices from the blackest hour of night; to leave clawprints in blood on the village streets, using the talons of a dead owl.

"You are our luck charm, Little Bat," Alzance said by the fire after a very near escape from a camp in the southern mountain pass where the cypresses grew thick as bristles on a boar. They'd been out to steal back a ceramic crock of sheep cheese that the men of Tar had stolen from the larder of an old shepherd's wife, and return it to the poor woman. Lillet was always sent up a tree as a lookout, for she was nimble and quick and her eyes were like a bat's hearing—sharp and uncanny. This time, her owl's hoot of warning had been drowned out by the bellowing of a bull being slaughtered without ceremony at the foot of an evening fire. A dog had spotted Spiros as he crept in the shadows toward the cheese where it sat in a cart of spoils. Lillet saw the dog, but Spiros did not, and on he moved, step by step, making himself a shadow.

Vris and Alzance meanwhile created a commotion on the camp's western edge by cutting free the tethers of three donkeys and tapping their haunches with firehot pokers to send them galloping. They took down two tents at least, tangling their hooves in the ropes. But the dog ran barking at Spiros as he made to snatch the crock of cheese. Lillet hooted and hooted again, knowing it didn't matter now because the dog had taken hold of Spiros' leg and surely any moment someone would notice and come with a knife to kill him.

The black dog who now preferred Lillet's company to any other's sat at the base of the tree. It took all of her power over him to keep him from barking too. She crouched with her back to the trunk, stroking and stroking his silky head, her eyes squeezed shut. Words her mother had once said to the Moon she repeated now, at random. Surely the brothers would all be caught and killed. Surely she would be left alone again. In her mind she made little cords like her mother's nets, one for each of the brothers, and in her mind the cords she made became a net that swept them toward her, safely, all unharmed.

What felt like a very long time later, she opened her eyes at the sound of Spiros' heavy breathing. Alzance and Vris were on his either side. Blood dripped from Spiros' leg, but it was a minor wound. There was no sound of pursuit, only Alzance's low whistle, and the sea's dusk wind blowing in the olive boughs. All of their eyes were at her feet. The black dog whined.

A thin white snake coiled there, its heading meeting its tail just before her toes. It seemed to be asleep, but when Lillet looked down and saw it there, it lifted its head and was gone again so quickly that later, beside a fire in the cave once more, Lillet wondered to herself if it had melted away right into the earth.

IN THE FOLLOWING WEEKS LILLET'S PRESENCE made them bolder, wilier. Something about her began to make them half-believe their own hauntings, and what the men of Tar whispered around their fires when they thought their commanders couldn't hear. That spirits, old spirits, haunted the southern valleys of Kefthyra. That they'd rather be back home again in Tar, where a shadow stayed a shadow and where the night kept its own silence. Now Lillet always knotted the brothers to her in her mind, though she knew not if it helped, twisting little pieces of autumn grass into knots to match the ones in her mind as she called her lookout calls from a tree.

Then one day Vris had a reckless idea, and Lillet, out of an impulse she could not fully explain, would not let him do it alone.

"I'll dip my own feet in blood," he said by a morning fire as Alzance stirred barley in a pot with goat milk. "And walk down the village cobbles, in the place where their commander sleeps in Samos. That will give them a bigger scare than any owl's claws."

"They will track the blood back to us, from your feet," said Spiros to his brother from over a rabbit hide which he was tanning with its brain. "Or a sentry will see you. It's a bad idea."

"But it's my own, and not yours. Our plans are always yours, and carried out by you," the boy replied. He was looking at Lillet and not at Spiros. Lillet sat on the fire's far side, mending one of her deerskin boots. There was a little line of concentration between her eyes and her black hair fell very straight and rough to her waist. "What do you think, Lillet?" His voice was strange and shy. The girl hadn't yet looked up, lost as she was in her work and her own thoughts. Alzance glanced at Spiros, who twisted his mouth in a broken kind of smile.

She looked up then, and saw that it was for her, his shyness. She didn't know what to say.

"I'll come with you Vris," she replied after a moment, and her sureness unnerved them all. "You know what a quiet shadow I can be. We will bring soft leather to clean and tie your feet so they will think we vanished into the air. Then they will really believe in demons." Her eyes went bright, and a little wicked.

"But Lillet," began Alzance, his tone a father's.

"I am your luck charm, am I not?" she said over him. Her quick, dark smile went right through him, into the cave's quiet.

LATER, WHEN IT WAS ALL OVER, Lillet cursed her own words, for surely there had never been any luck in her, nor any power at all.

Alzance and Spiros kept watch, one on a half-burnt rooftop, the other up a tree looking down across the village. Lillet and Vris crept barefoot from the olive groves to the cobbled way that led between the dwellings where the battalion commander and his generals slept. It was the third hour before dawn. Lillet's bat eyes found every bit of light. They'd watched for several nights before this, to memorize the movements of people to and fro, and particularly of the long-limbed village woman who slipped nightly into the commander's chamber and did not leave. They'd watched until at last the streets were still and only martens were abroad, rooting in the middens.

Now, even the martens were quiet. All Lillet and Vris could hear was their own breath. They walked very slowly, so that their footprints left no disturbances across the ground. Lillet carried the waterskin full of marten blood. Just where the cobbles began she opened it so Vris could dip his feet in.

Vris's bloody footprints were bright in the darkness. Their shape frightened Lillet as she padded silently beside him. They walked together the length of the village street, trying not to breathe too hard even though fear thudded through them. But when they came to the commander's shuttered window opposite the place they had agreed they would turn around and flee—up a lane that led through pomegranates back into the oakwood— they heard noises coming from within. A woman's high cry of pleasure. The lower noises of a man.

They both went very still in the middle of the street. Their arms touched at the elbow. The noises grew louder, more breath- less, then ceased. Lillet's arm felt very hot against Vris. She thought of that long-limbed village woman slipping nightly into the commander's bed. How it was she could give her body to a man of Tar, and why. Still neither of them moved, as if the sounds of that copulation had broken something in the night, broken the spell they had been walking through the darkness.

She realized sickly then that she had forgotten to pray to any moon or mother. She had forgotten to tie the knots in her mind. She tried to knot and twine their safety quickly, right then, but she was too nervous, and Vris was looking at her with too much trust for her to think of anything else except what was before them.

A creak of the bed from within and a padding of feet roused them both. There was no time to bind Vris' feet with buckskin and wool to hide their tracks. There was only to run. But the woman, coming out the oakwood door and into the starlight to relieve herself in private so that she could wash away the commander's seed, saw them both, and the red footprints, and screamed. This sent the commander running out, half dressed, calling in a frightened voice for his men. Torches were lit and with the speed of a warcamp half a dozen soldiers were armed and on their bloody trail in moments.

Alzance and Spiros saw it all from the rooftop and the trees, and came running without hesitation and without hope.

For there was little hope, three shepherds and a girl against the warriors of Tar, though they fought bravely to the last in the oakwood as the dawn raised itself golden out of the sea.

Lillet stared at the two women who stood in front of her, offering her their kindness. For a moment she was the girl before ever had come the men of Tar. Before she had seen death, and been split open by a circle of soldiers, shared as a deer that has been gutted and skinned. For a moment her brown eyes in their hollows, her sharp chin and sharper nose, quivered. Zola sat down beside her on one side, and Arete on the other, careful not to sit too close. The smell of a mother, her dark and silver hair flashing, her small strong hands taking over the spindle and distaff without effort or comment, her broad hip spreading out inside its linen skirts to touch Lillet's skinny haunch in a single place, came over the girl. She swallowed hard.

"I am no child," she said at last, stiffening herself away from that touch, clenching her body tight around the terrible cleft in its center. She remembered as she spoke another time she had said the same words, and how naïve they had been then, before she had known what it was men could do to a woman against her will. But that remembrance brought back faces too dear, and she bit her own tongue in grief.

"Ah," said Arete Her eyes were hard with understanding inside the dark lines of her face. She'd taken her hank of woven lace out again, and worked at a corner of it with thick hands, brushing back bits of soot.

"You are a woman, then?" asked Zola, careful to keep her eyes on the spindle, her hands steady. This child could be little older than her Tiln, though not as old as Essel. Eleven, maybe twelve? She'd meant to keep the names of her daughters buried deep in the tilth of herself, until she could find some way to escape this place and seek them. But now, beside this girl, they rose, barefoot in the oak forest as she had last seen them, where the purple crocuses had just bloomed out of red earth after the rain. *Please oh please oh mother may they live, may they be unharmed, may I find them, oh my children.* It was a scream in her, and it showed in her eyes, which she tried to hide by looking down. She saw her own fingers shaking, and stilled them.

Lillet watched Arete's sooty face, trying to find words that would not let the tears out around them.

"Yes," was all the girl could manage. With it she saw not her mother, hiding her swiftly inside the olive tree, nor the men of Tar over her and in her until there was only darkness, nor the day only a fortnight before she and the brothers were captured, when her first blood came in the night onto her thighs, and there was no one to tell, and she had crept down to the cold river to clean herself and bind a rag inside her smallclothes. No. What she saw was the brothers, her bandits, killed by the spears of the men of Tar—Alzance with the terrible opening in his neck; Spiros split open like an ox and everything vital coming out; Vris bleeding from a dagger in his shoulder where it met his chest, his eyes still open and bright with pain on hers as the soldiers took her away. Surely he was dead by now, her last friend, and the black dog dead beside him. She hoped he hadn't heard her screaming, after. She hoped he was already dead by then.

"They called me Little Bat, you know," Lillet found herself saying. But this wasn't what she had meant to say at all. The words came out broken at the ends, and choked. Then she was crying big warm tears that welled up from a great depth.

Zola took the girl's head upon her warm lap, and Arete stroked and loosed her wet, tight braids. The feeling of that little head in her lap, those young hands bunched in her skirts, made

Zola's husky singing break apart. Across the room of weaving, spinning women went a silent movement of tears. A gaunt old woman from the eastern city of Samos began another song. One of the younger women near her knew it too, about the goose-women who once lived in the blue cove of that eastern valley. How their feathered coats were stolen one by one by men. How they could turn to geese no more.

Tears were a dangerous doorway, but as the old woman from Samos sang in a high, strong voice made rough by a lifetime of olive smoke, the others who knew the song joined her, filling in the three parts so the room rang. More tears fell, new ones that had never been shed. They were a salt river that joined an old forgotten sea. Zola wept for her husband, and for her girls, for her twin boys and the milk that still made her breasts ache, but she also wept for the sea, for the lost freedom of her body each morning, buoyant in the gentle tide, and for her oak trees and her little mother kermes flocks, now tended by other, more cunning women, jealous, greedy women who she knew had sold her family and her name to the men of Tar.

Arete held both Zola and Lillet in her ropy arms, and the embrace smelled of olive wood and smoke. The lines and lumps of her old body were a comfort, as lying on the earth is. But the sudden uplift of tears lasted only a moment. Each woman mastered herself. Clung to wool and flax, to spindle whorl and loom weight, until the grief could be swallowed, battered back into its hatch, the key hidden deep. The song ended.

The fire was low. After a while Arete rose to stoke it. She was charwoman everywhere, now. She only removed her sooty apron to weave and to sleep. Her lace was turning black, from brushing against her blackened apron. Tonight, she understood that this was part of its necessary making, though she didn't know how or why she knew. Things had always come to her thus, she saw now. A clear voice, or word, or task done a particular way, with careful steps. They were part of a dark, unseen incantation whose pieces she was only just beginning to recognize. The fire in the prince's room. The woman Zola with the red on her hands, how the look that had passed between them, coming upon Lillet, seemed to be made of its own secrets.

The night the men of Tar took Arete as a slave, she had
been climbing the wall of the fortress called Kush to save
the last wild caper that grew from its cracks.

The fortress seemed to be part of the hilltop itself, extending
its height. From the walls one could see clear across the foothills
of Mt. Enos to the southern coast, west across a bay to the ruling
city of Kranea, and north over seven valleys to the foothills of a
smaller mountain called Calo. It had been built by three generations of Aget kings in their desert style, and the place was called
Kush in their tongue. No force could invade Kefthyra without
being seen from the fortress. But the power of Aget had waned.
So it was that although they saw the soldiers of Tar on the horizon days before their attack, the men of Aget could do little
from their watchtowers to resist them. Surrender was altogether
preferable to death.

There was a very small village around the base of the fortress.
When the soldiers came, they refrained from burning the cluster
of houses and goat sheds not out of any kindness for the residents,
but because they wanted the dwellings for themselves. It was,
after all, the most defensible place in all of southern Kefthyra.
Still, when Arete saw the soldiers of Aget raise the white flag
of surrender, and heard the boots and shouts and shields and
hooves of the men of Tar climbing the steep road to the fortress,
she dragged her cedar chest of dowry linens out into her olive
grove just in case they decided to set the houses on fire as they
had done elsewhere.

It was the chest where she kept her grandmother's bone needles and pins, her lace-knotting hooks, her fine-spun bedclothes. A woman's power lay in that chest and nowhere else. Once, it had been otherwise. Long ago, so long ago that even Arete's grandmother's grandmother's stories contained only stray threads and hints and seams of that other way. Still, Arete had been collecting those pieces, each a tiny, lost hymn of meaning, and knotting them away among her linens since her husband had died at the hands of Aget thirty years past, leaving her heartbroken and childless too. Corners of old tales. Words fringed in power from a lost language. A felt sense that came upon her sometimes—and more and more of late—of knots, one tied to the next, that were not of thread in her hands, but of life itself. Made of things she could not hold: a bird's flight, the shape of an olive root, a word seen in the random etches on a stone. All in her there in that place where a child had never grown.

The soldiers of Tar found her among the olive trees. She sat calmly on her cedar chest, ready for her death. But they did not kill her, only dragged her inside. There, they ordered her to cook and clean for the three stonemasons who would be lodging in her house while the fortress was rebuilt after the grandiose, clean-edged manner of Tar. She knew what would become of her if she resisted, or poisoned the food she served them. And for some reason she did not herself understand she knew it was not her time to be killed, that there was something more she needed to finish.

Spitting in their food she did do, out of sight. And she refused to house under the same roof, sleeping instead in the winter sheepfold. She used her dowry trunk as a table, and began to smell of lanolin and old dung. She was a very efficient housekeeper, having looked after her widowed uncle, mother, and an ailing sister in turn after the death of her husband, helping them with children and hearth and their household weaving, the ideal spinster. Cooking, cleaning and washing for three men took up only half of her time. Once, she would have spent the rest of it tending the sheep down the hills thick with oak and wild pistachio. But the men of Tar had slaughtered all the sheep in the village and salted them for their own stores.

So she began making an intricate lace hem to still her angry hands. It was an angry hem in kind, with strange sharp-edged stars and serpents. She didn't know where the patterns had come from. They were not patterns her mother had taught her. She sat for hours under her olive trees, hooking lace and listening at the yoke of her rage, listening to the lace in her hands and the earth under her feet for what she should do, for what it was that needed doing. She could see the fortress's wall from her olives. It had long been wild with capers. But all week men on rope ladders slung down from the fortress's walls had been clearing weeds from between the limestone cracks. Now there was only one caper left. It was around the north side, facing slopes of dry pine forest where cicadas rubbed their bronze wings during the heat of the day.

When the idea came to her at last, it was far too mad to resist, and so she set out that very night, before there was time to convince herself not to. Thus she found herself clinging barefoot to the fortress wall at the dark of the moon, her bent fingers and toes dug goat-wise into whatever stony purchase they could find, trying to save the last caper plant.

I am too old for this, she thought. The stars of the Scorpion were rising. Guards patrolled with torches dipped in olive oil. She wore black, as always, and a black scarf over her gray hair. Her legs shook as she found a new dip in the stone and pushed herself higher. The caper was now only a hands-breadth away. It grew in generous cascades, with round succulent leaves and trailing arms.

Really, I am too old to be behaving like a girl of twelve. But it was the principle of the thing, and the way it had come into her with its own unbound conviction, giving her limbs a strange and youthful strength. Arete touched the hank of lace around her waist for luck. Then she lurched up the final handspan. Her fingers brushed the round leaves. She thought she must be very high up by now. The caper had been nearly halfway. Good thing it was so dark. She could pretend the drop behind her was only feet, and not a whole steep hillside full of pines.

She'd brought a kitchen knife for prying the roots out from between the stones. Now she reached for it, shaking. Set it in her teeth. Inched, scrambling a little with her nails, for a better hold. *A fine sight I must be*, she thought. *A wide-hipped old crone barefoot on the wall of the fortress of Kush with a blade in her teeth like some pirate's mad grandmother.* She almost laughed. Fear and exhaustion made her feel a little drunk. Like an evening after sweet mountain wine. The stifled laugh set her knees trembling. She bit into the blade too hard, cutting her tongue, then cursed it for a pimp, a cuckold and a whore, and the wall too, using the most vulgar words for each. This steadied both her grip and her nerves.

There. The caper was before her, at eye-level. Her toes felt wet, and ached. They must be bleeding. All the better. She'd stain the wall red. A woman's first and last magic. Then light flared below her, and a sudden voice.

"Halt where you are and drop your weapon!" The voice sounded mildly incredulous, and young. Familiar, too. It was the voice of the stonemason's apprentice, the lad she'd been feeding from her own garden and larder this past month, the boy whose clothes and linens she washed weekly with her own, and the others', not quite able to break the laws of hospitality and do a poor job. Those laws were very old. There wasn't even any hair on his chin yet. She hated him now for the disbelief in his voice, and for his betrayal. She took the knife out of her teeth, and tasted blood. This time, she did not say the words in silence.

"Pimp, cuckold, whore's child, how dare you follow the old woman who feeds you, as if she were some criminal? Can't you see

I'm busy saving this old caper from the ravages of your masters?"

Her eyes gleamed, a little overkeen. He took another step forward with his torch and his dagger. She grinned. Genuine fear moved across his face. *He must think me quite mad, or a witch,* thought Arete, not loosing her blade. *Well, perhaps he is right to look at me so. Perhaps, after all this time, that is precisely what I am.*

He swallowed hard and said "a- a caper?" looking disturbed. All at once the hate went out of her, and she pitied the boy.

"What's that down there?" called a voice from the wall. Torches swept through the dark toward them, catching the wild edge in Arete's black eyes, the gleam of her bloody knife. *Bare-assed, fucked and shat,* came the silent curses now, but she didn't back down or drop her knife. Damn them, she was just an old woman with a cooking utensil and a fondness for plants. She'd done nothing but make lace and linens and wash them and help raise other women's babies and grandbabies and wash them, and wail for the dead and wash them, and milk her sheep for cheese, since she was a virgin of fifteen. She'd developed a vulgar tongue with age, and a certain untidy anger, but who wouldn't, in a land so often occupied? These were ways to pass the time, to light the way—laughter and rage, both.

"May the moon's owls piss on your wall!" she said, very clear and loud, so as not to be misunderstood. These men didn't speak the language of Kefthyra very well. "Do I look like I'm capable of murdering you all in your beds? I'm just here to save the caper! Leave me in peace to finish, would you?"

There followed a lean, stifled silence. Then someone snorted, and the stonemason's apprentice, red and stammering, blurted, "I followed her my lords. From the house where we're lodging. She crept out at midnight with a knife and made right for the wall. Her leaving woke me and—I followed. I didn't like the look of things. Seeing as she had the knife, my lords."

Arete changed her mind. She did not pity the boy. The hate returned, searing her. There was too much whimpering in his voice, a dog's desire to please. She spat at him, and on the wall, and threw her knife far into the pines. The Scorpion glittered above, bladelike. The wheeling Bear looked on with gleaming eyes. The north star seemed to blink, once, and then the soldiers of Tar had surrounded her, and were pulling her forcibly down to the ground.

"Crazy old bitch," the one who bound her hands hissed, ripping the black scarf from her hair and baring her silver head to the night. An owl passed on wings so pale and silent that only Arete looked up. She heard the crickets singing everywhere. She noticed the man who bound her only peripherally, as an unpleasant shape in the darkness. He sounded as though he spoke through many teeth, and smelled of burnt olive wood, and bronze, and days of wine.

"The prince needs more women in the capital. He is seeking slaves," said another, the one with his spear to her spine. He picked up her headscarf with his dagger and tore it neatly in two. Someone beside him laughed and made a lewd gesture. "For working *looms*," continued the other, laughing too. "Cloth making, and suchlike. Women's work." This was dismissive, a sneer.

"She hardly seems worth the trouble of bringing anywhere, old sack," said the first.

"The older the better, says the prince."

"Queer appetites, his."

"Better with the thread, you idiot. And he wants lots."

"Making a point to his father, he is. With all that red."

"Will the king even care?"

"Likely not."

"The old bastard."

THEY WALKED ARETE ROUGHLY OUT of the night's darkness and into the torchlight of the fortress. In the morning, they took her overland to Kranea.

The fire grew again, lapping its stone bed. It cast brief shadows across the cold flagstones, the tattered ocher rugs. On the women's looms brilliant tapestries grew, glowing in that fresh surge of flame, all from the red of Zola's dye vats. It was no good to make them poorly, out of hatred for the new men of Tar. It was better to avoid being beaten or raped. It was better to stay alive. Now and then they found a slavewoman hanging from the olive trees by a noose of her own sheets, a woman who had not been able to go on. But most lived in hope of escape, of finding family again, or lived simply for the sake of life, which was a gift.

One carpet, warped to the largest floor loom, was already half the length of the room and patterned all over with diamonds and bull horns in varying shades. A stern, precise woman named Tharne, with a prominent, curving nose and black curls that frizzed and slipped their scarf, wove it. Now, as the singing subsided and the fire blazed again, she paused, staring at those many vermillion threads. There were dry lines from tears down her cheeks. She wiped them, and wove again. Silence returned, save for the popping fire, the hush and click of shuttles, the clatter of loom weights, the whir of spinning wool.

Lillet had fallen asleep with her head in Zola's broad lap. It was damp where her cheek pressed.

Slavewomen slept in two long rooms off the weaving quarters on beds of rushes and rough linen. Some were kitchen maids or charwomen or sweepers, but by night all gathered to lend a hand with the making of textiles. A simple cypress stool sat beside each bed, and a red clay pot for water, but the women managed to make their corners their own, with small amulets hung on a pin, or a wreath of flowers from the courtyard, or a dove's feather, gray as dusk. Nineteen women slept in the room where both Zola and Arete—in opposite corners—made their beds. Another twenty in the room adjoining. The smell was always musky and warm, thick with oil from the lamps, for there was only one window and the walls were heavy limestone blocks. Dread roosted in the rafters at night along with the bats, and Arete rose very early to be away from it. The dark was always full of stifled sobs.

Zola carried Lillet to her own pallet. Her arms and back were strong. The girl weighed little. Arete brought a small black pearl of poppy resin from her corner, and lit it for a moment, burning it under Lillet's nose.

"For dreamless sleep, little dove," she said, and patted the girl's loose, dark hair. Zola pulled a woolen cover over her skinny legs, and smoothed her forehead.

"In the morning, we will give her a tea of cyclamen bulb." She didn't look at Arete while she spoke, but still at Lillet, her face a small girl's in sleep, soft where it had been sharp before. "You know how to make it safely, I think?" Zola turned as she finished speaking, her eyes very dark, and Arete was struck by the thought that this woman had been loved, very much, and not long ago. A husband would not look elsewhere from a woman like this. Love of life danced in her straight body, under her nails, at the roots of her heavy hair. Even sorrow as big as the sorrow that dreamed across the women's quarters at night could not snuff it, not fully.

"Ours is a dark country," Arete replied, and the words surprised her. "I know its lightless pathways well. They are growing in the olive grove beyond the courtyard now. I will gather them at dawn when I go for the firewood."

This was a strange reply, but Zola took it in like she had taken in that meeting of eyes over Lillet in the corner earlier in the evening. Part of a secret only just remembered, just known. A kind of riddle. She nodded.

Presently Arete left to stoke the night's fires across the prince's halls. Zola stayed beside Lillet, awake until the constellation of the Hunter set in the south before dawn. Then she slept, curled in a crescent halfway around the girl's legs, with a brown cloak over her shoulders. She dreamed of her children, and woke weeping.

Red the beginning
Red the end
In blood they make
In blood they mend

-*Of Red*, from the Old Language

At dawn that day in autumn when the men of Tar came, Zola had swum naked in the sea. Even with five children and a hill full of oaks to tend, not to mention the daily rhythms of her life—baking, weaving, mending, washing, nursing, tending, soothing—Zola always rose with the sun, took herself in silence down the narrow footpath through quince trees and between white stones, left her nightclothes in a heap, and swam. Today the sea was rough with the wind that came ahead of a storm. She poured out a little sheepsmilk as an offering in the tide. Her breasts floated, gleaming with the iridescence of the day. Salt buoyed them, made them alert and plump and unlined again, seemingly unchanged despite many years of breastfeeding. She loved how the sea made her skin feel endless, part of that much greater body. Her strong legs opening and kicking were flooded with salt and cold. She didn't stay in as long as usual, because of the wind. It splashed water into her eyes. She swallowed a mouthful, and coughed.

She walked back to the house slowly through the swelling quince trees, watching the sky. It was full of ornate and heavy clouds. A storm by late afternoon, likely. Inside, she wrung her black hair on the hearthstones and stirred the acorn porridge over olivewood coals. She lifted her twin sons from their cradle and set them to drink, one at each breast. They sucked noisily, fists in her wet black hair and little noses scrunched. Caster with his wrinkled brow, Coll with his smooth, and the traces of cradle cap. She'd make an oil infusion of mullein to rub there—later, after she'd brought some of the acorns in, and seen to her dyes. It wasn't urgent. One of the children could help her. Perhaps her daughter Essel, who was fourteen and her oldest, or Omerr who was twelve and so patient with his little brothers. Though at present he was still in bed. He was growing like a young oak, and his skinny legs kept him up at night with their aches. More and more he followed his father Oran to the hills during the day, for his home seemed suddenly full of girls. The twins were only a year old, and didn't count yet as boys to him. He was growing self-conscious of his own gentleness. Oran tended the sheep with the dogs, ranging them up as far as the next valley in summer when forage was thin. Recently Omerr had started to carve his own shepherd's stick out of a fallen olive branch.

Oran was a kind man, and loved his wife too much to ever question her morning swims, or to complain that it meant his breakfast was a little later than other men's, and that his children thought nothing of asking him to put the kettle on if Zola wasn't back when they woke up.

"The sea gives to me my good spirits, and my luck with crimson," Zola would say, and it was true. She worked dawn to dusk in good humor and high energy. The perfect wife, other men said to Oran in the village center, where they often met to smoke their long amber-mouthed pipes when the sheep and goats were in and the sun was going down. Whenever her nerves began to fray, or her mood grew weary, she had only to think of the feeling of the sea on her skin. "It is to me what I am to you," she said to her children. "That's why I bring it milk."

Besides being a good mother, a good wife, and a good housekeeper, Zola was also the most sought-after maker of crimson dye on the entire island of Kefthyra. Many women who lived where the kermes oaks grew—near the sea, on rough hillsides or windy headlands—harvested the kermes insects who fed on the oak sap and made the red dye too, but nobody's red was as brilliant, as colorfast or as abundant as Zola's.

Oak groves were passed on through the maternal line, and had been since the time before the first invasions a thousand years ago. Zola's maternal oak grove was very large and very old. The kermes insects had always been tended by women. It was, after all, the kermes mothers whom they harvested, after they had died laying their red-stained eggs. The oak groves of Zola's women had always produced the most brilliant crimson. She followed what her mother taught her closely. Much of it involved not the dye recipe or how she loosed the dead kermes bugs from the bark, but how she treated her trees.

And so she gathered their acorns and feed them to her family. Acorns left ungathered on the earth through the winter told the trees that their gifts weren't wanted, and they produced less the following year. None of the other women in the village did so. Acorns were called the food of the poor. Since the men from Helladia had come, there had been barley and wheat and rye to sow. Who wanted to eat acorns, when they could eat wheats? Zola did, and her trees were the healthiest on the island. And even though the men of Aget and the nomads of Helladia had changed the names of the old gods, Zola practiced the rituals that had been passed down to her without hesitation and without fear. She praised the kermes mothers as her sisters. She never harmed a single of their eggs. On the longest night of winter, she and her children and her husband and all the sheep and the sheepdogs too filled the oak groves with singing and dancing, with fires and bells and a whole barrel of dark wine poured onto the earth.

Other women had plenty of cause to hate Zola, and a handful did, but for the most part they only envied her from a distance. She was difficult to hate, being too good-tempered and generous and quick to laugh.

But after the solders of Tar came, and everything changed,

the women who had known Zola before felt only shame for their envy and their hate, and shame also at their relief—that after all they were not Zola, and did not possess her oak grove, her cheerfulness, her immaculate hearth. That perhaps so many blessings only court disaster and sorrow, and that it was better to be mediocre, and ill-tempered, and afraid.

ZOLA BROUGHT A BOWL OF PORRIDGE to her son's bed, rousing him with a low shepherd's tune. The half-carved crook leaned near his pillow. Essel and her younger sister Tiln were already up, washing their hair in rainwater from a bucket by the well. She could hear Tiln's chatter like a little bird, and Essel's solemn replies. Her eldest daughter had always been stern like that, a small mother. By the time she could walk, she was already tidying up after herself everywhere she went. Often, when Zola came in from her daybreak swim, Essel would fix her with a look near scorn, the kind of look some of the village women gave her. Women who hadn't stopped to exclaim over the sweet fullness of a pomegranate recently. Women who didn't let those red juices drip off their fingers, but rather cut them with a knife, and never stopped to put their weary feet in the sea.

Well. Essel. Maybe she would ask her to take Tiln and the twins out into the wood to hunt for mushrooms. There had been enough rain in the last fortnight. Purple crocuses were sprouting out of the red earth up the ridge. There might be chanterelles. They would be nice for supper. What was girlhood, after all, without such barefoot idylls in the early autumn wood, with the light gold and soft, and that scent of pine and oak and fallen nuts?

Zola saw the girls coming, and brought down the gathering baskets from their hooks by the door.

"Take your sister and the twins to the pinewood to gather chanterelles, will you my love?" she said when Essel came through, her hair very neatly rolled up in a linen cloth. For a moment Zola saw her as a grown woman, long-necked and long-faced and regal. Very dark, darker than Zola or Oran, dark like her grandmother, with small, deft hands and long straight hair she kept as neat as her linens, in a braid. She was off to braid it now, with Tiln at her heels like an unkempt lamb, and as curly, chattering still. Tiln was ten, all legs and flights of fancy. Just now she was saying something about hermit crabs, and the shell of one she'd seen in the tide all covered in algae, and how it was that they chose their homes. How she loved their slender, scuttling feet, the way their eyes peered out from inside the darkness, and their small pincered claws.

"Yes, mother," said Essel. She looked at Zola's wet hair, which had dripped twin streams down the front of her shirt, as she went to braid her own. "Though it smells like rain."

"Mushrooms!" Tiln ran to take the baskets from her mother and line them with clean cloth.

"Come home if it starts," called Zola. "Though I think it won't 'til dusk."

Oran came in after them for his porridge, and ate it in three swallows. He'd been out since before sunup to lead the sheep to water. Now he was off to the eastern ridge with crook and flute and a goatskin of weak wine to bring them to a patch of newly blooming thyme. Omerr, lethargic before, was suddenly at his side, dressed and neat-haired. Zola kissed them—her son's boyish cheek with its smell of amber and sundried linen; her husband's mouth, rough with beard but always warm, the resin of morning cold on his breath. He palmed her backside as he left, whistling.

"Isn't your mother beautiful, my boy?"

Zola let the twins drink themselves fuller, changing breasts for each, then tied Caster to Essel's back, and Coll, the smaller, to Tiln's. The girls took gathering knives, a waterskin, a twisted cloth of acorn bread and cold sheep cheese.

"Bring home some crocuses, good Essel," Zola said, kissing her daughter's head when she was finished braiding. "Beauty for our table. You have a better eye for such things than I." Essel smiled. The compliment worked. Give the girl a treat disguised as a task and she never argued back.

"Maybe cyclamens for their sweetness?" Essel said, taking one of the baskets. Her eyes were so big and black, thought Zola. Much moved far down in them, more than any mother could know.

"And for love-cakes!" added Tiln. "To attract true love. I'm making one if you aren't." She pulled her sister's braid and trotted out the door, tickling Coll's feet where they kicked at her back.

"Come home by noon meal, or before if it storms," Zola called after them. "The twins will be hungry by then."

She spent the next hour in the oak grove, gathering acorns. By midmorning, she was sweating from the late summer heat. The cicadas made a sleepy drone. The storm clouds had passed on without opening, and the sky was entirely clear. She napped briefly on a cloth under the trees, the oak leaves prickling only a little through the rough weave. Then she went to her dye house, a stone structure at the near edge of the wood, and pulled several skeins from the strongest vat. The smell was of rot. It was a hearty, healthy smell to Zola, and she smiled. The smell of earth was often rot too, of a thing being turned into something else. The skeins streamed red dye back into their vats. Zola rinsed them in a second bucket and hung them from a line between the dye house and a branch. Pink water dripped onto the ground. Then she went to examine the bark of her trees for pregnant kermes mothers.

It was their season, but early still. On the first trees, she found none. Deeper into the shade, where the cicadas cried out more loudly, she found three, all scattered along one bending limb. The mothers gave their lives for their eggs. It was their last effort, climbing up from the earth to a branch, sucking at the oak sap, producing that crimson which protected their eggs from disease and from any small predator. The crimson seep smelled sharp and resinous.

She crouched in the low oaks and said the harvest words, praying abundance upon the eggs, calling the mother Red Moon in the few words of the old language she had been taught. Then she gathered them, one by one, with her fingertips. They held on tight to the bark, even in death. Their carapaces gleamed and stained her hands.

Later, Zola could never be certain which came first—the sight of that crimson on her fingers or the sound of men's boots crunching toward her out of silence through the wood. Later, she remembered the two things simultaneously, the dye on her fingers a kind of premonition. Usually the red stains left by the kermes mothers reminded her of menstruation. Only on that day did the sight of red make her think immediately of slaughter.

Still, she rose to her feet with a steady, slow grace, the copper gathering pot in one hand with its three red carapaces. She smoothed her black apron and her black hair with her free hand, composing herself. Spined oak leaves and an acorn cap fell to the ground.

Twenty soldiers of Tar surrounded her, spears raised.

Kefthyra had been an occupied land for her whole life and before, but there had never been soldiers in her oak grove. Blood, the same color as her kermes, stained their swords. Elaborate breastplates and plumed helmets gleamed in the long light through the trees. Oran had heard word in the village that the Prince of Tar had taken the capital from Aget a week past, but this was expected, a kind of political handoff. There had been no further news that any battalions were continuing north of Mt. Enos. How had these men come here so quickly, and without warning?

"Men of Tar," Zola said in a low voice. "Why are you here in my oak grove?" She did not mean to, but it came out a growl. "Are you seeking refreshment?"

This had happened now and then with the soldiers of Aget, when the people of Kefthyra were not inclined to pay their taxes. She did not allow herself to think what other kinds of refreshment these men might seek. Nor what kind of blood it was on their swords.

"We've already availed ourselves," said a sinewed man with very straight teeth. His nose flared when he spoke. "Your land has provided—much refreshment." Something in his broad eyes made Zola think, with a wild, sick lurch, of her daughters. The red stain on the oak tree spread across her lids as she blinked, swallowed, tried to reply.

"Ah." A croak, with none of her usual strength. Why had one of the villagers not sent word? Were these men so swift, so silent, that no one had seen them? Had they travelled all that way by night? Had they killed any messengers who might have warned them? Oh mother, oh gods, where were her girls, and the twins? *May they be out still in the pinewood. Oh, may the chanterelles be plentiful. May they hide in some deep root. May the twins not cry out.* But which way had the soldiers come, and which way would they leave? *Mother below, not the pines, not her children.* And where was Oran? Why had he and Omerr not run to warn her? Why had the dogs not barked from the far ridge? Her thoughts flashed, red and stained, the crimson on the bark, the mother dead across her eggs.

She knew then, without knowing how she knew, which way the men had come. Why there had been no barking from the dogs, nor warning from her Oran or her Omerr. She looked again at the blood on their spears and couldn't breathe. She knew without evidence and without hope that the blood was her husband's, her son's, her dog's.

"What do you want." This came out with more strength, each word spat, and not a question. She clung to her copper pot, the little tree where she'd left her harvest prayers, trying not to fall to her knees.

"We've already taken it," replied the sinewed man. Another flash of straight teeth. Their commander, he must be. She noticed, as if from a great distance, that his plume was red while the rest were white. He spread his hands, indicating the oak grove. Though its oaks were small and ragged by nature, they were robust, and spread across the entire valley and hill-side overlooking the north-facing cove called Ateras, where the village perched. The oaks? That's what they had come for? "Everything, that is, but you. The women of your village were most obliging, directing us here. Orders from the Prince of Tar. He requires a personal dye-woman. He means to monopolize the flow of crimson across the White Sea. You, he was told, have the reddest. Your village women will be happy to provide shipments of the stuff to the royal palace. He requires the capital to be robed in red."

"You cannot." It was a snarl. "No other women may touch my grove. Only I and my daughters may handle the kermes. It is an ancient taboo. I would not advise you to break it." Red was the color of women, of birth. It was not the color of soldiers or kings. So her mother and her grandmother had taught her.

A snigger passed among the men. Zola saw their faces only vaguely, undifferentiated, a circle of white teeth and bronze. They were not men, but demons. She was not a woman, but a bear. She could feel every inch of her own skin, and their eyes across it. Her breasts hurt with pent milk for her sons. She curled back her lips.

"We can establish a trade arrangement, nothing more." The words came from elsewhere, between her teeth. She did not have the heart for words. Her husband, her children, her trees. She could smell the smoke now. Was it their house? In her mind she saw the pomegranate by the low door, in flames. "You will take neither my trees, nor me."

"It is pleasant to watch you talk," said the commander, lazily, flicking a fallen oak leaf from his wrist guard. "But we seem to be getting nowhere." He turned to his men. "Seize her. And don't enjoy it too much, not before I've had my bit. Easy on the eyes, you are. No wonder the village women wanted you gone and your trees for their own."

There were too many hands and too many spears. They had her before she could move, rubbing at her breasts and her haunches with hot hands, hissing and calling in their own language, dragging her until she was beneath the red-plumed commander, who had loosened his pants with the same laziness with which he spoke. The copper pot had fallen from Zola's hand in the struggle, but somehow one of the kermes mothers was there still, in her palm. She fought, kicking, crushing the carapace into her clenched hand until the red seeped out and dripped on the earth. The commander watched her struggle and smiled. He liked a disheveled woman. He lowered himself toward her.

Old words were in her throat. They came from nowhere, from the place where her neck pressed into the red dirt, into the oak leaves and acorn shells. The crimson in her hand felt hot and powerful. She screamed out the words. The sound was full of death and of power. They were not her words, not any she had been taught from the few that were remembered. There were bears in them, and serpents large as caves. The oak leaves moved above her.

Every trunk dripped vermillion. Every trunk bled. And she bled the same dye from her milk-taut breasts and from between her legs where the commander had pushed back her skirt. Not blood, but kermes.

That was enough to terrify them all, and in the slackening of hands she leapt to her feet. Red dye dripped everywhere from her. The kermes carapace that had been pressed into her hand was nowhere; not on the ground; gone. On her hand was its mark. She thought of Oran and of Omerr, dead under their swords. She thought of Essel. Abruptly the red was gone, and she was mortal again, standing in a shadow that was not dye, but only leaves. Still, beneath her feet, she felt it. Whatever it was that had given words to her. The men of Tar, despite themselves, felt it too.

"Tie her," snapped their commander, when he could speak. Lust was gone. Only disgust, now, and fear. He tried not to look afraid, but he was for a moment more terrified than he had ever been in his life.

The power did not come back into her, though she fought them and their ropes. Someone struck her hard across the brow. Then there was nothing but darkness, and a stain of crimson, spreading across her eyes.

Lillet swallowed the tea of cyclamen bulbs without a word when Arete handed it to her in a clay cup over the women's sunrise meal. They ate out in the walled courtyard in fine weather, and it was a warm October day. White crocuses with yellow tongues pressed up along the footpath that led out into the olive grove where Arete and the palace's other charwomen gathered firewood from tall stacks under wooden shelters. Soon, men would bring the piles in, but for now, the early autumn sun continued to cure them. The mauve-flowered cyclamens sprang up around the bases of the oldest trees, in shade. Their upblown petals made small vortices of perfume. Pregnant women knew the danger of stepping over those flowers in bloom, and kept well away for fear of miscarriage. Lillet had watched her mother do the same, but she had miscarried even so, and more than once. Lillet had seen the blood. It scared her, but then she had been a child, and had known nothing worse than a goat at slaughter under the shepherd's skillful hands. Now, she drank Arete's clay cup of bitter tea and was not afraid, though Zola had whispered to her at dawn of its purpose and effect. How her own blood would clean her.

Swallowing, she tried not to think of Alzance, of Spiros, of Vris, but failed. Mostly she saw Vris, the dagger in his shoulder and blood in his teeth, and the amber eyes of the dog, gone dark in death beside him. She would do anything to be clean of what had happened there, and the guilt she felt at its happening, foolishly thinking herself a lucky charm when she was anything but; how she had forgotten, that final time, to pray. She would do anything to be cleaned of the touch of the men of Tar, but feared she could not be. She drank more quickly. Even if she died of it, she didn't mind. Better than the dreams that split her every night. Better than the sickness in her belly, better than the memory of her mother's voice lifted up with her hands to the moon.

She ate only a bite of the barley porridge and a swallow of sheepsmilk. Already the tea was starting its work, sickening her. She looked a woman again in the strengthening light of morning, and not a child as she had in sleep. A sharpness sat around her, and some of the other women eyed her almost with fear. Her face had that cast to it, pointed as bat wings. The early sun played odd tricks, and for a moment a horned moon lay in shadow over her black brows. More than one of the women saw this, and later they whispered over their oakwood looms—was she the Lady of Beasts, Our Virgin of the Wood, Huntress and Keeper, come to test them, come to avenge her lost maidenhead upon the men of Tar? Would it be best to keep their distance, and save their own if it came to it, or treat her as a hidden goddess with all the kindness in them, and earn her blessing? But that was foolish, Vela cut in. There were no goddesses and no gods. So the Prince of Tar ruled, and so it was. What goddess had looked out for them, the fallen, the spoils of war? Lillet might be a witch and dangerous in her ways, but surely there was no Lady, no Huntress, no Moon, or they would be with their husbands still, their lands and their bodies unruined.

The women gossiped on over their work, and the sun reached noon. By then, Lillet lay limp upon her pallet with a seep of red across the rags between her legs. In it was a tiny child no bigger than a pea who passed away unseen, fishlike in his nature still, and mostly dream. Arete wiped at the sweat on the girl's cheeks and forehead with a rosemary-soaked cloth. She'd pressed a poultice of crushed yarrow inside the girl because she couldn't keep down any tea. The bleeding slowed, at last. The pulse under Arete's fingers quivered, then settled. Lillet slept. The old woman cleaned the blood from her thin legs. Later, Zola would come. Now, she was at her dyes by the prince's decree, and seeing to the girl's spinning besides.

The blood that pooled from Lillet was its own dark country, spreading across the rags. Something moved in it, a vision. Stones and water and great, terrifying depths. Arete sat back.

"Cocks and cuckolds, but I'm getting old for this," she said aloud, and made herself hoot a little with laughter. It had been a while since she'd laughed. Since that climb up the wall for the caper.

She looked again into the drying blood and saw stones with secret hollows below them, lapped by sea. She knew that place. It was at the bay's harbor, just beyond Kranea's walls. The Swallowing Stones. That was what they'd been called when Arete was a girl. A place of potency in the old days, dangerous to visit at night or in winter, for fear of what their darkness, compounded, might take from you without your knowing. A place where women left offerings to the underground, and only women. For into those hollows the tide went, and did not return. Swallowed with a lap and echo like some inverted bell, the opposite, the empty spaces ringing out instead.

The old ways taught that the water, thus swallowed, traveled under the island in hollows and rivers through the limestone. It travelled entirely in darkness for all the moon's waxing, new to full. Then it emerged in the bottomless lake on the furthest eastern edge of Kefthyra, there above the city of Samos. Bottomless because its bottom was the whole labyrinthine underside of the island, its lightless passages where only water and darkness knew the way.

How anyone knew this, the unseen movements of water in that black and the precise place of its reemergence, no one could say for certain, as with all the oldest tales. But Arete remembered her grandmother's words by some smoking olivewood fire in the stone house up the flank of Mt. Enos where she lived all her days, speaking in secret to her sheep so they produced milk of surpassing sweetness, collecting carefully the cyclamen bulbs in autumn for the girls who might come to her in need. Her grandmother had said: *in the caves they burned laurel leaves and the resin of the poppy, and saw inside the earth. Do not doubt that women have travelled there with the parts of themselves that can fly free of the body. Do not doubt the stories are true, and that a woman's soul has floated down in darkness in a laurel leaf for all the moon's waxing, until she reached the other side. What do you imagine birthing a child entails, or burying a lover?*

That lore was old and nearly forgotten by the time Arete's grandmother told her this. It had been old two hundred years before, when the men of Aget first took the cities of Kefthyra. It had been lost long before that to the men of Helladia. It was easy enough to change the words for things, the hymns sung out at shrines, but harder to change what sat beneath the names and the stones in the memories of women, the women left behind when the men were killed. It was well and good to be a hero for a day, but heroes do not remain, like wives do, who are never called heroes though they have kept what might have been lost from going, hidden there between linens in the cedar trunk, or out in the fields as a word whispered to the budding olive.

But why she, old Arete, should see a vision of those holes in the stones at the edge of Kranea's harbor was not immediately clear. She finished cleaning the blood and watched Lillet as she dreamed, her forehead brown and clear. Magic worked obscurely. She could wait to understand its meaning. Something was moving, earthwise. In Lillet's bat-wise face; in Zola's redstained hands. In herself, too. That was all she knew, but she knew it surely, at last.

"Grandmother," the girl croaked, reaching for Arete. New

cramps wracked her. Arete was quick with a tea of viburnum bark now, and the leaves of yarrow. Sitting up to drink woke Lillet sufficiently that she said, "why do you let that lace of yours go black with soot?" because the dark hank was in Arete's lap, a lengthening coil which never seemed to be far from her hands.

Its dirtiness had been bothering Lillet all through her delirium and even her pain. A white snake it was, rolled in soot. A seam of light, blackened. It was now as long as three women, worked on a needle-fine hook in patterns of star and horn and lunar eye, traditional protections from evil. Such a band was usually made to go about the hems of skirts, at cuffs and necks, all the openings in a garment, so that no evil could slip in. But there was something odd about Arete's lace to Lillet's eye, the kind of weirdness only the fevered notice, or women in their bleeding. In her sickened dreams, she seemed to be washing and washing out the soot, but the lace wouldn't come clean and the black covered her hands and the hank became a real snake, white as the snow that fell but rarely on the top of Mt. Enos. It coiled and coiled around her belly until it seemed to vanish into her. Now, awake, sipping at the tea, Lillet saw the lace idle and limp in Arete's lap, and was relieved.

"Magic's a strange business, dovie," replied Arete after a silence, thinking of stones and of blood. She patted Lillet's arms with warm, bent hands. "You have to be willing to feel about in the dark. Otherwise, it's a danger and not a gift. I listen for it, and let my hands do its bidding. So it seems I'm doing with the lace, and the soot."

"But what is it? Whose bidding?" Lillet's dark eyes were darker for the pain, but also bigger now with interest. Was it magic her mother had taught her in the cave of Drakaina? Magic or just women's matters, keeping what might be lost alive? Was it magic her mother had done over her father's fishing nets with her deft hands, or just care? Was there any difference? And that feeling Lillet had sometimes known as a young girl, and again with the shepherd bandits, was it magic too? A wild freedom in all her limbs; a glee at moving and living; the sense that the water slipping down its stream, the olive leaves silver in rain, the hawk circling with sun on his wings, all were in her, of her, or she of them, and she knew each from a knowing outside herself. What it felt to be the olive leaf slick with rain, and the wheeling hawk, and the water running and running without fear and without end until the sea.

All at once she remembered the cause of her delirium, and the blood that had left her. She looked, but Arete had taken away the rags. There was only a trickle now, caught in yarrow. Whatever the men of Tar had put in her, it was gone, though she could feel something else there still, something intangible.

"Well," replied Arete, watching Lillet's face. "The pattern beneath the pattern. A thing felt, but not seen. You take my meaning, I think, though you can't know it in your thinking, or by the clear light of reason. It makes the flax grow, and the barley, but it isn't summer, no. It's more root than that. The pattern beneath the pattern. And it has nothing to do with kings." The old woman snorted. "Thankfully. The shitting bastards."

Then without ceremony she lit a little hand-packed cone of amber resin and the leaves of thyme. Lillet, laughing at the old woman's vulgar outburst, and surprised at how good it felt to laugh, settled down to sleep once more.

THAT EVENING, ZOLA AND ARETE wove twice as diligently as usual, to make up for the girl's absence. There was enough cloth now for a new wall hanging in the feast hall, and curtains for the prince's bed. Fresh sails for his ships were almost finished. All crimson, just as bright as wounds. When two serving men rolled a barrel of dried kermes mothers from Ateras into the women's quarters and left them by Zola's vats, she kept her face still and unmoving. But when they were gone she wept—for the little mothers, for the eggs beside them that the women were harvesting despite the taboos, despite all the promises she had made to her oak forest. She wept for her children, and her husband, and the weeping was the kind that sears, too deep almost for tears.

Three nights later, Lillet rejoined them. She was very pale. She sat near Arete, spinning slowly, her spindle skittering back and forth on the floor.

Zola stood hunched over her dye vat, peering into its red. The steam was making words. *In a season, maybe two, we may be no more*, the husked insects whispered to her from their vat. *Our children may be no more. Gone from your forest, gone from your trees. We may remain only in this, our crimson. By the time your daughters are women, we may be gone from all the trees of Kefthyra. Help us, mother. Help us, daughters of Ateras.*

Things like this often wafted up from Zola's dye vats as she stirred them, adding the necessary ingredients—fat of a hedgehog, eelgrass, a single handful of sheep dung—and said the ancient words. Auguries; sudden words of truth. Word that the kermes were dying made her sick but did not surprise her. But this sudden image of her daughters made her stop altogether, and stare down into the pot, searching desperately in its whorls of oil and red and steam for the faces of her children. Was this a truth spoken by her oaks? Or a longing only? Could they be alive, somewhere safe and hidden?

She made a little cry and staggered back, trying to breathe for the sickness of hope that wracked her.

In the woods, the mother
In the mother, twins

Born out of darkness
Out of long dreams
Into light

Long ago
An old mother
Walked out of the oakwood
Into the darkest part
Of a winter sky
For her final hibernation

She is the one
Who points true north

She is the one who sees
With stars for eyes
The dying
The ending
The forest full of spears

When it comes
She will walk
The oakwood on feet
That leave no pattern

In the woods, the mother
In the mother, the woods

Fawn and acorn
Marten grouse and stone
Stream and cyclamen
Waxing moon and new

Always she dies
To save the child

- *Of Bear*, from the Old Language

It was the bear who found the wounded man beneath a wild pistachio bush, covered in leaves and very fevered. But it was Essel who pulled him out and felt his pulse and kept the bear from licking at his blood. Essel's arms had grown very strong in the month since the men of Tar had killed her father and brother and taken her mother away. She and Tiln climbed trees for shelter in the daytime, and she was often carrying the twins, though lately she'd fashioned a kind of saddlebags out of rushes that slung over the bear's shoulders. The twins preferred this, one on each side of her great belly, holding fistfuls of her fur, gurgling and sometimes shouting with pleasure. Then, Essel had to silence them with her sternest words; they were fugitives, she told the babies solemnly, though surely they couldn't understand.

Tiln did, and took it all very seriously, though before she'd been a silly, dreaming child who never could complete a chore without forgetting it at least twice, distracted by a beetle with furred legs, or a snail shell speckled white, or a stick that looked like a horse. Now, her knack for spotting small details was a blessing; it was Tiln who could find mushrooms where no one else saw them, and who saw the boot prints of men in the forest humus when to Essel there were only leaves and acorn husks. This way, they kept out of sight and did not starve, though barely.

For a moment, looking down at the wounded man, Essel thought coldly that she should leave him there since he was already so nearly dead; and what good was a wounded man to them, she and her little sister and the babies? They had the bear to protect them—the Lady of the Hunt in disguise, Tiln whispered—and that was better than a man. Besides, men wanted things from women, frightening things, and Essel was afraid after all they had seen and heard, hidden deep in the forest, traveling mostly by night.

But then the bear began to lick the wound at the man's right shoulder, cleaning away the blood, and Essel, horrified, thinking the bear was going to eat him, moved to push her away. The man let out a whimper so childlike, so full of pain and terror, that she dragged him out from under the bush in pity. This made him groan more, so she left him and brought one of the reed mats she'd made as a bedroll. She managed to get him onto it, and dragged the mat into the cover of the oaks to their makeshift camp in a thicket of young trees.

The saplings were twined with a thorned, blooming clematis that caught at Essel's shift. Their smell was of honey. A small stream ran nearby. She brought water from it, soaked in a rag from her skirt. She cleaned the wound at his shoulder, a deep dagger gash that had partly healed, but had opened again and now festered. She cleaned the dirt from his face until it was smooth. Then she saw how young he was—little older than she. A boy, and not a man, though bearded. He slept in fever, and sweated through his clothes. A dirt-darkened white shirt; the goatskin pants of shepherds. Caring for him made her feel no longer a girl, but a small woman. She supposed that she had been for at least a year now, since her first bleeding, but she'd never cared for a boy who wasn't one of her brothers. It made her feel capable, and a little flushed.

A day and a night passed, and the boy did not wake. Essel washed the wound with a tea of wild thyme from the hillside beyond the wood every few hours. She tried to remember all the things her mother had taught her, and wept, thinking of Zola.

Tiln came with olive leaves from an old tree growing alone at the oaks' edge, and these they got him to drink as a tea, drop-wise, from a cloth. The bear suckled the twins and did not try to come near again, but watched with small golden eyes, eating acorns. Tiln gathered fingerfuls of cobweb from dark crevices. Essel did not laugh, now, when the girl apologized to each spider. Life was much more precious to her than it had ever been before the men of Tar.

They tried to press these in the wound to close it, but Essel thought they might have made it worse. Tiln also found the body of a worm snake, hollow and dry on the sunny hill, its bones picked loose and clean, its skin a dark and shining tunnel. She brought three vertebrae back and laid them beside the boy's head. He slept on, and murmured, and once cried out. Essel thought of her brother and her father. She had seen their bodies up in the hills with the sheep, their throats cut cleanly and the dog's too, as if they'd been attacked from behind. Now, as she could not then for the absolute terror in her, she sat rocking with grief. This boy had her brother and her father in him. He was dark like them. He had a shepherd's kidskin boots. Beneath the sweat and sick, he smelled of goat, and wool. She would not let him die. Why had she found him, if only he was to die? Why the bear, why their own lives saved, if only there was to be more death?

A big moon lit the night. All the shadows moved in silver. Skeletal hollows sat under the boy's eyes. Small owls called in high, blue voices. Essel and Tiln tried to sleep, holding one another and leaning against a tree on their single sleeping mat, but could not. They ate handfuls of acorns Essel had leached in the creek, bland and a little bitter, but food. The night smelled of autumn's coming cold, and the cyclamen flowers that had grown after the late summer rain, and the bear, who slept with the twins so buried between her paws and fur that only their feet were visible. Essel worried that they were losing their humanness; that they were losing her, and Tiln, and their own names. Already they hardly looked up when called. Already they turned to the bear first in everything, and showed no inclination for walking. But they were alive, *alive*, and any aliveness was its own gift.

Essel looked at the boy. The moon had turned him ghostly. He breathed shallow, infrequent breaths, only a small flutter of his shirt. She got up to watch that he was still breathing several times, and to change the cloth on his wound. He no longer felt hot, and the wound no longer oozed. Did that mean his fever had broken, or that he was dying? She didn't know. At last she slept with Tiln's head on her chest and her cheek on Tiln's hair. When they woke there were little prickly oak leaves on their wool capes, and the air was chill.

"What will we do when it gets too cold?" Tiln said, picking oak leaves off Essel's arms. The fires they lit were always very small, for fear of smoke. But Essel was looking at the boy, and didn't seem to hear. The boy's eyes were open. He was looking at the bear. Caster and Coll drank at her belly. The bear looked back at him with her strange eyes which in the dawn light were bronze and not gold. She made no movement.

The boy wondered if he was dead, and at the gates of the Old Mother. Two girls watched him. Naiads? For they had come up to him again and again with clear water. A tall one and a small one. For a moment the small one looked like someone he had lost. But then his brothers' faces stormed him, and he let sleep take him again so as not to think of how he had left them, of how they had died.

The bear shifted. She licked at Caster's feet, which made the baby giggle. The boy started again from his half-sleep. Essel leapt up at the motion and came to him. She had gone terribly shy the moment before, seeing his amber eyes open, fixed on the bear, full of their own secrets. Before, fevered and asleep, he had been hers. She had saved him. The Boy, she called him in her mind, and imagined his life, his family, who he had loved. He was dear to her, asleep. A piece of her father, her brother. Awake, he was a stranger. She did not know what to say.

"You're awake," was all she could manage. A blush too, which she hid by laying her cape over him. His knees were trembling with the morning's cold. "I'm Essel," she added, not looking at his face again. "We found you in a bush and dragged you here. Well—the bear found you. Who are you?" That was a lot at once. She bit her lip. He stared at her, hard. It took most of his strength to hold onto her words. Then she saw tears in his eyes.

"Thank you," he said after a time. "My life is yours I think. And hers." He nodded toward the bear, going a little paler. "I'm Vris."

His own name was a terrible doorway. It opened out into memory. He closed his eyes again. This time his dreams were not hallucinatory, but clear. Mercifully, his brothers were not in them. Instead, he dreamed of the girl Lillet. Her name had come back to him with his own. Lillet, Little Bat, with her witchface and her quick hands. Lillet, who had been his only friend, besides the dog and his brothers, who were too much more than friends to think of, not yet, not now. Lillet he could manage. Lillet, because he had not seen her die. The last thing he had seen was her in the arms of the men of Tar, carried off with the other spoils—Alzance's dagger, Spiro's heavy wool coat and their grandfather's bronze arm band. What had happened to her? Had they killed her too, later, after—?

He found that he was awake, and sweating. The girl Essel held a cool cloth to his forehead. Now a leaf-full of acorn mush mixed with something sweet—a crushed wild apple, a bit of late blackberry Tiln had found. He tried to swallow and managed, coughing. It was Tiln who peered at him now. The expression on her face made him want to laugh. A look of wonder and of disgust, both. Like he was a strange creature washed up out of nowhere, and stinking. She had a long face and lips that naturally pouted, which made her look always thoughtful. Her eyes were oddly pale against her black frizz of hair, which was matted now with sticks and oak leaves. He grinned at her. She squeaked, and clung to Essel.

"The bear," said Vris, trying to sit up a little. Both girls darted back. The bowl of thyme water spilled. "Are you her nymphs? Have I trespassed, and am to be killed?"

Tiln giggled again, and then turned red with it, looking younger than her ten years. Even Essel grinned, though her eyes remained solemn.

"Of course not, silly! Why would we save your life only to kill you?" said Tiln, rocking forward on her heels again. She liked the darkness of Vris' face, and the earnest way he spoke.

"The bear," said Essel. Her expression unnerved the boy. What had she seen, to fix him with such gray eyes? Then he thought that maybe his own eyes looked the same. "We don't know where she came from, only that the twins would be dead if she hadn't. Now they might end up part bear, which is better, I guess." Her look changed. "It wasn't long after our father and brother were killed. Up north. In the valley called Ateras. They took my mother for her dyes. Her crimson was always the best.

"We hid a long time in the forest until we were starving and the twins were screaming and we thought surely we'd be discovered, and then the bear found us and—she left us a rabbit she had killed. We ate it raw. She let the twins drink from her. We could smell smoke from our house, burning. After, we ran together. We haven't been near to a village since. We don't know what places the men of Tar have taken. Or if they've taken everywhere. I think the other women—they gave my mother away. I'm afraid someone might give us away, too. I think the bear talks to them. The twins, I mean. They're so small they could only say silly things, nonsense words, before. Now they are quieter. They make sounds like she does. They watch her like she's speaking to them. We would be dead, I think, without her. She won't let us drink from her though. We tried, but she pushed us away. See?"

There was a thin line on her cheek, which she pointed to. She hadn't spoken so much in a long time. Since she'd been her mother's daughter in the oak grove. Since she'd had a father and an older brother. Her chin was wet, and cold. She felt it and found tears there. Tiln stared at her sister's tears. She had never seen Essel cry before, and it made her feel small and frightened and alone. Vris sat all the way up on his strong arm.

"I've lost my family, too," he said. "I am no one now. You're why I'm alive at all. I'll be a brother to you, if I can be."

Saying the word *brother* stung him, and it stung Essel too. She opened her mouth to say something hurtful, but Tiln, who was younger and simpler still of heart, pulled a small snail shell from her pocket and pressed it into his hand. It was the color of an olive leaf, with white spots. Her eyes shone like little oil lamps. They'd found a young hero, a forest god, she was sure of it. Maybe he would turn into a long-legged fawn. Or a fox. Mother had told a story once, from the northern mainland she said, where there were men who could turn into foxes and who sang songs that made trees pick up their roots and walk. He looked a little bit like a fox, a shaggy dark one. His face was sharp enough, but kind.

The snail shell in his hand was a wordless affirmation. An acceptance. He understood it, smiled, put the shell in his pocket.

"There is a safe place I know of," he said. There were tears in his throat but he swallowed them. "We could hide there for some time. Until—until it seems safer. It's not far from here. It's not far from Kranea, either."

"Shouldn't we stay far from Kranea?" asked Tiln. But Essel was twisting her hands, thinking. A low luster came across her face.

"We could seek news of mother," she said. "Oh, do you think we could?" Her eyes shone on Vris. It was against the code she had made for them, the rules she and Tiln had kept to out of necessity, and the bear with the twins by nature.

"I was a bandit before, you know." Vris shifted, laying back again and groaning. But there was a little smile on his face now. "We spied on them, and stole, and tried to haunt them. That was Lillet's idea. My—friend. I think she was taken to Kranea too. Isn't it better to at last try a brave thing, and die at it, then stay forever hiding while the world burns?"

"Mother would like us to try to live," said Essel, keeping her voice steady. Oh, how she wanted Zola near! How she wanted to lean on her wide hip, and feel her hands smoothing and smoothing her hair, and smell her smell of seawater and sweet rose oil, with the musk of dye beneath.

"I'd like to be a bandit," said Tiln.

A rete and Lillet looked up from the whirring of their spindles at Zola's cry. She stood hunched over one of her great copper vats, her head halfway inside, her black hair engulfed in the stink of the kermes steam. At last she raised her head. Her face was pink, and dripped.

"My children are not dead, but somewhere hiding!" she said, recovering enough to speak. Her eyes were bright. Tears welled there, then fell down her cheeks. She did not lower her face or move to brush them away.

Arete thought of the Swallowing Rocks. That name and vision had crouched for days now in the holes in her lace, in the fire, waiting for her to pick it up, to handle it, to carry it somewhere. As she had tried to do with the caper. The girl. The snakes in the fire. Was it desperation that made these feelings come, these visions? Was she only going senile after all? For it felt as though some other force outside her own mind had come to dwell inside her. She had thought, perhaps foolishly, that it was the Earth's. But maybe it was only madness.

The name of the Swallowing Rocks rose up now as she looked at Zola, and she thought that at last she knew its purpose. But still she could not quite believe that such a thing was possible. Maybe loss had only maddened them all, and Zola no less, standing there with her head inside the dye vat.

"How can you know this?" she said to Zola, tenderly.

"My kermes." It was a wholly lucid look, the one in Zola's

eyes. "There in the vat. They are whispering. Of my daughters when they are grown. They have never lied before."

"Once I was good at sneaking in and out of anywhere," said Lillet, wanting to help, wanting to make Zola happy. She stilled the sheepswool that spun at her fingers. Her tone was light, but the look on her face sickened suddenly, remembering.

"I must leave this place," said Zola, hardly hearing the girl. She set aside the long bronze ladle and it pooled with red. "Tonight! My children—" She swayed. Arete was there to catch her, to sit her down, to hold her while she crumpled, and wept.

Across the room shuttles clattered, loomweights clicked, spindles whirred and ticked, thread and cloth swelling and swelling into the night, and the women murmured or sang or sat quiet, keeping themselves and their work apart from Zola's weeping, for fear it would undo their own.

"I had not dared any hope," Zola said after a time.

Lillet held onto her hand, but she was ashamed of what she felt as she looked on Zola's strong, tear-burnished face. Jealousy. She didn't want Zola to be anyone else's mother. She didn't want Zola to forget her. And yet she knew with the sad clarity with which a woman knows, and not a child, that Zola's fierce affection for her was borrowed. It belonged at last, and first, to her children.

Arete watched Lillet, knowing, and Lillet looked up into that knowing. Something in her eased. *I am no one's*, she said to herself. *That is who I am. I am my own.* Her own blood had cleaned her. That's what Zola said. She was motherless, fatherless, childless. Only Lillet, Little Bat. The Moon's. Then she heard her own mother's voice saying *Look to her, and I am there*, and she knew that she was not alone after all. She smiled a little.

"We will go to the Swallowing Rocks," Arete said. "There are pools there, for seeking visions, and holes that know no bottom. That would be a beginning, I think, though I know not how it will end."

THEY MADE THEIR ESCAPE BY NIGHT A WEEK LATER, under a full moon so they need light no torches. Lillet taught them the owl cries she and the bandits had used, though it made her choke with tears. They filled a heavy linen sack of food between them, slipped from their daily meals. It had been difficult to hide their plans from the other women. Arete suspected that Vela knew something, and watched them keenly. But after all it was madness, and a death wish, and for that reason Vela could not anticipate what it was they planned to do. They did not all rise from their beds at once in the night's quietest hour. Arete stayed by the hearth in the weaving room and feigned sleep. Lillet pretended a stomach illness and begged Zola in whispers to come out of doors to help her.

Lillet and Zola did not creep out of the sleeping chamber, but walked calmly, Lillet a little hunched over her belly, Zola patting her arm. This was Lillet's counsel, for she had seen it work many times among the war camps of Tar. Look as if you are supposed to be there. Look as if nothing is amiss. A few women stirred, and slept again. Only Vela watched them from her bed with slitted eyes, and was not sure.

Outside in the walled olive grove they took up the cloaks and boots they had hidden among the stacked wood, and the bag of food. Arete met them shortly. The sooty lace was in her hands. Even as they walked, following the inner wall's shadows, she hooked and knotted nervously. Lillet wondered if what she did with her fingers on the thread was the same as she had done in her mind for Alzance and Vris and Spiros. She did not try it now, but only breathed her body inside the shadows, holding Zola's hand.

There were no guards in the slavewomen's quarters, nor beyond the olive grove and along the fields of wheat and barley that now stood dead in anticipation of winter. Slaves came and went throughout the city on various errands; it was only Kranea's outer wall that they could not breach. Their three shapes made quick, strange shadows that were hardly distinguishable from olive trees, and stalks, and bay shrubs. Only when they were in sight of the outer wall did they hear the sentinels, walking up and down its length in boots that rang on the stone. They could see the torches from a distance, and smell their smoke. The moon sat straight overhead, and the limestone of the wall was so pale in color it looked as if it had been quarried there, from some great crater.

Each stone in the massive wall was as broad and as tall as an oxcart, and cut polygonally. The result was impregnable, and heavily patrolled. Still the three women kept their calm, and followed Lillet's counsel. Breathe inside the shadows. Walk as a shadow. Empty your mind of fear. Empty yourself of doubt. You are a shadow, you are a shade, you are nothing at all. Instinctively they each held a part of Arete's lace as the open end grew under her fingers. She hooked it ceaselessly inside the shadows as they went, binding them to each other and to the night. There were a series of knots at its far end, which Zola held.

They came near the gates of Kranea and stopped in a pool of darkness to wait and watch. Three men stood with spears crossed, guarding the entrance. The white plumes of feathers on their helmets shone in the moonlight. Lillet quailed, remembering, and clutched at the lace. She thought of the redness of her own blood between her legs. Zola hissed her husband's name between her teeth, and her eldest son's. It was rage she felt, not fear, rage so hot she thought it might break their hiding with its heat.

"Untie the knot," said Arete, without a sound, only her cracked lips moving. Zola calmed, and obeyed. She untied the first knot, murmuring the names of her children and her husband in the cadence of an incantation.

Lillet thought the stars had shifted and were falling. Then she saw that the sky brimmed with bats, thousands of them flying on tapered and delicate wings. The collective cries of their echolocation rang crosswise through the dark. Lillet's head spun. She held on to Zola and to Arete. The old woman had started to laugh, silently, her whole body heaving with a laughter that had long grief in it. The bats descended in one dark and flapping mass upon the guards. All along the wall there were shouts, and several arrows shot, but these did little good against so small and deft an enemy. Now Lillet was laughing too, with joy, for she loved bats, loved their dusky furred feet tucked up against their bodies, loved their strange mouse faces, the tapers and hooks of their wings. How they could curl up and make a home so safely in any darkness. And how fierce and quick they were!

"Now!" hissed Arete. They ran together inside that storm of bats, right between the three guards at the gate, who were so shrouded in little wings, so busy shouting and lashing out, that they could see nothing at all but the faces of bats.

"A little bit of lace!" Arete chanted under her breath as the gate opened without effort under their hands, a single bolt easily lifted by three. "All this time, and all you need is a little bit of lace!" Her chanting sounded half mad, and free.

Bay water lapped under the moon against the stony shore of the harbor beyond the city's gate. Fishing boats crouched at anchor, a few lit amber from within by fishermen readying themselves for a nighttime hunt. It was easier to catch the little schools of smelt by moonlight.

The Swallowing Rocks were not far, nor the harbor's mouth where it met the greater sea, but they had to go very slow inside the shadows. The bats had drawn many guards toward the gate, but not all, and their torchlight far above made rings of danger that moved at random down into the shadows where the three women crept. And yet for a time they felt beyond the reach of danger as they moved in the night's air outside the wall, in freedom, the friends of bats, the keepers of some miracle they didn't fully understand.

They heard the water being swallowed before they could

see the rocks. The sound of little wavelets hitting stone, and a deep undulation when the water did not return. Lillet thought it sounded alive, and in her mind she saw a great creature coiled there, swallowing the sea.

Their skirts trailed in the water as they clambered down over the sea stones to the very edge. Zola looked back along the wall, then out across the bay toward the flanks of Mt. Enos, the northern rise of Calo. Even under the last of the setting moon, she could see the new scars where trees had been cut. How the whole western face of Enos was turning to stubble, to stumps, to stone. She looked away, and down to the pools in the rocks at their feet, where the night crouched and moved. The rocks were limestone, like most of the rocks of Kefthyra. Sea and rain pocked them, so that their surfaces were grooved, rivuleted, whorled, little labyrinths that mirrored much greater labyrinths far underground.

"Here," said Arete, close to the bay's edge, where the stones made tidepools and a barrier to the sea, so that the water was swallowed only little by little. The old woman squatted by a moonwhite stone oddly unblemished by weather. A hermit crab carrying an ancient shell scuttled on purple feet away from her shadow and into a deeper pool. The sound of swallowing was very loud. Arete was laughing again. Lillet felt uneasy, watching her laughter. It had a fraying about it, an unraveling, like the edge of something.

"By all the cuckolds, but I haven't a clue what comes next!" she cackled.

There was a terrible silence. Panic crept all through Lillet's body. She remembered the men of Tar. She remembered capture. She began to feel dizzy with the memory of fear.

"Old woman, are you mad?" Zola snarled, breaking through the girl's dread. Her tone was cold, furious. It was ruthless with need. "Why did you bring us here, if you do not know? What of the miracle of the bats, if you do not know? Are we to be sacrifices of Tar here in the stinking tidepools, before ever we have a chance of finding my children, of being free again?"

"I know nothing. I know only what comes to me, when I am listening. I know nothing of bats. I know nothing of power. Only I felt those things in my hands, in the lace. I saw it, our coming here, but I did not see what came next. A pattern, only. Many shapes in the dark. I know what my grandmothers told me, but it wasn't much, and those women who journeyed through the underground lived long ago, when the old language was spoken, when magic was known. I have no knowledge of how one seeks a vision, only that they come."

Zola turned away without reply. She would not meet Lillet's eye. Her own were cold. "Essel. Tiln. Caster. Coll," she murmured, bowing her head over the pools of water where they were swallowed. "Essel, Tiln, Caster, Coll." She tired to feel what she had felt in the oak grove when the kermes rose red through her body and made her powerful. But she could feel none of that now, only sorrow. In her mind she could not focus on the memory of her children's faces, but saw instead the flanks of Enos, torn, and her husband and her Omerr, killed. But this she quickly stifled in her heart, a scream that was silent but did not end. She had not seen it with her eyes, but she knew it in the blood on that sword the day she was taken, and in the boasts of the soldiers later, when she woke, slung over one of their horses. *Easy to butcher as their sheep, that shepherd and his runt and bitch.* The words burned her, rising in her memory. They would break her. She stamped them out and turned back to the other women.

Arete untied a second knot in the lace, muttering, her laughter gone. The surface of the pool shifted for a moment, opening into some other darkness that held no stars or moon. Zola gasped. But the vision did not hold.

Lillet sat back on her heels. She watched both women, thinking of what Arete had said about the old language, thinking about her mother and the Moon and the cave called Drakaina.

"It's a place of the old faith," she said at last in a small voice behind them. "So it must be hungry for the old words. You said they used the old language here, long ago. Well, I think it wants to be praised. Then maybe the water will show us something it knows, something about your children."

Both of the older women turned, staring. Lillet's face was long and angled in the moonlight. She did not blink.

Stone. Bear. Red. Moon.

Snake. Snake. Snake.

Lillet began to say them, over and over, the words that came to mind. The ones she could recall. Then the words fell from the three women all together into the water, like tears. They came without memory or effort, as if they had been given from elsewhere. They waited, and said the words again and again until the night was made only of those ancient tones.

The smell of the bay rose in musk and salt between the words and the women who spoke them. The water lapped. The stones swallowed. The night was endless, spinning through them. They waited, kneeling, faces close to the pool and the place of swallowing.

Without warning, after a long time, the water changed. Zola understood the pattern of its changing first. She cried out, an animal noise.

"Essel, Essel!" she cried, and her voice rang through the darkness above the sound of the swallowed tide. The face of her child peered up at her from the pool, bright with recognition, the same as she remembered but older, thinner, with infinitely more distance in her eyes. Above her was the beginning of a sunrise, the same sunrise that was above them here, by the bay. Lillet and Arete leaned close to see Zola's daughter, and something inside of Lillet caught at the sight of Essel's solemn, quiet face. She felt an almost frightening recognition. Like she had always know that face. She held herself, and looked away.

Boots clattered over stone, and several men shouted. Essel's face vanished, and Zola saw only her own, weeping.

"I see them by the water!" a voice cried across the distance, near the wall. "They are by the water!"

A group of soldiers was coming toward them between the moored fishing boats along the harbor. There was a woman with them, cloaked against the cold. Arete recognized Vela's small, thin form, the shape of her hatred, and knew they had been betrayed. The lace fell from her hands into the pool.

"Oh my daughters," she whispered, taking Zola and Lillet by the hand. "Oh my daughters I have done us no good this night. I have wasted what was growing—"

"No." Lillet put her own little hand over the old woman's mouth. It was cold, and soft. Her eyes were not afraid. "Look."

In the pool where it had fallen, the lace was loosing its soot and turning very white. More than that, it seemed to be moving, writhing. Lillet remembered the white snake of long ago. She reached for the lace, her fingers gentle.

"Witch!" came a woman's scream behind them. "The little one is a witch, I told them all! Look how they crouch there doing ill!"

Soldiers surrounded them along the harbor stones. There was nowhere to run but into the sea.

"I will not go to them again," hissed Zola, readying to swim, her body heavy with ending.

But Lillet and Arete were not listening to her, or to Vela, or to the barked orders of the soldiers, commanding that they surrender themselves once more to Tar, or be killed like animals in the tide. The men raised their bows and notched their arrows.

Then they saw what was growing in Lillet's hands. It was a snake white as limestone swelling with the light of the dawn, growing and growing until its body filled the pool and coiled around the rocks. It grew as fast as that sunrise cresting over Mt. Enos. The soldiers faltered another moment. It was Vela who screamed, "What are you waiting for? Kill it! Kill it! Kill them!"

But the snake had already opened its mouth. The scent was cavernous, the fangs stalactites. Its great head swayed above them. Then it plunged down to swallow Lillet, Zola and Arete whole.

A dozen arrows clattered useless across the stones. As fast as it took an arrow to fly, the serpent had vanished into nowhere, into the ground.

Beneath stone
The snake sleeps

Hers are the tunnels
Through the underworld
Hers the caverns and the pools

Every age, she sheds entire
A sheath of star and earth
The oldest lace

There are words
To call for her skin
To pray for an end

These words are also blades

Take care
For they will open
A doorway
Into the darkest country

Where words themselves
Are made

- *Of Snake*, from the Old Language

The children stayed several days more in the camp in the oak thicket until Vris was well enough to walk. He mended quickly now that he had a small thing to hope for, Lillet's name a warm stone in his mind. He held it there, touching it often. Tiln continued to bring him treasures, now she knew he cared for them in the way she always hoped Essel would. A bit of bark covered in strange green lichen that stood up and flared out like snouts. The tea-gold husk of a cicada, light as paper and gleaming with ridges and empty eyes. The rest of the worm snake, that strange dark tunnel of scales, which they wound together around the base of a tree, and laid with cyclamen flowers. For this, Tiln loved him, a puppy love that turned her clumsy all over again, and for which Essel teased her as they fell asleep.

"What do we know of him, Tiln?" she whispered into the dark. "Besides he lost his brothers, and was a shepherd. He says he was a bandit, too. You would marry a bandit, Tiln?" But her tone was teasing, light, and it made Tiln wriggle closer, just to hear that lightness. It was so rare a sound, now. "You are too young to marry anyhow. And what would you wear? A crown of oak prickles and rotten snakes?"

"A dress of spider silk!" Tiln replied, half asleep and grinning.

"Oh, Tiln."

THE NEXT DAY THEY LEFT, TRAILING OAK LEAVES from their fraying hems. They kept to goat and deer paths. As before, they let the bear lead the way. Caster and Coll dangled from her haunches in their saddlebags. They kept silent, watching the sun flicker over the rocks. There they passed quickly between sage and stone and wild pistachio. Vris walked beside the bear, and altered their course a little now and then. They were passing around the eastern flanks of Mt. Enos, where there were no villages, only sheep herders and their infrequent huts, and where the land in the mountain's long shadow stretched out in strange hummocks of green that grew around the scatterings of limestone. There were tiny oaks no bigger than Tiln, their trunks shaggy with dark moss, and little cover save the small trees and the stones. They kept low in a slight valley where a dry riverbed lined with plane trees wound, but there was no one at all to see them save a herd of wary-eyed goats whose long, spiraled horns cast elaborate shadows.

They spoke little. Vris kept his teeth closed around the pain in his shoulder. Essel thought that every distant, unusually shaped rock was a man, and ducked. Her palms were sore from tripping on the uneven ground. Tiln had filled one pocket with moss, and found them a little cache of almonds at the base of a crooked tree mottled yellow with lichen. They cracked them with rocks for a midday meal. Caster reached for his own shadow across the strong green earth, humming and burbling. Coll discovered a sound in his throat that was like a growl, and practiced, alarming Essel several times that he might be choking, until she understood that he was speaking like a bear, and left him to it in some despair.

The bear caught a rabbit, skinned it and ate it whole, leaving behind a wet, bloody pelt that Essel gathered up into her pack for cleaning later. She had several skins, thanks to the bear. In winter, they would have at least one fur blanket. Frost hardly came to Kefthyra, but sometimes snow dusted the top of Mt.

Enos, and certainly a night when the stars were out was too cold to spend unsheltered.

By dusk they were parched. Most of the streams were still dry. The autumn rains had yet to start in earnest, and their two waterskins were empty. Vris recalled a small, cold lake in the eastern foothills above a dry riverbed. The lake was near a very small village that had been burned by Tar. Coming near it, they saw a single stone house lit from within, half-singed though it was. Two bent figures moved back and forth, casting tall shadows. There came the sound of an end-blown shepherd's flute. It played a sad, low song. Vris thought they might stop and show themselves, ask for a cup of water, a warm bed, but Essel couldn't bear the music, and she was afraid. Anyone might betray them. Even Vris. She watched him then, sick at heart, as they climbed a small hill through old cypress trees that reached up into the night, darker even than it, and at last came to the lake.

There they all bent their heads like the bear did. They put their faces to the cold water, and drank. The noise of their slurping made Tiln laugh.

"We sound like sheep," she giggled. "And look like them too!" Essel's hair, like her own, was a wild and curling mass, a black sheep's coat standing on end. Vris' young beard was stuck with leaves and dust. Tiln's laughter caught the others, and they all laughed, choking a little, snorting water from their noses. Even the twins, who didn't understand, made noises of glee.

The stars and moon were in the water. There was a sheltered place to sleep where several stones made an uneven circle. Vris thought it safe to build a hot fire there. He knew well how to make it smokeless. He had been gathering dry twigs all day. The fire was a small star on the vast earth. They roasted a quail Vris had killed with a stone. Tiln laid the bronze-edged feathers in a circle on the ground.

They slept close, for warmth. The open sky was cold above, and the lake breathed out a coldness from its depths. Even the bear slept beside them, and Vris beside Essel. Tiln and the twins slept in the middle. All night, Essel woke when Vris moved. She could feel his heat without touching him and worried he had a low fever again. Or perhaps she was just very cold, and careful not to let any of her limbs touch his. And yet the cold and the distance woke her. Once she found her foot was brushing his. A thrill went through her, quick as lamplight. She quelled it. But she did not move her foot away, and slept at last without stirring.

Just before dawn she woke. This time Vris had rolled so near his breath was warm on her. She rose abruptly, shedding her sheepskin, and went to splash her face. Her body felt strange and shaken, awake to some other longing that had nothing to do with the boy's body near her in the night. It confused and troubled her. A long slender light lay across the eastern horizon. Stars still shone above: the final, the most bright. Everything smelled of darkness, of dry oak leaves and dry stones dampened by night.

Above all, the lake's smell rose with an earthen, freshwater clarity. Essel crouched over it, inhaling, and the scent alone cleaned her. She splashed her face and gasped with pleasure at the coldness, how it woke her skin. The lifting light made the lake seem to rise into being before her. Its color was an indigo so dark, even as the sky grew light, that Essel wondered at its depth. It was not a very big lake, but quite round. Perhaps it was really a cave on its side, mouth facing the stars, swallowing the night. The lake looked back at her with eyes of similar solemnity. There was enough light now to see her own face in the water. It was very still, without wind.

But it was not her own face she saw. Her own face had become three. Had water dripped from her chin, refracting her? She saw the face of a girl near her own age, but with eyes much older. Sharp-chinned, sharp-nosed, a thin, unnerving face that arrested her restlessness and her longing for a moment entire. Beside her was an old woman wearing a black headscarf. The third face was very beautiful, wide-eyed and wide-lipped, the most beautiful woman Essel could imagine.

She cried out. It was her mother. A word was on her lips. A word was on all of their lips. The three said it together, and it seemed to fall from their mouths like a pebble into water. A word of f's and i's. The water wriggled.

"Mother!" Essel cried, reaching out her hand. Where was she? How could she be here in the water? Who were the two beside her? Surely the vision was too clear to be her own dreaming; the great stone walls behind them were wholly unfamiliar. And there—her mother's face had changed, going slack and stunned with recognition. *Essel! Essel!* She saw her mother's lips move with her name, though she couldn't hear it.

Her fingers brushed the water, but her mother vanished. Only the dawn was there, glowing, and something in the center of that glowing, beyond her own reflection, something moving below. A fish? She leaned nearer. The movement broke the water's surface, and something ghostly leapt between her lips, onto her tongue. *Fithi*, she said aloud. The old word for snake, but changed, somehow. Sharpened. She swallowed, afraid of what had happened, and the word seared her throat going down.

She edged back. The water dripped from her chin. Tiln had always been the dreamer. The one to talk to frogs and hermit crabs. The one who listened to their mother's stories, and believed them. Not Essel, who did not dream and did not speak to trees, preferring what was sturdy, and practical. Even the bear she had accepted as such. Not the Lady of the Wood, as Tiln believed, come to help them in a time of need, but only a mother bear who had lost her own cubs, and had turned her maternal sorrow on the twins.

Essel shivered and edged away from the deep water, suddenly very afraid. Surely her mother had not been in the lake. Surely she had not swallowed that snaking word.

The bear was standing right behind her on the bank, so close

Essel felt her heat, and understood her size. She stood as tall as Essel's shoulder, but three times as broad. Her coat was thickening for winter. Her small eyes were amber this morning, and Essel felt them looking into her, beyond her, as if they could see the place the word had gone, the place it rested. Essel lowered her eyes. The bear did not. She started to feel afraid. Would the bear kill her, and all of them, at last? She looked up again. The bear's eyes followed her, and there was some expectation in them, some gleam of meaning that Essel could not understand.

"Arktous," said Essel. The bear blinked, and took another step, and bent her great head to drink from the lake. It was the word for bear in the old language. Essel did not know where it had come from. *Arktous*, she said to herself. The bear turned to look at her again. Water streamed from her black snout. This time something in Essel thrilled at the look, the power of the bear, her broad, shaggy paws.

Who are you? she thought.

I am the old stars, came a reply in her mind, but she didn't know if it was the bear's, or her own, for the twins began to wail then, and the bear turned away.

The need to weep rose up in Essel, and this time she could not stop it. She crouched by the water and let the great sobs heave her until she couldn't breathe.

LATER IN THE DAY, LEACHING A SMALL SKIRTLOAD of acorns in the lake, Essel decided that it was only hunger and fear that had made her think she was swallowing words, and talking to bears, and seeing her mother in the water. For Zola was not in the lake now. The bear ignored her once more. Essel's stomach was a small, hard fist of hunger. Tiln was gaunt too. Her arms were sticks. How would they make it to Kranea, let alone survive the winter? Meat came only with luck, and rarely. Acorns would soon be gone, eaten by deer and martens. Essel sent Tiln and

Vris to collect acorns for the remainder of the day. She took off her undershift and made it into a sack. Better cold than starving.

The next morning they moved on. Vris had little use of his right arm, but he still carried the sack of acorns they had gathered. They climbed through a valley. There they saw burnt vineyards and half-ruined olive groves and Tiln wondered aloud at the intelligence of these men of Tar, for burning up good food. They kept out of sight, and saw no one save a group of old women over a fire pit, making olivewood charcoal. At midday they passed the village called Pore. Men of Tar lived there openly now. Their tall oak ships sat in the harbor with new red sails. Essel saw the sails from a distance, and thought sickly of her mother. Men in the bright and gaudy dress of Tar moved along the streets. The hooves of their horses rang. Tiln held very hard to Essel's hand, and almost screamed with fear when she stumbled on the path, afraid of alerting attention though they were far above the town.

Before dusk they reached a dry riverbed that cut down the middle of a gorge.

"Here," Vris said, pointing up. "The cave is here, far up."

The walls of the gorge were sheer and jagged, with raw places where great heaves of stone had fallen during earthquakes. Small oaks and the pale, furred sage of the island grew where there was purchase. Essel swallowed. Tiln reached again for her hand. It felt warm and dry in Essel's, and she squeezed it. The bear snuffed her nose once to the earth, and began to climb the narrow track. The twins did not shout or gurgle, but only watched the small trees, the blue dusk, the bats, with big eyes. Essel and Tiln did not speak; fear sat too tight in their throats. They followed, leaning forward and walking on their toes like they had seen goats do. Vris did not speak because in the dusk, in his heart, he saw his brothers, how together they had leapt down the path like goats, and the black dog bounding behind. How the girl Lillet had leapt in front of them all, her long young legs flexing like a little doe's.

Halfway up, Tiln slipped in loose limestone and shrieked, her leg skidding out and kicking stones off into the darkness. She grabbed at Essel, and Essel lunged for an oak limb. They heard the loose stones clatter at last to the riverbed far below. The small oak bent, but held them. They kept climbing without a word or a look between them. A word or a look and Essel thought she might sit down there on the gorge's edge, and not climb any higher.

The last part took them over bare rocks. Essel froze once, looking down, her breath coming too hard, but Vris grasped her hand and told her where to put her feet. They all reached a ledge and the cave mouth at last, panting, hearts juddering. Grass grew on the ledge, and wild sage, and a single, stunted oak. It was a young cave compared to some, its opening only just beginning to show the mineral drip of stalactites in lines of chalk-white and rose. Inside was only darkness, and the smell of old fires. Vris choked on a cry in his throat at the smell, and the memory. He didn't make a sound again until he had lit a fire in the old hearthpit.

"We will be safe here for a time," was all he said.

The fire made quick, long shadows on the walls. Essel saw an alcove full of figurines and offering cups, dancing. The bear lay down with a pleased sigh, and the twins crawled all over the floor, trying to eat the stones. Tiln followed after them, loosing the stones from their fists, smiling. Essel set the bag of acorns near the fire to dry them.

They slept in the dark's folds, and their dreams were in darkness.

Vris dreamed of the place his brothers were, a place of water and shades. Tiln dreamed of the tunnels of small animals, and the warmth of their lives. The twins dreamed of eating stones, and the bear's fur, and the water of the time before their birth. The bear dreamed of the cold, vast distances between stars. Essel dreamed of the lake, and her mother's face in it, and breathed out again and again the word she had swallowed there.

Fithi. Fithi. Fithi.

It slipped out between her teeth. It slipped down between the stones, between seams of mineral and wet. It slipped away from her into the earth. The bear woke, and watched it. The stars moved, little by little, until it was dawn.

Into snake into stone into earth there was no beginning and there was no end to their swallowing and for all the moon's waning the women called Zola called Lillet called Arete were swallowed they traveled the underground rivers of Kefthyra in a white snake sometimes they were inside a dark wet hot body pressing and pressing but other times they sat in the prow of a long white boat that passed through caverns of limestone dripping and humming in the earth's darkness they were completely naked the crone the mother the girl their breasts heavy their bones heavy their hearts entirely light they did not say a word for there were no words in them except the ones they had spoken into the ground stone red bear moon snake snake snake these words rang without speaking in the place they had come from before ever humans found them on their tongues the women had no names in the underground inside the island where the limestone ran its clear black rivers the invisible opposite of that bright upper world there was little air and sometimes only water but what bore them onward was an older justice than air or even water and like salt they had been swallowed so that only in namelessness could they be borne each seeing her own death her own birth the place of entry the same and only place and although there was no light but blackness red moved on their eyelids in eddies in aureoles the form the cosmos took upon its making the form a planet takes upon its end for the earth was swallowing them and swallowing flesh is not the same as swallowing words you do not come out unharmed and sharpened no you are transfigured wholly digested transformed you are made part of the snake the water the labyrinth the stone the earth's own dream for she values not names but the continuation of life of which bodies are many and same and holy all woman to water to acorn it is no different and they had already given the words they had done their part they had loosened the snakes they could be minnows now or birds or stones so still and dying the water bore them where their words had gone there where they had been directed by a mother's love to the lake with no bottom among the cypress trees and there the white snake thought she might rest a while deep in the stillness in the cold of the water to digest and dream and turn them three to eggs to nothing more to a birth of baby snakes dying lay the three women three whorls of human memory in the belly of the tunneled dark and only the youngest the smallest of them all could remember anything of herself before because she kept holding and holding the Moon remembering that another mother had given her the oldest light the Moon's

Sit on the earth
All whole things
Have their darkness

What you have accomplished
And what you have not
Are One
Darkness is cupped by light

Everything is always
Somewhere on the path
Of being made
One soft edge
And one sharp

Grow full with the fullness
Of your own being
Follow and keep the oldest light

This is how to
Swallow the brightness
Of the great turning

- *Of Moon*, from the Old Language

A heavy storm kept them in the cave the next day. Water streamed down the cliffs and made the mouth a veil. It was a snug place in the rain. Vris set out a wooden pail that he and his brothers and Lillet had left in the cave's recesses and it filled in minutes. Essel used the water to cook porridge for them over the fire with the acorns she had leached the day before. With a fire lit and rain moving outside, the cave walls softened to liquid and glowed. Later, very warm, Essel combed and braided Tiln's hair with her fingers, and Tiln turned pink in the fire's light, watching Vris. He had not smiled at all since they had come to the cave. He stared into the embers as he had been doing all evening, holding his shoulder where it ached. Tears stood in his eyes.

"Do you think there are ghosts here?" Tiln whispered very quietly to Essel when it was her turn to braid her sister's hair. Her eyes were still on Vris She whispered it close to Essel's ear, a tickle like warm moth wings, the smell of her girlish breath the same as it had always been, the smell of Tiln—milky and clean but a little sour, like she had been chewing on earth. That smell made Essel smile.

"No, my Tiln. Only shadows, only the memory of his brothers," she whispered back. "It is safe here." She said it surely though she wasn't sure of anything now, and squeezed her sister's hand. And yet she felt safer here than she had felt anywhere since before everything had been taken away, since the stone house of her childhood with its pomegranate tree and the oak grove all around, since the sound of her father and brother whistling sheep calls down from the ridgetops, since the sight of her mother cooking acorn bread in the olivewood coals and singing a kermes song with the twins drinking from her breasts.

But she didn't let herself think of home and of before for more than a moment. Only the things that would keep them alive. Only the acorns, the water, the fire. Where they might gather more wood, and dry it. How they might store more water than a single bucket. Whether Vris or Tiln or the bear might catch another rabbit for their winter blanket, or a marten. Whether they could really make it to the city of Kranea, and what they would do then, and if they would die there.

Tiln nodded like she always did when Essel said something certain, but still she watched the crouching shadows, and wondered. When Vris looked up at her at last, she blushed, and then felt very silly and young and stupid, and said, loudly, "look, the rain is letting up," so that she could run to the cave's mouth and stick her face out into the stone's dripping, into the night still purple with lightning.

The bear made a noise where she slumbered in the cave's darkest recess, the kind of little bark she used when she was tired of nursing the twins. Her smell of musk and fur and milk filled the place. Caster and Coll, milk-smudged, clambered away from her great belly and toward the fire. Caster stopped to put a piece of charcoal in his mouth, and Essel darted up to take it from him, to try to urge a little acorn porridge down, so that he might have a taste for something other than bear's milk. He nipped her finger, hard, and she almost dropped him. Tears came to her eyes, and she wasn't sure if they were from pain, or fear. She set him down and kissed his dark and growing hair. She smoothed her fingers over Coll's plump cheeks.

"At least you are keeping fat," she said to them both, trying not to cry. She sat down near them, and Vris. When she looked up at the boy she saw that he was watching the twins and that tears had fallen down across his face.

"It was our fault, you know," he said, taking her by surprise. "Mine, really. Not Lillet's. Mine. I wanted to impress her, and she…" He choked. Tiln crept back to the fireside, closer now, her face dripping with the last of the rain. "She was too good a friend to let me go alone. I wasn't ready, I wasn't as good or as fast as my brothers, or her. But my brothers—they were wise. They had to let me try, to make myself a man. They knew they couldn't stop me. But it was too dangerous. It was stupid. What did it matter, making a few of the men of Tar believe in ghosts for a night? Why didn't we just do our best to live for each other, and not revenge?"

VRIS SPOKE FOR A LONG TIME. About what had happened in the hills above the town called Samos. About his black dog, and Lillet. About his brothers, and the goats, and their names. Late into the night they sat by the fire. Words came that Essel had never meant to speak. Tears which she had never meant to cry, not in front of Tiln. But Tiln, leaning on her sister, was relieved to be able to say at last that she missed mother, that she wanted papa to be there, that Omerr had been carving his own shepherd's crook that day. For once, Caster and Coll were happy to sit quietly in Essel's lap. They chewed on her wool cloak. They patted at her chest with their little hands, looking for breasts with milk. They fell asleep curled against each other in her skirt.

It felt terrible at first to say their names, the names of the ones they had loved. It felt terrible to cry so loudly, without being able to stop, in front of others. But after a while, as the fire fell away to the faintest coals, and they rolled up near it and each other to sleep, what Essel felt was a strange and miraculous lightness. As if she were the rocky face of the gorge, stripped clean by rain. She fell asleep believing that Zola's face in the lake with no bottom was only a figment of her sadness. That such a thing would not happen again, now she had said it, now she had said her mother's name.

But the dreams that came to Essel in the cave's dark were full of her. They were not dreams of the past, of the hearth and the acorn bread, her dark wet hair, the twins in her arms, or even dreams of what might have happened, the kind of dreams that move too slowly and with silent violence. What Essel dreamed was far stranger, and more frightening, and she woke from it in a sweat to pace the cave's deep corners where the bear slept. In her dream, her mother was in the belly of a long white snake. There were two other women with her—the girl and the old one Essel had seen in the lake. They seemed to float inside that snake, curled around themselves, fetal and naked. The snake moved through a narrow watery darkness, along tunnels that bent and turned and branched in a hundred directions, tunnels as white as the snake's skin, the white of ancient limestone. It was unclear whether they were dead or alive, for they drifted in an amniotic silence inside the snake, inside the stone, inside Essel's dream, and Essel for a moment drifted with them, but then she couldn't breathe and thrashed her way awake, gasping.

That was no dream, a voice said far away inside her as she paced. But she silenced it, and tried to think, to reason, running her hands on the cave's cold, rippled walls, trying to take some solace, some power, from the other women who had found shelter here before her, leaving behind their broad-hipped figurines, their vessels for sacred wine.

The bear was awake now, watching her. Essel could see the bronze gleam of her eyes. That was no dream, the voice in the darkness of herself said again. But Essel was caught in the bear's gleaming look. A vast intelligence watched her from those eyes. She felt she was staring into the night, into the face of a star. The words she had known when she stood by the lake were gone. What was it she had swallowed? What was it she had called the bear? But they were gone, and only the cave remembered. In silence, in its depths, the words snaked down and far away, following seams and veins of mica, of hematite, of quartz, seeping like water across the island, connecting stone with stone, beyond where roots or minds can go.

Suddenly the bear snarled. Essel jumped away, but the snarl seemed only a warning, the kind of snarl she directed at the twins when they were pulling her fur too hard. And yet Essel did not know what kind of warning. Bears cannot speak, she told herself. Neither do lakes. She crawled back under her cloak, and tried to sleep again. But the dream only returned, more vividly. When she woke again at dawn, she felt as though her head was full of stones. She felt as though she hadn't slept at all, and yet she knew she would find no more rest. So she rose, rubbing her eyes, and went for wood to build up the fire, and to splash a little water on her face from the rain bucket. Tiln and Vris were still asleep, curled close together near the embers. Watching them in the pale light of dawn, she told herself it would be silly to share her dreams aloud. What would be the use? They should talk of practical matters instead; of Kranea, of winter.

After a little while the fire was crackling again, and a thin pot of acorn porridge bubbled. Essel sat with her hands close to the heat, stirring now and then.

"Where is the bear?" Tiln sat up from her tangle of wool cape and rabbit fur, her dark hair knotted, her nose smudged with ash.

She was not in her corner, and nor were the twins. Essel ran to the cave mouth, calling out their names. Vris, awake now too, went out to the little grassy plateau, peering closely at the earth and then at the stones on the narrow goat path.

"She's gone," he said, pointing down. Sea dew had darkened the stones overnight, so that the places where they were loosened or moved showed lighter. "There, you can see where her paws pushed the rocks away."

"Where has she taken them?" Essel cried, wildly. "Has she

eaten them?" The acorn porridge began to burn. She crawled the length and breadth of the cave, searching for any sign of the twins—some tiny handprint in ash, some soggy pebble, but found none. "She is a murderess, only a hungry old bear after all, tricking us!"

"Quiet," hissed Tiln in a tone she didn't normally use with her older sister. Her small brow was furrowed. "Don't speak like that of a bear. Maybe she is trying to tell us something." Her eyes looked very keen to Essel, as if she knew something her sister was hiding; but maybe that was only the older girl's guilt, rising.

Essel clenched her teeth and her fists, thinking of her dreams, of the voice in the night, the strange intelligence that rested in the eyes of the bear. The snarl. *That was no dream,* the voice had said, challenging her and all she thought she knew.

"Listen," Essel began, but Tiln was already gone, scrambling barefoot down the goatpath, calling for her sister to follow.

Through Kefthyra something began to move. In the north on a rocky homestead a man slaughtered a goat and the blood that ran across the ground sank into the earth before his eyes as he prayed to the goat's soul to be forgiven, like his father had taught him, holding the body until it was still. The blood went right into the earth like water, and was gone.

On a stone-laid footpath past a round well between villages above the eastern cove called Effemia, a woman gathered bay leaves into a basket. She cut them carefully with a little bronze knife, muttering the words her aunts had taught her. Everywhere she cut welled a drop of blood. When she noticed its brightness staining her blade, she didn't run, but sat down in a crouch and laid the knife on the ground, remembering an old story about the laurel tree.

In the long, narrow bay between Kranea and the far western arm of Kefthyra, a young man out fishing in a small boat dove overboard at the slow height of noon to cool off in the milky green of the sea. He floated on his back, held by salt. He thought of a young man who he had kissed in the sand only yesterday; a first kiss, a dizzy thing. Clouds left by the lightning storm drifted with great pearlescent flanks overhead. There was a sudden rush all around him, and a sea turtle with long, tapered eyes and a shell as green as summer huffed out of wide nostrils, watching him. The young man kept very still. The turtle had the eyes of his mother, who had passed away in winter. He wept, and his tears fell into the sea. When he climbed back into his boat much later, the hold was full of thousands of perfect, silver sardines.

In the foothills of the smaller mountain called Calo, an old woman set fire to her summer garden, now only the last brown stalks of peppers and corn. She had done so every year since she was small. She lit it at dawn, with the dew wet and five buckets of water lined up from the well, in case. The smoke glowed in shafts of early sun. The smell reminded her of every autumn of her life, and that continuity brought her peace. She watched the flames, and the black that followed. She offered wine and honey in the fire's wake, admiring the fine, cool morning, the sight of the mountain and its rocks rising up behind her house as they always had. That evening, when the fire was all the way out and the ground cooling, she came to admire the ash, and found it full of baby snakes. They flickered and writhed with happiness in the warmth of the ash. She watched them, on her knees, until night had fallen and the earth was cold. Then the snakes left, making a pathway of their bodies up the mountain and into the crevices between the stones.

On the west-facing, pine-clad flanks of Mt. Enos, where the men of Tar were lumbering wood for their ships and their cities back home, hacking with sharp axes and without prayers or offerings of any kind, the workers began to suffer debilitating nightmares. Dreams that were constant with screams. When one very old tree was felled, a narrow, bottomless pit opened where its roots had been. A man fell in. The others could hear his screams for hours. They tried to cover the hole with stones, with wood, anything to stop the sound, but everything laid near its edges was pulled in, as if by a great gravitational force.

The bear's trail led all the way back across the foothills and scrub slopes to the lake with no bottom. At no point was it difficult to follow. Her pawprints lay heavy across the land.

"It's as if she made them clear on purpose," said Tiln, her face very long and still as they caught their breath under an old twisted almond tree and cracked a few of its nuts. A gleam was in her eyes though. A fierce look. *She is the Lady of the Wood,* her eyes challenged Essel. *I know it. Mine are not always a little girl's fancies.* An unseasonably warm wind clattered the almond branches. There were still a few autumn crocuses across the earth, white ones with golden marks on their petals. They rippled.

"She is only running heavily," said Essel. She tossed a nutshell and rose to her feet. "She has a heavy load, and she is rushing." Even she could hear the falseness in her voice. Vris eyed her, and Tiln, but said nothing. They were going the opposite direction of Kranea, and Vris' spirits dropped with the distance; the imagined nearness to Lillet had lifted them more than he had known. He focused on the bear's tracks, her rough marks across loose stones and mud. Their clarity made him uneasy.

They came to the lakeshore in the early afternoon under a fine warm autumn sun. Green was springing up wherever it could, between stones and cypress trees, flushed with rain. There was a buoyancy to the earth that surprised Essel. Then she saw the bear's broad back in the lake. She was swimming. The twins were slung in their reed saddlebags. Caster wriggled, and Coll shrieked at the cold that was starting to ride up his tiny legs.

Vris was already wading into the water. Essel and Tiln ran after him. As the cold pressed Essel's knees, and then thighs, and then engulfed her, breathlessly, all the fullness of her dreams returned. The bear was paddling in circles. There was a look almost of irritation in her golden eye. Of weariness. She swam carefully, keeping the boys aloft, though Coll was wailing from the cold. She swam as if she was looking for something, hunting, waiting.

It can't be so, Essel thought, thrashing through the water toward the bear. The white snake. Her mother, the old woman, the girl. And yet when she tried to peer down into the water to reassure herself, she saw a terrible smooth white gleam far below. She choked on water, then pressed her head under and opened her eyes. The word seemed to course out of her from where it had been lodged, biting into her throat.

Fithi

Fithi

Fithi

The water surged.

"Mother!" cried Essel.

Vris grabbed Tiln to him as the water heaved. It was a sheet of indigo, of darkness. It broke open its fathomless cold upon them. The bear was nowhere.

"Mother? Where?" Tiln screamed.

But Essel couldn't hear her. She was at the leading edge of that unfathomed surge. Indigo first, then suddenly white—as limestone, as bone, as stars. It rose from the lake, not water but the oldest word, the beginning, the dark's snake, she whose mouth was the earth's first cave, and last.

She had not expected to be called again. The light and the day and the winter sun were not her world. She was made of silence and the dark spaces that live in stones, of the unmaking and the made. And there was one of the three in her belly who pained her, who had not forgotten her own name, who had not lost her selfhood entirely in that pythian stillness. Who clutched Lillet and Moon to her breast like stones, whose womb had taken in the snake's own children in that unwinding darkness and was swelling with them now.

The white snake's rising pushed the water shoreward in a heave. Essel, Tiln and Vris were thrashed under with it. The snake's head was a flat shining triangle in the light, vast and beautiful, with tiny exquisite eyes. She plunged down again toward the place of her dreaming, jealous of the three in her belly, hoarding their deaths, pained by the knifing consciousness of the smallest one.

But the bear waited there in the center of the vortex, where the snake's body rose and readied to fall. She was no longer bear-sized but vast, the twins two stars of light at her hips. Her paw struck the snake's white body, lightning to a great tree, rending. A shower of brightness fell everywhere. Scales, ash. Into that scattering, that shower, that brightness, that ash, went both bear and snake, unmade.

The lake settled into the vortex where they had vanished. Three women and two babies floated there among the moon-white scales. The earth shook, everywhere, as it swallowed. The shaking sent rocks tumbling down the slopes, and a cypress came crashing green and brown to earth. The lake water moved again, all as one, this time in a single direction, surging east toward the softest shore.

In the rush of it Lillet's limp body surged against Essel's swimming one, so that she found herself heaving and paddling another weight to shore, an entirely naked girl with a swollen bright belly and a face as sharp as a bat's. Her arms and legs engulfed Essel, nearly drowning her in the tangle, but she fought her way to shore, pushed by the water, pulled under once,

wracked suddenly against sand and smooth limestone grit with
the other girl's body over her, warm despite the lake's cold. It
was the strangest feeling Essel had ever known, the feeling that
split hotly through her as she scrambled upright, rolling the body
from her, cradling it as she did. She was for a moment in a kind
of lover's embrace. It was as if she had already held this girl, had
always held her, in ways she could scarcely imagine. Every bit of
her skin flared where Lillet's touched it. Every bit of her native
solemnity broke.

She leapt to her feet to get away from the feeling, her young
body coming wildly alive, upswept as the autumn cyclamen, soft
as the gold-streaked crocus that opens in red earth, alive as she
had never been before. Is this what it felt like to be Tiln, always
ecstatic over strange little lichens or finch eggs, a special acorn
cap, a stone seamed with crystal? But those were girlish ecstasies.
This was a woman's.

There were white scales across the shore. Tiln sat in a blind
terror, weeping, picking the scales desperately from her skirt, her
hands shaking. Vris lay on his back, Caster and Coll clutched in
his arms, trying to breathe. An old woman and a younger woman
lay naked at the lake's edge, the younger woman's head between
the old woman's long and wrinkled breasts, childlike in her stillness, her smooth brow.

"Mother!" This time it was no dream, no vision. Essel stumbled, dripping, sobbing, to lay her hands upon her mother's brow,
to kiss her cheeks, to feel at her pulse. It was very slow. Her
mother looked distant from her, laid in the old woman's arms,
apart, a woman separate from the mother Essel had known. It
frightened her. For a moment Zola was a complete stranger.
Then Tiln was there, clutching her.

"Is she dead? Oh Essel—what's happening? Who is that old
woman?"

"No, not dead, but cold. We need to build a hot fire, dry our
clothes, wrap them, warm them." Essel's solemn practicality

returned to her all at once. She tried not to look back at the girl with the swollen belly as she went to search for wood. But she couldn't help her eyes. She saw Vris crouched at her side. The twins were still in his arms, a little squashed. He had his forehead to hers, and was weeping. A cold wind swept across them all, tearing at the lake. Essel tried to think what to say, what to ask; why was Vris there, holding the girl? Then she heard him murmur "Lillet," and understood. How had her mother come to be with this girl whom Vris had known? She turned back to her mother and the old woman, her arms full of wood. She crouched by her mother, setting down the wood so that she could stroke Zola's cold face. Both women were so still, in a sleep deeper than dreaming. How could it be that her mother was here, now, at last; that she had been inside that darkness, that snake?

A terrible, rending cry came the girl's limp body, and Essel whirled upright to see what had happened. Vris leapt back. The twins began to wail.

"What have you did you do to her?" Essel yelled, flying to his side. Her own voice frightened her, and her fury. She snatched the twins from him, kissing their wet cheeks desperately. Lillet opened her eyes. They were two sharp wells. She writhed.

"What have I done to her? What did they do to her?" Vris spat. The anger in him made Essel step back. It was bearlike, and black.

"We need to build a fire," Essel said, softening, feeling older than her years. "Let's keep them all warm. This is a woman's matter." She turned back to the girl. "Is this your Lillet?" she asked, more softly still, feeling the strange weight of that name on her tongue, and the possibility that she was already promised, that she was his. But Vris was gone at the forest edge, breaking cypress boughs for Lillet to lay upon. Tiln darted close, helping to build up the fire to warm her motionless mother and the old woman and this strange screaming girl.

It was a quick, agonizing, animal birth. Lillet refused Vris' touch, shying from it as from some anticipated violence, and let only Essel touch her, mop her brow of sweat, squeeze her hand, push her palms against her back or belly, gently, to ease the child down. Essel had helped her father with the birth of lambs and goats, and once the sheepdog with a litter of pups, but never a human woman. Still, she somehow knew what to do, pulled into the vortex of the birthing, hardly conscious of anyone or anything else, Lillet her own world. Somewhere at the edge of their yoked awareness, Vris hovered, holding Coll, and Tiln fretted, holding Caster, touching her mother's neck for the pulse, both feeding the fire until it was dramatically large. The flames leapt at the dusk. Vris built another bed of cypress boughs under the old woman and Zola, and dragged them near the warmth, though they did not stir. Tiln kept by her mother's side, touching her hands, untangling her dark-matted hair.

Lillet knew little but the contractions through her body, the warmth of a certain pair of hands like amber through her. She clung to their simple heat, half-dreaming still, half snake, half moon, hanging to the pieces of herself that she could remember, and her name. Somehow the snake's children had become her own, in that timeless time in the dark country inside the island's tunnels. At last the first head breached. It wasn't a human head at all, but a serpent's, tiny and bright eyed, skin new as the newest leaves on olive trees.

Essel stood back. At that moment Lillet was hardly human. Some other presence sheathed her, hovered round her, shadowed but whole, as the moon is.

Lillet birthed a hundred baby snakes onto the earth at the edge of the bottomless lake. They went forth from her without looking back. She had been only their vessel from elsewhere to here, and now they slithered unsentimentally away in every direction across the rocky ground, over the heavy, dreaming bodies of Zola and Arete, around the lake, into the trees, up the cliffs and away.

Later, both the next day and when she was a very old woman, Essel recalled their birth and their leaving as one swift motion, like a sudden torrent of autumn rain which turns the olive trees to a rainbow of droplets in the flash of sun, blinding. So the snakes, and Lillet opening to birth them, blinded her. Never before and never again would she behold so near a likeness to time itself. It was like seeing the moon touch down to earth and flash the whole motion of her cycle, then leave again as quickly, and Lillet only a small woman who the moment before had still been a girl, wracked by forces far beyond her and left husked—kermes, barley, acorn—on the ground.

Snake-touched, Zola stirred awake against Arete. The cypress boughs rustled. She felt the fire's heat and heard, before any other sound, the whimpering hunger cries of her own baby sons.

E arth was not merciful through her snakes. Hers was a terrible justice when it came. All day the newborn serpents streamed across the valleys and mountains of Kefthyra. All day their cool bellies pressed the cool stones, their tongues tasted the air. They knew where they were going. Their mother told them through her stone. They went where the circle had been broken, they went where the oldest justice had not been kept. Some passed through the houses of goatherds and farmers, of beekeepers, weavers, tanners and fruit sellers, through their olive groves or sheepfolds, blessing them with flickering tongues. Old women scooped up the dirt they had passed over to place in clay vessels, or sprinkle with water from a mountain stream. In the years to come, that day in early November became a holy one, the Day of the Snakes' Return, and people left offerings of honey on their thresholds.

The newborn snakes were adders, and they grew larger as they went. By the time they reached the lumber camps of Enos, the gates of Kranea, the docks of Pore, the village of Ateras, they were tawny, sinewed, and grown.

It took only a single bite at the back of the ankle to kill a grown man. They curled in perfect circles around the feet of the ones they bit. Just there, the earth opened, taking in each victim, and for many days after, the round places where the ground had opened were smoking and black, like rings where fire had been. Some women and men of Kefthyra who had betrayed their own people were bitten and swallowed too, and some folk of Tar were spared—a hapless iron smith's apprentice, a ropemaker, a captive tea merchant, several whores, a soldier who had laid down his weapons and gone native for a beautiful boy of a mountain village near Ateras. Those who had not enacted violence upon others or Earth's own ways were spared. Those who had were not.

The Prince of Tar they left for last. By the time the snakes found their way through the city's stone walls, courtyards, and corridors to the prince's inner chambers, there were no soldiers left to guard him. Slaves and visiting traders wandered the empty streets, dazed and skittish, terrified and awed both. A warm breeze blew everywhere across Kranea, smelling of cyclamen flowers. In the slavewomen's quarters, shuttles hung from looms, wool was cast sidelong from spinning wheels, spindles lay across the floor. All the women were outside, holding onto one another, talking with strangers about what had happened, peering at the black and smoking rings that pocked the perimeter of Kranea.

The prince did not believe in bewitched snakes, nor in a swallowing earth. Still his men had been coming to him all morning with reports of strange and terrible disappearances that seemed to burn the ground, and a tide of snakes, until suddenly no more men came to him with reports, and all he heard was the silence of the city around him. The sudden emptiness of the walls. He smelled a strange, unholy burning. Despite himself he grew afraid. He crouched at the door with knives, waiting. Surely it was easy enough to kill a snake if you saw it coming. What was the big fuss anyway, a few rampant adders? Where was everyone? The fools. He yelled for his servingman, a maid, anyone. But the halls echoed horribly, though he denied the horror of that echo as it came back to him. A log fell to embers. A snake came out of the embers. It did not make a sound as it circled his shaking ankles and lifted its sinuous body to strike.

The hole left in the wake of the Prince of Tar smoked for days. No one would go near the room until at last an old woman was brought in who claimed to know the language of snakes. Wherever she lay her new white hank of lace, the black rings vanished.

Sing a word of making into the cleft in the rocks at the bay's edge. Drop it down swift to the sea's water, a secret ship. The stones will swallow it, not back into the bay but into the island herself, into her cloven, tunneled dark. That word, sung in the old language known to rock and sea, will go the way the water goes, joining rivers that snake through the dark and endless limestone. Half the moon's making, from dark to full, that word will travel in utter blackness, lit only by the pure river's melody. West to east it will flow on the dark waters of Kefthyra. From death to life. From dusk to dawn. Moonwise, unbound. Watch carefully the waters of the bottomless lake on the island's eastern coast. Watch daily at the water's shore as the moon comes to full. Listen for the rattle-song of the kingfisher, lady of storms and blue. Do not swim inside the moon's light on that lake of no ending. Only wait, and at the edge of fullness, at the hem of night, the word will come bobbing up from that underworld. It will have changed. Listen closely to what the island's dark and unseen rivers have made of that word of making. Listen to how it has grown, and how it has stayed the same.

That word is a needle now, ready for the thread.

-Instructions for Making, from the New Language

E ver after, Kefthyra was both feared and revered across the White Sea. Women came on pilgrimage to gather ash and earth from the black rings left by the snakes who had unmade the world, and to visit the caves and temples where the old language was being made new. Only boats of peaceable intent made berth in Kefthyra's harbors, decided not by fishermen or soldiers or sentinels but by the shores themselves. Lightning, wind and sudden rip tides had their way with those they did not want.

The cave called Drakaina became the seat of the first Oracle in a thousand years, in a tradition almost entirely forgotten, and Arete was its first priestess. She had two handmaidens, and the women on pilgrimage came as much to glimpse them as to seek prophecy from Arete. She Who Had Birthed Snakes, and She Who Had Called Them Forth—that was how Lillet and Essel were known in distant lands. But to each other they were only ever *love*, and their days were measured by the sweetness of thyme and artemisia incense as it smoked in its little bronze tripod; by the fetching of water from the smooth white riverbed in the gorge; by the spinning of fine pale silk for Arete's auguries; by the dances they made nightly around the fire, snake-dances they invented as they went, laughing, touching, making light of the power in their bodies, and so nurturing it.

Separate, Lillet and Essel might each have remained tight in their own inertia, their own pain and solemnity, like two lonely fists. Together, they bloomed; they were two wild vines frothed with white clematis flowers, impossible to keep apart. They slept together outside under the stars and left Arete to the silent peace of the cave, so that they did not have to stifle the sounds of their pleasure. They made in life, between their two bodies, what Arete made with her hands on white threads, twisting them into Oracles, into New Words, into Knowing.

Much later, when Arete was gone and Essel and Lillet the keepers of the cave, their auguries were made not of thread but of a twinned dance and the patterns their bare feet left behind in the fire's white ash. Women came from farther still to consult them, and to learn from them. Always, snakes came forth from the cave's crevices to dance with them and vanished when they were done, leaving behind their own sinuous lines.

AT ATERAS, ZOLA WENT BACK AMONG her kermes oaks and for many moons did nothing but nurse her sons and her dying trees. Her milk, which she had feared dry, ran impossibly. Her breasts weighted her. She had more than enough to feed both her trees and her boys. For her oaks had indeed begun to die, and there were no new kermes mothers for many years.

Vris came with them to Ateras. He had seen how it was between Essel and Lillet from the moment Lillet woke, and found that he loved the twins and Tiln with a kind of painful brotherly tenderness that was the only true thing he had left inside himself. He did not leave again in spring as he planned, but stayed a full year, and a second, and then a third and the beginning of the fourth—first to help mend the ruined house, then to hunt deer and rabbit for the larder, and later to grow a flock of sheep so that they might have milk and wool again, though at first the sound of bells made Zola weep.

He stayed away in the hills for a time then, and slept out among the blooming summer thyme. The twins were boys of four, and wanted to come with him, but Zola hardly let them leave her sight, though they were wild things. They still did not speak well, bit each other often, and could not keep a pair of shoes between them for more than half an hour.

A few times that summer among the purple thyme and red earth and stones Vris thought of leaving Ateras for good. Perhaps it would be better for Zola and her family if he struck out on his own at last. He had burdened her long enough; she should not feel charged with him. Alone, he longed for Lillet though what he longed for in her was only his memories, and the proximity of his brothers.

He did not know it then, but it was for Tiln he came back down the mountain in autumn, chased right to her doorstep by his sheep. His pockets were full of treasures he had been setting aside for her, hardly realizing he did; it had become so natural to both of them by then. A striped sheaf of wasp's papery nest; the wishbone of woodlark; a fistful of thyme flowers; a tiny mouse tooth like a crescent moon.

He found her in the kitchen by a ceramic crock, looking very grown for fourteen, her girlish shift suddenly not covering much of her dark legs. There was something wider and fuller about her, in the way of Zola, her dress tight in places that it had not been before. Still her wrists were as girlish as ever. She was feeding milk from a cloth to a baby snake she'd found sleeping in the crock the day before. Her hands were stained red from work with Zola in the dye house. The kermes had started laying again at last while he was gone. Coll and Caster ran hollering to Vris. They clutched at his legs with pleasure and stuck their noses under his shirt to smell him like cubs, gleeful at his scent of hills.

"Look," Tiln said to Vris, as if no time had passed, not aware of what was in his eyes, nor of the long, owlish beauty of her profile as she turned. She held the little white snake in her hands. His pink tongue flickered. "Do you think it's one of Lillet's? Should we call all snakes her children now? Or grandchildren maybe?"

And she laughed, delighted by the thought, a laugh that released what was unfinished in Vris' heart, released it wholly and without regret, like a pair of good scissors would.

He wanted to give her everything at once then, and found himself stammering, fumbling thyme flowers and wishbones and papery nest into her hands. This frightened the snake, who wriggled free onto the floor and out the open door, where Kefthyra's autumn shone golden and Zola was coming in past the huddled sheep with a basket of red wool in her arms, singing.

EPILOGUE

The Garden

*Down in the garden just beyond the fields we know—those fields
where the grass is going to seed and the apples are falling early,
bruised with heat—the small and gnarled men rise up from
the shadows of dusk to do their nightly work.*

I went out walking for no other reason than to clear my head,
as I often did on those days when an idea had held me fast
over the notebook all morning. It was my usual walk; I'd
done it almost every day save in very hot or very wet weather
since we'd moved to the island from the city five years before.
We'd moved for the sake of quiet, and fir trees, the clean air
and innumerable stars. We'd moved to raise our daughter in the
woods. Coming, we left behind our mobile phones and wired a
landline. Internet was only available through a little cable. The
clarity that came with what we'd left was immense.

Looking back, I can't remember anything unusual about that walk from the outset, no premonition of the uncanny lurking in the shapes of alder crowns or the creaking of limbs. No vast and unusual silence in place of the summer thrushes and robins, darting for red huckleberries. No eldritch cast to the shadows. There'd been a bear recently, come down the mountain due to summer drought. I'd seen her on my walk a week before, rearing up in surprise out of the salal. She huffed, but ran, a thicket of darkness. My skin hummed for the rest of the day at having been so wholly seen.

I wish I could say I had some intuition of what was to come as I made my usual round through the fields and firwood. I could embellish the telling if I was that sort of man, but in truth the only hint of the otherworld about my thoughts was the small, bright eyes of the bear I'd seen, and how they'd reckoned me, and where she might be now. My mind had been so tired of late; nothing I put down on the page seemed to sit right, to unfold with ease, as it usually did. Everywhere a false start. My days seemed measured by the worth of my pages, as if that was all life asked of me, all it wanted. As if I was only a mind, and a pen. It was hard to climb down out of my mind, after. Walking helped.

I was lost in that thought, of my work and of the bear and where she was, only half-aware of the fir trunks and the long gold light of late afternoon. Still, something made me come to a stop in the middle of the path. I was near the place I'd seen the bear. A tall stand of huckleberries grew thick to my left. Wild roses twined in among them, bright with hips.

I fretted over that moment later, trying to deduce what sensory force had stopped and turned me thus—the sound of the gardeners' dark feet? Petals, falling? A scent, near unbearable, of nectar? But no, those scents and sounds came later, as I drew nearer. I can only say, half-incredulous still, that it was my soul moving swift and breathless just a little ways ahead of me that made me stop and turn my head. Such a thing had never happened to me before. It has, however, happened since. But first I must tell you what it was I saw gleaming through the rosehips and the firs, before you will understand why it must have been my soul that moved me just to the place where I might see it, like a shaft of sun refracted through dew, which only at a particular angle will reveal the full spectrum of its light.

It was a garden, sitting there in a clearing within the young firs, a great jewel full of sun. It sat there in the peak of its bloom, luminous with color. Deep purple larkspurs leaning against the white froth of umbels; the lemons and mauves and creams of gladiolas raising great budding spears between the dusky cosmos; calendula too bright in its oranges and yellows to look at long; nasturtiums and dark pink morning glories and elaborate nigella crowns and a tower of dark sweetpeas hedged in cornflowers; zinnias of a vermilion which made a strange unbidden nostalgia press my chest; strawflowers glossy and bright as women's hats from some lost world; and the dahlias, heads lifted above the others and thrown back to the sun—burgundy ones like dark blood, yellows tinged with tangerine, and greatest of all, the blooms big as faces open so fully they made planets of themselves, each petal a full spectrum of pink.

These depths of color I learned later, when I moved closer, when I walked among them, trying to memorize each curve and pattern and shape, trying to make them part of my own soul. That is why I can tell you their names now—I spent weeks after, years, with gardening volumes, discovering every name.

In that moment though I knew only an overwhelm of color. I struggled through the wild roses, the tangled salal and sharp-leaved graperoot. Had someone bought this bit of land and turned into a garden while I wasn't looking? But that wasn't possible; I would have seen it, heard the earth movers and the voices of the workers. I did, after all, walk this path near daily. Even I, lost in thoughts as I often was, would have noticed something so significant. But I wasn't bothered by such thoughts for long. Something else in me was too full, too giddy and gleaming, to work out what was possible, what was logical. I kept on through the underbrush. The garden had not seemed very far when I saw it from the path, but now it was always one stand of trees distant, a shining patchwork of color and light, and the heady intimation of many bees.

At last I stopped, weary of the scratches on my legs, a little unnerved by my own fervor. I began to worry that I might get quite lost this way, that I'd seen some fata morgana, some trick of light and heat over a pond I never knew was there, though fata morganas occurring in forests I'd certainly never read about before. But as I started to fret and wipe at my brow, a thrush made the sound of water in her throat, and the firs around me released a scent of sweet almonds. I looked up, straight ahead, and there was the garden not more than three paces away, rimmed with a hedge of dark mauve roses, their centers gold with pollen. Their scent opened around me in the sudden sun, and I almost came to my knees before the gate of that place, weeping.

But just then I saw three things which so astonished me that I kept my feet out of pure wonder. First, just at the gate's threshold sat a dog the color of creamed honey, with wild fur that curled just slightly at his paws and tail. He regarded me with dark, intelligent eyes that, had he been a man, I would have called compassionate, but as a dog I thought carried something further still. Second, a very clear voice came into my mind when I saw him. It said, "leave your concerns at the gate, dear sir. You have no need for them here." The voice was so patient and so kind, just like the eyes of the dog; as if the follies of humans were long known to him, and impressed him very little. I did not know how to reply, or to whom—aloud, or in my mind? And could it be that great shaggy dog, could it truly?

As I stammered and hesitated I saw the third thing. In the garden, beneath the twisted old apple and pear trees which grew along the far edge, and in and out of raspberry canes, many small men the color of earth worked, patting here and there with hands like roots, crooning small husky songs that stirred a pure note of sorrow up from somewhere entirely unknown in my body, which pierced briefly through my breast and then was gone. Now tears fell across my cheeks freely, but I did not notice them because the dog had led me through the gate and into the garden, and no human being could walk in such a place without weeping.

A quality of light struck me, the shadows cast delicately behind the incandescent blooms. In among the petals, in the light and the shadow, I saw the forms of my own life, an effervescent movement like some ornate shadow puppetry—my daughter being born from my wife, both pink and screaming; my wife dancing in a winter field of snow in a blue dress when we were very young and had only just said *I love you*; my grandfather dying in his old dark bed and a priest and candles beside him, the first death I had known, and how hard he clasped my hand; the cherry tree in the garden of my boyhood and a small me laying across a limb, belly plump with cherries; my mother's face, very close, kissing me at dusk and her heavy string of glass beads falling out of her blouse against me, warm with the smell of lilies; my own daughter down by the sea watching the little purple crabs on the rocks with perfect delight, chanting *bug bug bug* as they scuttled away.

Then, as if they had always been so and never my own memories at all, these shades and sylphs of light among the tangled stalks and blooms became others, not my own life but another life, or many, and yet I knew them well and clearly—a slender woman with heavy hair opening a carved box, and all the sorrow and need and pleasure I'd ever felt pouring out it with a rush of pollen into the air; a man in a hundred pieces and his wife, weeping, more beautiful than any woman I had ever seen, gathering his pieces up one by one into her arms, her dress dark as river silt; a man with a golden instrument in his lap paddling a long thin boat in a very dark place, turning back just once to look on the ashen face of his beloved, losing her there, and the red poppies in the upper world where he returned; a man with a lantern inside the belly of a great beast, singing; a lovely girl, falling and falling from a hole in the clouds to the earth far below which was only just being formed; a woman in a garden, speaking to a golden snake in an apple tree; a hunter with his bow, a pond full of beautiful long-necked women, the shore lined with feathered skins; a little box full of embers and a hummingbird darting away with one in his beak; a young man following a ball of golden thread as it rolled across mountains; a citadel, a whole gleaming city of gold and silver and bronze at the edge of the sea at sunset, and a woman in red opening the gates to an inexorable tide; a great savannah and in the center a woman holding her newborn son up to the stars, asking for one to fall into his heart so that he, too, might walk among lions; an old wounded man and a young shining one and the cup between them, and outside the land all wasted and dead for the question the boy did not ask, the question that I, now, standing there among the bees, knew with perfect clarity for one long instant. But coming back fully to myself I could not recall it, and to this day cannot recall it still, though I have known it when I dream.

I had wandered further in to the garden, trying to get closer glimpses of those phantasms at once intimate and strange. Now, the flowers engulfed me, chest-high, as if I had waded in to a lake of inexplicable phosphorescence—great dark red blooms of perfect geometry; spires of mauve and yellow and rose; white umbrellas nodding pollen; a profusion of fragrant orange pinwheels at my ankles, stumbling with dark and velvet bumblebees; the broad-hipped pear trees, a single cherry; the hedges of rose and raspberry. It was like being inside a single, unbroken moment of creation— a rose, opening—and also all of them at once, a beauty so sheer and so unmanageable that I felt myself trembling. I was close to terror. I feared that behind all of these bright petals I might actually glimpse the One Who Made

Them, and whether that force were simply a great light, or a great shadow—an old and radiant man or a woman as broad as the earth, or none of these, or an unseeable crossroads of matter and spark—it would destroy me where I stood. It would undo me, unmake me, unspool the story of my life.

Then I had the sensation of a long, long arm cloaking my shoulder, a wind that carried a solar heat, the scent of warm amber. A very tall being urged me with unspoken tenderness toward the garden's far edge, where the pear trees dreamed in silence their swollen fruit. I didn't dark look, not full on; I was still afraid of some essential combustion, some annihilation, if I turned and stared directly at the one who guided me. In the corner of my eye the being was the color of blue in northern summer skies, where darkness never completely falls; a face neither male nor female, but both, and gleaming with little thorns of stars, with translucent dust as on the wings of moths.

"Come," said a voice, and the white dog was at my other side, watching me with a compassion that only dogs know.

I found myself before the oldest, largest pear tree. The beautiful, terrifying being and the dog were gone. That tree might have been as old as time in its broadness. Its gnarled trunk was flecked with lichens in every hue. Its fruits hung near, shrouded with their own heavy scent—of marzipan, of sun, of the warm necks of woman and the inside of the earth. One of the small dark men emerged from the branches, clambering down quick as a squirrel. He carried a perfect golden pear in his hands, freckled red from the sun and utterly unblemished. He held it out to me, and I bowed, I who had never bowed to anyone or anything in my entire life. There was no other way to accept such a gift except with such a gesture.

The sun moved behind an old fire. When I rose from that deep bow, holding the pear out in front of me, the garden was gone. I stood knee-deep in salal, clutching a great and golden fruit. The pear had not lost its luster or its scent. It gleamed there in my hands. All the colors of the garden shone in its freckled skin, and all of its shadow too. I sat down there in the thicket and wept for what I had witnessed, and what I knew I would one day lose.

I NEVER ATE THAT PEAR. Of course I didn't. How could I? I did try to explain what I had seen to my wife and my daughter, and I think they worried for my sanity, though they did not say so aloud. Only when a season had passed, then two, and the pear still sat untarnished and unaged on my desk on a little silver stand meant, I think, for teacake, did they begin to wonder. I know this because they studied me, each in her way, and asked me sidelong questions about my work. For I had become obsessed, a scholar overnight, sending away for expensive antiquarian volumes on the sacred gardens of India, of Japan; for horticultural encyclopedias and historic treatises on the rose, for books on the Persian gardens of Shiraz, the poetry and folklore of English flowers, biodynamic principles and the arcane philosophy of alchemists, the lore of elementals. It did me some good, I think, to be thus immersed, though in the end it would have been better if I had simply planted my own garden sooner, and made a place for my wife and I to sit under fruit trees after our daughter had grown and moved away, so that together we could have watched their blossoms fall in spring, their leaves return, their fruits ripen, and cut them open together to share that sweet fruit. Instead, I sought the garden only in my mind.

I might have gone mad if not for the golden pear that never diminished on my desk, and the memory of the feeling of that place—a place where neither regret nor worry touched; where time seemed to well from the blossom, and tell itself in light and shadow every story that ever was, all held inside a single one.

Many years later, after we had become grandparents and a terrible war had come and gone from the world, my wife fell very ill. Then I thought, with a great surge of hope, that I understood at last what purpose I had saved the golden pear for all these years. I brought it to her with a little knife and bade her eat it, certain it would save her. But she only smiled, my beloved, and refused. *I do not want eternal life, my love. That is not for human beings. We have had more than our share of sweetness here; now give it back to the world, and me as well.*

She made me promise to clear a space and plant the golden pear in the earth. I could not bear to, while she still lived, in case she might after all decide to take a bite. But she was much wiser than I, my wife.

After the funeral, I brought her ashes with me to the firwood because I did not know what else to do. I was crazed with my sorrow. I brought the golden pear too. I went to the place I had so many years ago seen the garden. My frequent coming and going, seeking it, had cleared a path to that place which was still only an opening in the trees, thick with salal. Very gingerly, I began to dig a hole, and then another. I'd brought a shovel. I cut the pear into three pieces, a seed in each. Inside, it was still wet and fragrant, dripping sweet as the day it was picked. I buried each piece. I licked the juice from my hands without thinking. I spread my wife's ashes in each hole. Then I laid down on the cold ground over the three mounds I had made, and wept, so many tears for an old man to weep. I wept violently and long until my whole body hurt, and then I slept all through the spring night without stirring, dreaming of my wife when we were young, and our daughter a baby still.

When I woke, I understood. I spoke to my wife, and the pear seeds, and the fir trees. In a shaft of early sun, I saw a figure. Dark as earth, with gnarled hands and tender eyes. Then another, gleaming as with the dust of moths. But there was no garden around me that morning. I began to weep again. Then I began to dig.

ABOUT THE AUTHOR

Sylvia V. Linsteadt lives in the bishop pine forest of Inverness, on the Point Reyes peninsula, with her husband. She is the author of the novel *Tatterdemalion* (Unbound, Spring 2017) with artist Rima Staines, and two books about the local and natural history of the San Francisco Bay Area, both published by Heyday. Sylvia is also the creatrix of Wild Talewort, a tales-by-mail project that ran from 2013 to 2016, in which rewilded fairytales and myths were sent out to subscribers around the world. More about Sylvia and her work can be found online at her website, www.sylvialinsteadt.com.

ABOUT THE ILLUSTRATORS & DESIGNER

Rima Staines uses paint, wood, word, music, animation, clock-making, puppetry and story to attempt to build a gate through the hedge between the worlds. She lives with her partner and young son in Hedgespoken, a travelling storytelling theater. More about Rima's work can be found on her website: www.rimastaines.com

Nomi McLeod is an artist, mother, occasional model and once upon a time circus aerialist. More about her work can be found on her Facebook page.

Catherine Sieck is an artist, potter and gardener; her art practice is in conversation with her work on land. More about Catherine's work can be found on her website: http://catherine-sieck.format.com/

Ashley Ingram is the lead graphic designer at Heyday Books, where she worked with Sylvia on *The Lost Worlds of the San Francisco Bay Area*, as well as a freelance designer. More about Ashley and her work can be found on her website: http://www.ashleyingramdesign.com/

Lightning Source UK Ltd.
Milton Keynes UK
UKHW041201140620
364910UK00006BA/1075